**Quest for Glory:
Crystals of Power**

by James Mann

Table of Contents

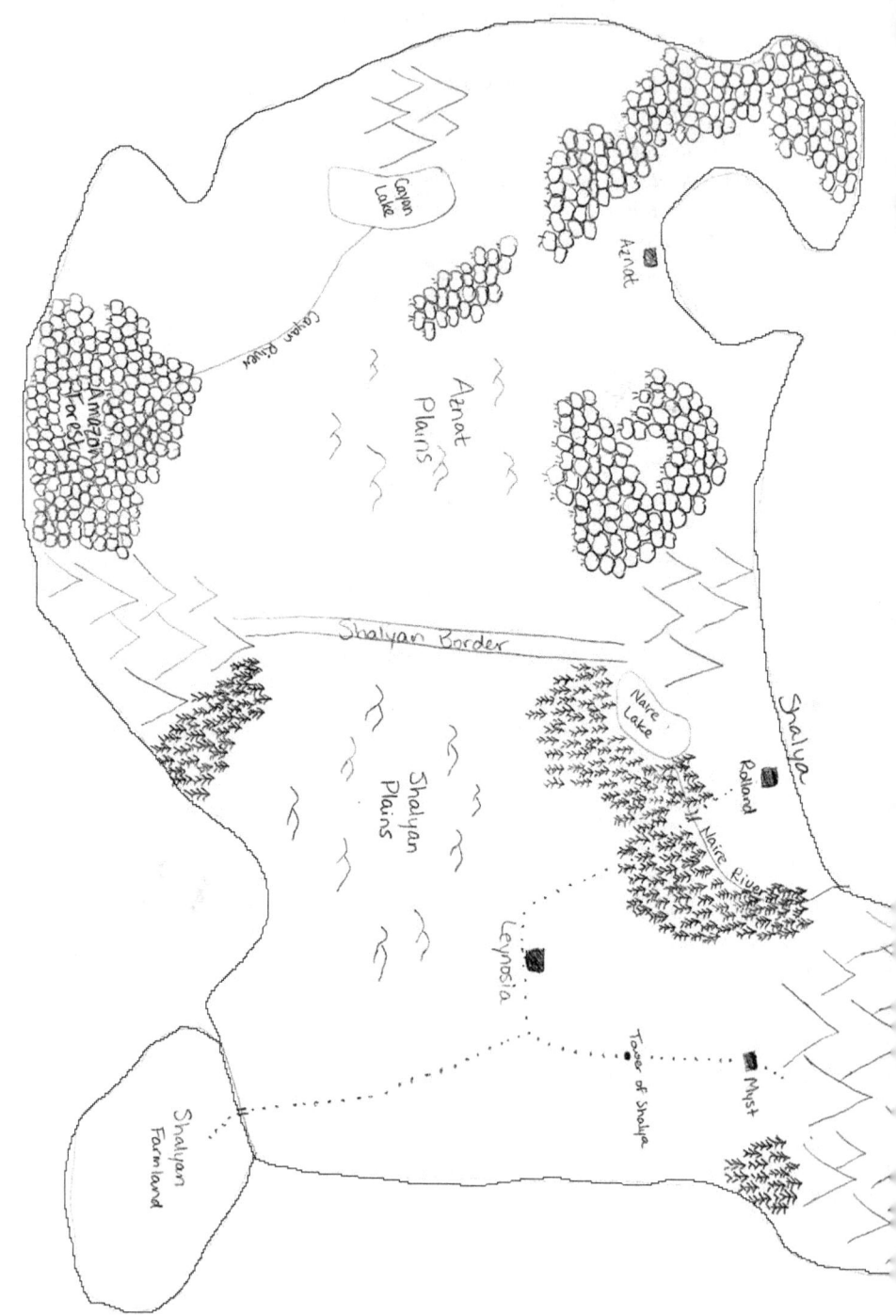

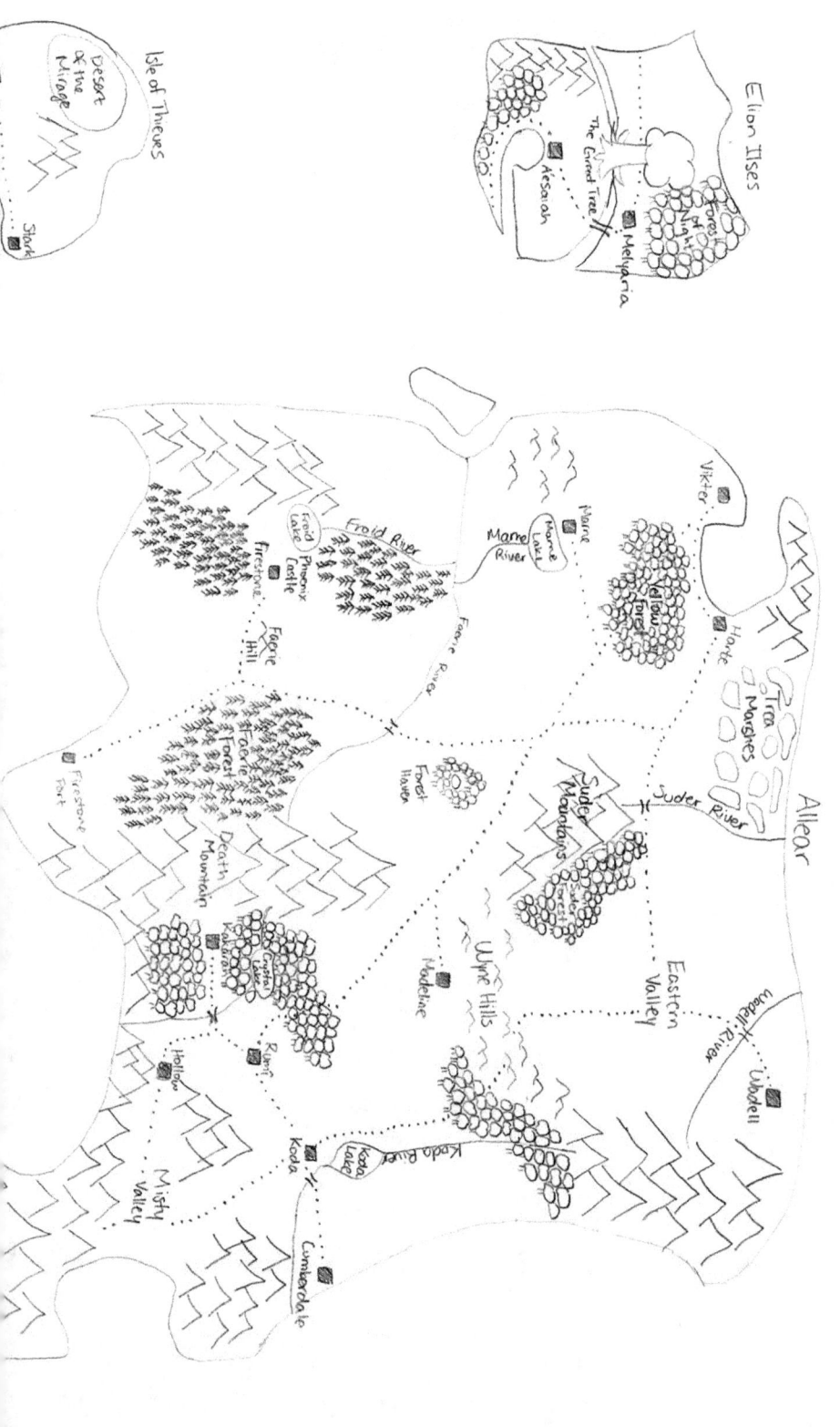

Isle of Thieves

Desert of the Mirage

Shark

Elion Ilses

The Great Tree

Aesarah

Melvaria

Forest of Night

Alleor

Froid River

Fred Phoenix Lake

Firestone Castle

Firestone

Faerie Hill

Faerie River

Faerie Forest

Death Mountain

Firestone Fort

Marne River

Marne Lake

Yellow Forest

Vikter

Harte

Tree Marshes

Suder River

Suder Mountains

Suder Forest

Forest Haven

Wyne Hills

Madeline

Eastern Valley

Waddell River

Ubadell

Crystal Lake

Hollow

Rumi

Misty Valley

Koda

Koda Lake

Koda River

Cumberdale

Allfor L

Norya

Noryan
Wilds

Hoarfrost

Divia

Caverns
of
Nora

Noryan
Tundra

Forgotten
Isle

CHAPTER ONE

The Call

Carter's hand brushed against the stems of the freshly bloomed lilacs, pinching a stem between his fingers. As Karen was walking behind him with soft steps on the tufts of grass, Carter looked back towards her smiling face and placed the flower within her auburn hair. He grabbed her hand and led her around the large growth of lilacs and found a quiet spot amongst the beauty of the green and shades of purple.

"Beautiful," Karen said.

"Only because you have come to brighten this place," Carter replied as he kissed her forehead.

"How did I get so lucky?" Karen asked, grabbing Carter's hand. She set the basket of flowers next to her as she sat down with Carter.

"I am the one who is lucky," Carter said. "You are the epitome of beauty."

They held each other's hand as they stared, as if in a trance, into one another's eyes. A breeze blew and the fragrance of the surrounding lilacs brushed against their faces.

"I don't want this moment to end," Karen said.

A roar filled the air. Carter looked up and saw the sky covered with clouds, now hiding the sun. A black shadow flew by, blowing fire from its mouth, followed with malicious laughter.

"What's going on?" Karen asked.

"I don't know," Carter said. He stood up and pulled her up with him. "Look out!"

Karen screamed and ran out of their haven and into the open field. A large dragon, with black scales with a crimson hue, stood before her and Carter. It had ten horns on its large head and its jaw was strong, able to crush bones to dust. Carter grabbed Karen as the dragon blew a shadowy fire over the lilac field, extinguishing the beauty.

"No!" Karen screamed.

Karen ran from Carter's arms toward the fire as she watched the bushes burn. The dragon circled overhead and swooped down, plucking Karen up into the air. Karen's screams could be heard echoing among the clashing of thunder in the sky.

With a loud snap, a charred branch crashed against the path, blocking Carter in. There was no way to escape the inferno as the flames vacuumed the oxygen from his being. His eyes could barely make out the crumbling stone of Phoenix Castle in the distance.

"Peace," said a voice.

Soothing rain began to fall on Carter's face. He looked around as the water fell from the heavens to extinguish the destruction. All that remained of the field was ash. He felt a strange peace as a beautiful voice sang out.

"Carter Lockwood," said the voice.

"Who is there?" Carter sat up and looked around but found no one.

"Carter."

"I am here!" Carter said. "What do you want from me?"

A white being, descended from the clouds and stood before Carter. He was a beautiful creature, in the form of a man, with gray eyes and flawless pale skin. There was a discharge of white smoke that wisped from the being, filling the ground with a haze. Carter's eyes could not look upon the radiance that was emitted.

"Fear not," said the celestial being.

"Who are you?" Carter asked as he stood up, keeping his eyes down.

"I have come to see if you are worthy."

"Worthy?" Carter pondered the strange being's words.

"The dragon you have seen is the demonic spirit known as Baelin."

"The Dragon, he took Karen!" Carter yelled, shielding himself with his arm. "We must rescue her!"

"Take my hand." The man extended his hand out. Carter looked up and took it, finding himself within halls of Phoenix Castle. It was demolished now with only a few pillars standing.

"Why did you bring me here?" Carter asked. "If you are here to help me, we must save Karen."

"Karen will be taken by Baelin but she will not die. Phoenix Castle will fall prey to Baelin's power and there is nothing that can be done to change the future."

"So none of this is real?" Carter looked around. "But it will happen?"

"Follow me."

Carter was led down the hallway toward a thick wooden door that was unhinged. They passed through the threshold and made their way down the dark corridor of the dungeon until they found themselves at a dead end. A musty smell permeated the room. In the room, there was a table with a sword lying on a satin pillow.

"You have faith in the light, Carter," said the man.

"I do," Carter said.

"You are to be tested by the Creator, but I must ask if you are willing to help rid this world of Baelin. Will you accept this quest?"

"How can I decline serving the Creator," Carter replied. "I yield myself to His will." He reached out to grab the sword, but it had vanished.

"Glory shall not be obtained so easily young Carter Lockwood."

"How shall I stop Baelin?" There was one thing that motivated him and that was Karen. He knew there was no way he would allow this beast to harm her.

"You must be trained and equipped to be one of the few Holy Warriors this world desperately needs. Extinguish the darkness with your faith and seek the truth."

That doesn't answer my question, Carter thought.

"Do not fret my dear Carter. Your quest is yet to begin."

***

Carter sat up in his bed and had a strange peace after what seemed like a nightmare. He looked outside and it was still late into the night. After his chores around the monastery the next day, he would discuss this dream with Father Isaac.

As daybreak came, Carter rose up to complete his tasks. A fresh snow had fallen on the ground. He put on his fur-lined coat and went out to gather the logs he had split the day previous. As he placed the last log onto the pile near the stables, he heard an uneasy snort coming from one of the horses. Investigating the noise, he found there was little hay for the horses to feed upon and quickly fed them before he mucked out their stalls.

It was a very long day with the snow to add extra work. As Carter entered into the hall, he heard the monks reciting their afternoon prayers. He walked past Father Isaac's study and noticed the door was cracked open. He looked inside to find the father busily writing on one of his parchments.

"Father Isaac?" Carter asked, as he pushed his head through the crack.

"Carter my boy," the old man said, taking off his glasses and setting them down. "Come sit." He gestured to one of the chairs on the other side of his desk. The old frail man gave a comforting smile as Carter sat down.

"I wanted to ask you about a dream." Carter said. *I hope he doesn't think I am crazy. Concerning the spiritual aspects of life, he is very wise.*

"Oh?" Isaac replied, raising one eyebrow.

"There was this dragon. I believe it was the Creator speaking to me. But that isn't the first time He has. When I was sixteen a voice spoke to me. It told me to journey here and train at this monastery. This recent dream, however, seemed as if I was specifically chosen to do some great thing."

Father Isaac, with dilated eyes, looked at Carter. *He looks interested in what I am saying. He might know the meaning of my dream.*

"Interesting," Father Isaac said.

"Please, tell me your thoughts. I don't know if this means I am destined."

"You are destined!" Isaac said, "I knew the first moment I laid eyes on you, the light told me you were special."

"You heard the celestial being's voice too?" Carter asked.

"I have always sensed the light ever since my dream when I was a young boy around your age."

"Tell me Father. I need to know."

Isaac slid his chair back and stood up. As he walked toward a closet, he took out a brass key from around his neck and unlocked the door. He reached inside and pulled out a sharp, double-edged sword with a beautiful hilt. There was a strange white gem etched into the bottom of the blade.

"This sword I shall pass on to you, as my mentor passed on to me when I was ready to take responsibility to wield it."

"What do you mean?" Carter asked, "Are you saying that you will train me?"

"The light brought you here to train and I must fulfill the duty. You shall be one of the few Holy Warriors left on this earth."

"I would be honored to train under you Father."

Isaac put the sword back into the closet and locked it, hiding the key around his neck. He took his place promptly in his beautiful upholstered chair. He looked at Carter and smiled. "You must be prepared to obey my teaching, Carter, and some of them you will not like," Isaac said. "I am well aware of your knowledge of the Creator and his standards for living but you shall be stretched in a way that proves your worth to obtain glory."

Obtain glory? Carter thought, *the celestial being said this.* "Tell me, what is glory?"

"In due time all will be revealed," Isaac responded, "The Creator's way is perfect and beyond our comprehension."

"What shall be my first task Father?"

"Go to the basement and clean some robes that need to be washed."

He can't be serious. How can I train to be a Holy Warrior by washing a pair of wool robes? Carter stood up from the chair and had a perplexed look on his face. He didn't know whether Father Isaac was serious or was attempting to make Carter sport.

"I knew you would not like some of my training." Isaac laughed.

Carter wanted to slump but held his shoulders high and walked out to accomplish the Isaac's odd task.

***

Karen looked out the window hoping to see Carter

coming down the road. A rush of perfumes flooded the room as Eleanor walked in from her workshop. Karen looked at her mother and smiled.

"Still looking for the boy?" Eleanor asked. "I need some Ice Pixies from the banks of the ponds."

Karen ignored her mother's comment about Carter being a boy. He was a man at the age of nineteen. She looked out hopefully one more time before answering her mother. "It would be my pleasure."

"Manners?" Eleanor replied. "Where is the Karen who gripes and complains about every little task?"

"I am that same Karen." Karen smiled mockingly. Maybe Carter would be out working near the monastery. She planned to do her task given by her mother and hoped to see Carter. "Where is your list?"

Karen snatched the parchment from her mother's hand and rushed out the door. She returned to grab her coat and slammed the door once more. Eleanor stood there shaking her head, arms folded, with a smile on her face.

***

Carter was on the roof of the stables brushing off the snow when he spotted Karen at the nearby pond. He quickly climbed down from the roof and headed toward her. She was gathering Ice Pixies that were growing near the banks of ponds in the area. Ice Pixies were a fuzzy blue flower that grew on the banks of frozen ponds and were often used for medicinal purposes to prevent hypothermia.

Karen dropped her basket as she ran to let Carter embrace her. Her chilled lips quivered when they touched his and caused her pulse to increase. She smiled and said, "My mother thinks that I am a love-stricken fool."

"Then let us both be love-stricken fools together," Carter said.

"I am glad that I came when I did. It took me awhile to

get out as I forgot my coat and then my basket." She laughed.

"I am always delighted to see you," He looked down at the basket, "even if you are doing errands."

"I love my errands because it's how I found you."

"I have great news my love!" Carter was smiling. "Father Isaac has agreed to train me."

"Train you? In doing what? What brought on this change?"

"I will be a holy warrior. I have proven myself and Father Isaac will train me in the way of combating the evil within the world." *I better not tell her my dream. She might worry.*

"Oh, darling!" She kissed him again. "How exciting! You make me proud to be called your betrothed."

In the distance there was a snap of twigs. Carter looked over and saw one of the royal couriers with a letter in his hand. "Do you live here at this monastery?" the man asked Carter.

"Yes I do," Carter replied.

"Please deliver this to Father Isaac."

"What happened?" Karen asked the courier.

"The King is dead."

CHAPTER TWO

The Coronation

Mianya sat in front of her mirror, brushing her light blond hair. As she stroked her hair with her brush, there was a knock at the door. "Enter!" Mianya said.

"My Princess, your mother requests your presence," said the Elf guard.

"Very well," Mianya looked at him, with the piercing gaze of her blue eyes, through the mirror. "Let her know I will be right down."

Her hand tensed as sharp pain came from her ankle. She lost control of her muscles and dropped the brush. The pain was spreading up her leg like a poison. As her hands trembled, she grabbed her pendant and shut her eyes. *Creator! Please end my afflictions,* she thought. A handprint appeared upon her raw skin.

My beloved, you shall endure and find rest.

"Rest," Mianya said to herself as she gazed into her flawless reflection. She stood up from her gold satin chair and swiftly exited her room.

***

Queen Thalandria sat on her throne as her brother, King Thulian, and daughter, Mianya, entered the room. Thulian approached Thalandria first with an Elven salute and stepped aside as Mianya approached her mother with a bow.

"I have called you both here to discuss a severe change in leadership regarding the nation of Allear." Thalandria said in her authoritative tone, "King Phillip III has recently died to unknown causes. As soon as the ships are ready, we set sail to the coronation of his son Phillip IV."

"He is just a boy," Thulian said, "Surely his sister Bethany is more capable to lead such a large nation."

"I do not have a comfortable feeling about this mother," Mianya interjected, "You believe it wise to journey so far? I fear dark times have fallen upon us once more."

"Dark times never left," Thulian said.

"Silence Thulian," Thalandria said. "Bethany has opted to not become Queen and the only rightful heir is Phillip. We must attend the coronation to show our support."

"I do not support this!" Thulian said.

"You do not support a lot of things but they are so!" Thalandria said.

"I trust your wisdom mother," Mianya said, "You know my thoughts and I feel we will be looked upon as a heathen nation without the proper focus of truth in the eyes of the people."

"We will worry about that when the time comes," Thalandria replied.

Thulian saluted his sister once more before he scoffed and stormed out of the throne room.

"Mianya," Thalandria said, "Fear not. I will not let darkness take you once more."

Mianya bowed and exited the room. Tears formed in her eyes as fear crept into her soul.

***

Mianya looked out over the fields as their carriage led

her, Thalandria, and Thulian down the road. They had journeyed miles over seas and the closer she knew she was getting toward Phoenix Castle made her uneasy. Her heart was beating fast. *Calm my troubled soul*, she thought. Her hand braced the wall as the last bridge was being crossed before their timely arrival.

"I do hope Hendor is well." Thalandria said. She turned to Thulian who was sitting, frowning. "Thulian, cheer. Your grimace look is going to make you look older than you already are."

Thulian continued to stare out the window.

"Mianya, are you ill?"

"I am fine, mother," Mianya replied.

"If there is some evil in this place, we will not tarry long."

Mianya bowed her head to her mother's words. The castle came into sight. The sun was shining brightly on the snow-covered towers and walls. As they passed the gates to the city, people turned and stared.

The gate to Phoenix Castle was heavily guarded and not many people lingered in the courtyard as ice covered the stones. The carriage stopped and Mianya looked out. The doors opened and a handsome man walked out with a smile that made her skin crawl. His black hair reminded her of Baelin and the proud look he bore concerned her.

Her eyes shot up to one of the upper windows as she could sense she was being watched intently by Phillip. A shadow from the window quickly vanished from sight and Mianya's eyes were now fixed on this man. He was strangely beautiful and this frightened her, reminding her of the dark days.

The driver opened the door upon the young man's arrival. Mianya was closest to him and feared to get out first as he stretched out his hand toward hers. His eyes were black as night and she was reluctant to reach out to take his hand. Slowly she extended her hand and when she touched his cooled skin, she became lightheaded as painful memories pierced her soul.

Please not again, she thought. Mianya found herself in the arms of the strange man, who was staring down at her with a vindictive smile. Mianya hastened to escape his touch, her ankle now burning with pain. Her eyes met his and she knew instantly who he was. "How?" she asked.

"Pardon my lady?" the man said.

"I know who you are." She removed herself from him and backed towards the carriage.

"I am Lord Sebastian," Sebastian said.

"Mother, we must leave," Mianya said, "It is not safe."

"With haste!" Thalandria commanded the driver as Mianya got into the carriage.

The driver got into the seat and they rode off down the road through Firestone and out of the city gates. They did not slow until they reached the first bridge.

"Mother, his cold eyes," Tears blinded her vision, "Baelin...."

"The council shall decide our next action upon our arrival to the Elion Isles."

Mianya continued to nurse her ankle. She could remember the vivid memories of that dark castle. She had tried to destroy it but something in the darkness burned her as it latched to her skin. She knew Baelin's castle had been found and that demon had released Baelin, but how? She had found a crystal before and released one of the Creatures of Old by shattering it with her pendant.

"Do you have something you would like to say Thulian?" Thalandria asked.

"Nothing that I didn't already say before," Thulian replied.

"We must find out how he escaped." Mianya said.

"What use is it to us now?" Thulian said, "It would be wiser to hide in the ice caves of Norya."

"We will continue to lie calm until something drastic

happens."

I fear that Shalya is in grave danger, Mianya thought. Mianya gave a faint whistle and a white dove flew into the carriage. She kissed its head and watched it as it flew south toward the nation of Shalya.

CHAPTER THREE

Baelin

Karen stared out the window, watching carriages contained with noblemen and women from around the land flock toward the castle for the coronation of Prince Phillip IV. She remembered when she was accompanying Phillip at his sixteenth birthday. She had felt like a princess but reality was more precious to her. Carter was everything.

"Karen, I know the streets are crowded but I need you to gather some more herbs from the northern forest," Eleanor said, walking in, as she dried her hands on her apron. "I have a feeling business will do well."

"Why search the northern forest?" Karen asked.

"I know you prefer Faerie Forest because the monastery is there, but I need you to hurry back and help me with this new pot of perfume." Eleanor grabbed a few vials from the shelf and walked back toward the door to her shop. She turned back to look at Karen before leaving her and shooed her with her hands.

Karen gathered her basket and put on her fur-lined coat before heading out. *Why can't mother just let me rest for one moment?* She stepped outside and the chill bit her nose quickly. She was thankful that spring would come soon. The beautiful lilacs were what she missed most when gathering herbs and flowers for her mother.

Karen saw her father walking toward her. He was holding something and she wondered what it was. Thomas was trailing along behind holding some supplies as well.

"Good morning father," Karen said, noticing that he was carrying linen. "What beautiful fabric. Did you make it recently?"

"Made from the best ewes in all of Western Allear," he said.

"May I ask who it is for?" She wondered because she knew he had agreed to make her wedding dress.

"You are too curious Karen." He smiled and kissed her on the forehead. "Now I know your mother needs your help with her new perfume. Run along so we can make the sales."

Winter was the most difficult time of year to make and sell perfume. Peter Proudmoore made most of his money during the winter as a tailor while Eleanor made the money during the warmer seasons. With five children, they were doing their best to provide for the family.

Karen continued to walk down the street and heard the ringing of bells and horse's breath behind her. She walked to the edge of the street and looked back. A magnificent carriage rode up fast with white steeds pulling it. She stared; and, as it passed, sapphire eyes within the carriage pierced through her soul.

"Magnificent," Karen said under her breath as she watched the carriage continue on. She had uneven breaths, and her heart raced as she had never seen an Elf before. She loved the flawlessness of her face. She wished she could have seen her whole being and not just her face.

Elves were the chosen race of the Creator. They had direct access to the Creator many years before Baelin's reign had corrupted the hearts of many men. Karen had so many questions she wished she could ask the Elves. She had faith in the light just as they did.

As Karen reached the edge of the city, she looked at the

two paths, one leading toward the monastery to the east and the other, north. Her heart yearned for Carter but she knew that her family's livelihood required her to do her part to help keep finances in order. She turned to look back at the path twice and then continued on her way north.

She spent the next hour gathering as many Ice Pixies as she could. When she filled her basket, she returned home. Upon arriving, she saw the twins, Adam and Susan, walking toward her.

"Karen!" Susan said. "Have you seen all the nobility? What a wonderful time to be in Firestone!"

"Karen, we saw Elves!" Adam said.

"I think I even saw the fat king from Norya." Susan exclaimed.

"You both need to come inside before you catch a cold," Karen said, "Your noses are red. Mother will not be pleased."

As they entered the warm room, Susan wouldn't stop talking. "The weirdest thing happened Karen. When we saw the Elves from a distance, that creepy man Sebastian came out to greet them. There was a beautiful Elf that emerged and then she just collapsed. It was the weirdest sight."

Karen smiled so to seem interested. She walked into the perfume shop next door and Susan followed after her.

"She looked frightened," Susan said. "I had never seen anyone look so terrified. I always assumed they were so calm. At least that is the way they appear in books and pictures. But that wasn't the best part. When the Elf stood up, she entered in the carriage and it took off toward the gate from where we were watching it.

That's why they were headed away from the castle, Karen thought. She wanted to go to the monastery and do some research now. She assumed that the Elf was the Princess Mianya. There was a book on her from when the Heavenly Knight purged a terrible demon from her body during the great battle.

***

Carter was headed out the side of the stable, to grab firewood for the monastery. He saw the silhouette out of the corner of his eye. Eliza was watching him from the window.

"Carter!" Karen waved. She grabbed up her skirt and trudged through the snow toward him.

He let out a deep breath. Karen ran into his arms as they embraced. He continued to glance toward the window.

"Is something wrong?" Karen pulled back and looked into his eyes.

"I have been doing a lot of work lately for Father Isaac and he hasn't attempted to train me once."

"Give it time my love." She brushed his face and entered into his warm embrace once more. She could feel the heat radiating from his body and hear the pulse of his heartbeat. There was so much of him to consume that she never wanted to leave his arms.

"Come inside. You are freezing."

They entered into the Narthex of the monastery. It was drafty but once inside the kitchen, the heat from the stove warmed them.

Eliza was in the kitchen. She glanced up to see Carter with Karen and blushed. She was stirring something and glanced up again.

"I need to finish my chore and then I will help you find the book you are looking for," Carter said to Karen.

"All right," she replied, taking a seat on the stool nearest to her.

Eliza looked at Carter as he exited the room. Karen noticed the way Eliza was acting flustered when Carter was around. "Hello," Karen said. "I don't think I have seen you before. Have you recently moved in? My name is Karen."

"Eliza," Eliza said. She continued to look at her bowl and kept stirring.

"You are very pretty," Karen said, "and I love your hair. You must take good care of it and brush it often. It's black as night, but the light still shines off it."

"Thank you," she replied. "So you know Carter?"

"Yes, we are to marry."

"Oh." Eliza continued stirring but now it was more rigorous.

"What brings you to the monastery?"

"Self-actualization one might say."

"I bet its nice being so close to spiritual men like Father Isaac. The Creator has truly blessed this place."

Eliza put down the bowl and smacked the spoon against the side of it. She set down the spoon and wiped her hands on her apron. She began to walk toward the door.

"I'm sorry if I offended you with my questioning," Karen said.

Eliza stopped. "No, you are fine. I must go finish washing the sheets."

"If you are ever in Firestone, stop by my mother's perfume shop. It's off the main street toward the castle."

Eliza stopped and looked back with a quick smile. "Thank you."

Karen slumped into the chair near the oven. She felt defeated and wondered why Eliza was so cold towards her. Maybe she was jealous? She was looking at Carter with some intent. Maybe that is why he was looking at the window, she thought. She warmed her hands near the oven as she waited for Carter to return.

Upon returning, Carter walked toward the oven and began warming his hands. He looked at Karen and smiled as she had dozed off in the chair. He kicked her foot with his and she opened her eyes and smiled at the sight of him. "Nice rest?" he asked.

"How long have I been asleep?" Karen asked. "Mother

will be worried. I told her that I was going to get some religious books from you."

"It has only been fifteen minutes." Carter laughed as he pulled her up from the chair. "Follow me."

They entered into the library. The monk in charge of organizing the manuscripts nodded as they passed by. They went to the section where the older books were kept. It looked as if no one had been in this part of the library for ages. Dust covered most of the books and they seemed unorganized.

"I thought it would be…" Karen brushed away a cobweb, "cleaner."

"I guess Tim had not reached this part of the library yet." Carter said. "Now, what is it that you are looking for?"

"A book on Princess Mianya." Her eyes scanned the room.

"May I ask why?"

"Remember when I went with Phillip to his birthday ball?" She began moving books around and blowing dust off the covers.

"How could I forget? Phillip looked at me with shock and I thought he was going to cry when he found out that we were to be married."

"The Elves were there and they were so calm and serene. Phillip's mother had just died and I was there for him. Sebastian was also there and was very polite and kind."

"Where is all this coming from?"

"I am concerned. I am terribly frightened for Phillip's safety."

"He seems to be in good hands."

"One night months ago, I saw Sebastian riding from Firestone and then when he finally returned days later, he had a dark spirit about him. He has changed and I don't trust him."

"I don't think that I follow still."

"I don't think that King Phillip's death was a coincidence." She brushed off another book and flipped through the pages.

"Are you telling me that you think that Phillip's father was murdered?"

"It is just a suspicion."

Carter laughed and grabbed the book from Karen's hands. He set it down and cupped her face between his hands. She looked up at him and her heart beat faster and her palms sweat, as he stared into her eyes. "Do not worry yourself over such trivial ideas. You told me that the King hadn't been himself lately."

"Carter!" She brushed his hands away from her face. "I am being serious. Sebastian has changed and that scares me. He brought fear into the Elves and they left before the coronation. Phillip is not himself either."

"I think you are over-thinking all of this. You have spent too much exposed to all that perfume." He grabbed her hands again.

She made fists and pushed into Carter. "Let go of me!"

"Karen," Carter said softly. He attempted to stroke her face but she brushed them away.

"I do not appreciate you making me out to be a fool, Carter Lockwood! I need to know what the one thing the Elves could possibly fear."

"Baelin."

"Baelin?"

"He was a demon. He was a man that struck fear into the hearts and souls of every creature that faced him. He was a terrible demonic dragon in his ultimate form. There are accounts of the great battle. Mianya used to be one of his minions. The Heavenly Knight purged the demon from her body."

"How do you know all this?"

"I have a book in my room that tells the accounts of that

battle."

"What happened to Baelin?"

"The Heavenly Knight trapped him in his own crystallized prison like the ones he put the Creatures of Old in. He took Baelin's crystal with him and rode off to the east."

"Creatures of Old?"

"Powerful beasts with unique powers. Somehow Baelin managed to capture them all within these crystals that he harnessed more power from. When he encountered the Heavenly Knight, they were scattered throughout the world. No one has heard of what happened to them. Nor has anyone heard of what happened to the crystal that Baelin was encased in."

"Do you think Baelin might have escaped?" Her mind was actively thinking of all the possibilities for Sebastian's strange and frightening behavior. "Maybe the knight didn't destroy the crystal but put it somewhere and someone found him and released him."

"Karen, maybe you need to go home and rest."

Karen glared at Carter and pushed him away. He just laughed as she stomped away from him. He reached and grabbed her hand to stop her from walking away. She turned and struggled to get her hand free and when she did, she turned once more toward the exit with tears in her eyes. As fast as she could manage, she escaped before Carter could intercept her again.

"Darling, please!" Carter called after her.

She turned around to look at him. Her cheeks were streaked from crying. "I am going home and resting. Go do some more chores. I am done talking to you!" She just wanted for him to listen to her. All she could think about was how frightened she was for the safety of those that she cared about most.

***

"My King, Karen Proudmoore requests a presence," said the royal courier.

"Let her in," Phillip said, waving his hand.

Sebastian was standing next to Phillip when Karen entered the room. Her eyes met his and she stopped dead in her tracks. Her heart was beating violently. "Phillip, may I speak to you?" Her mouth was dry and she swallowed a lump in her throat. Her eyes darted to meet Sebastian's and then went to the floor again.

"Is that not why you requested an audience with the King?" Sebastian asked.

"Alone." Karen continued to attempt to avoid Sebastian's gaze.

"Sebastian, please leave us," Phillip said.

Sebastian nodded and walked toward Karen, keeping his eyes on her until he passed directly past her. She looked forward and did not speak until she heard the door open and close behind her. She let out a deep sigh and unclenched her fists.

"How are you doing, Karen?" Phillip said with a smile. "This King stuff is hard. I am expected to be all calm and proper but I am really nervous. What if I fail the people…?"

"I am worried Phillip," Karen interjected. "I think that Sebastian can't be trusted."

Phillip began laughing. Karen glared and looked down. "Please listen!"

"I am listening. I just find your comment humorous."

"Why do you trust him? I remember how Sebastian used to be when I first met you both in the fields where I was picking flowers for my mother. He was quiet and disengaged but polite and kind. Now, I feel something evil has taken root in his soul. His hair is black when it used to be blond and his words are laced with bitterness and hate. He treats you like some puppet when he should respect you."

"He is my best friend, Karen!" Phillip stood up, "The truth could not be said for you. You have your precious Carter!"

"I… I…" she stuttered. She knew that Phillip had feelings for her that she could never reciprocate. She honestly wanted to be there for him in this difficult time of his father's passing but she knew it was not healthy for him. She only had his best interest in mind. It hurt her for him to be so oblivious to truth.

"I'm sorry, I didn't mean to snap." Phillip walked toward Karen and grabbed her hand. "Sebastian has been there for me through the toughest times and I know you have been there too but I am the only person he has since his father passed. And he has graciously returned the favor to me since my father's passing."

"I am concerned. I know that the Elves left when they encountered Sebastian. Didn't you find it odd that he brought fear to the Elves? When they came for your birthday, they did not fear him then and he was at the same table." Karen looked up at the high ceiling of the room.

"I watched the event take place myself. I asked him about the encounter and he assured me he did not know why they left. He greeted them with open arms and they retreated. He suspects that they do not find me worthy of the crown."

"Why would the Elves covet your crown?"

"I am unsure of that myself. Sebastian is investigating them right now. He also feels that Shalya is attempting to attack. We are a weak nation with this transition from my father to me and Sebastian wants to help me protect Allear."

"Please listen to me. There is no threat. Sebastian must be lying. The Elves are good and kind. Not to mention Queen Alphira. She is your cousin. Why would she covet your crown? I thought that she was currently struggling to suppress the wild men attacks from the Aznat tribe."

"What do you know?" he said. "You know nothing! You aren't even a noble!"

Tears formed in Karen's eyes and she stepped back. Removing her hands from Phillip's grasp, she turned to leave. She ran toward the door and opened it, seeing Sebastian standing there with a smile on his face. She ran past him as fast as she could and headed home.

Both of the men she cared about thought she was foolish. She wanted answers from the Elf princess but had no way to find her. She was probably already home by now. "Creator, please help me understand!" She cried out.

CHAPTER FOUR

The Fall of Shalya

The great wall had crumbled, protecting Shalya from the wild Aznat men. Men poured into Shalya from the west. The wizards stood no chance with the power that Sebastian had within his grasp. It was a bloodbath. There was an army of Shalyan men ready to defend their land, but they had not seen war before and were unprepared for the new threat facing them.

Sebastian rode past the masses of men fighting and headed east toward Leynosia. The city was quiet with all the citizens within their home, thinking that they were safe. He rode through the city and made his way toward the castle.

Alphira's guards ran from their post with their swords drawn, ready to defend their Queen. Sebastian quickly disposed of them and headed inside the Castle where more men were ready to face him. He used magic to disarm them and they fled. The throne room was just a few feet in front of him.

The doors flew open and sitting there, Alphira was trembling upon her throne. She had a tall slender body with fiery red hair that draped over her shoulders and back, contrasting with her pale skin and giving her a chilled demeanor.

Sebastian smiled and approached her. No guards were left to protect their beloved Queen. Sebastian put his sword away back in its sheath and approached her. She sat there as he outstretched his hand and stroked her cheek. "What tender skin," he said.

She took a deep breath. No words came from her lips as she sat there shaking violently. Sebastian grabbed her by the arm. Tied to his right arm was cloth to blindfold her. She willingly complied. "This is going to be fun." He pushed her along to the center of the room. She stumbled and fell to her knees in the center of the throne room. Panting heavily she began to weep.

Sebastian took his sword out and with one quick swipe, her body fell to the floor. "Scapegoat," he said. He laughed and slicked his hair back as he exited the throne room.

In the distance, from the entrance of the castle, Sebastian saw a flicker of light coming from the tower due north of the city. He mounted his horse and rode swiftly toward it.

He smiled as he approached the threshold of the tower. Dismounting, he was met by four Shalyan soldiers who he defeated. He fought his way up to the top. Opening the door to the upper chamber, he saw Alphira standing there. Her eyes were opened wide and her knuckles were white as she gripped her staff.

"I was pleasantly surprised to find your little trick you left for me," he said. "I sensed no power radiating from her body so I knew she was no magic user."

"What do you want from Shalya?" Alphira asked.

"What rightfully belongs to me." He cautiously took a few steps closer. "The power radiating from you is amazing."

"I do not know what you are talking about." Alphira kept stepping back as Sebastian approached.

"Lies!" he snapped. "You know that I desire the crystals and I thank you for finding them for me. It makes my job much easier."

"Who are you?"

"Why Sebastian of course. Who else would I be? Are you suggesting I am someone else?"

"There is something evil within your soul."

"Do you fear me?" He took one smaller step closer.

"How could I not after what you just did? If I happened to have what you are looking for, is it worth all this bloodshed?"

"Absolutely, I get more power from other's misery. Being trapped for a thousand years and then to be stuck in this mortal body, I need more power!"

"How can it be? You are just a young man."

"I am not who you think I am. If I could show you who I really was, you would bow before me."

"I would never bow to a demon such as you, Baelin."

"You are wiser than I had imaged." Sebastian clapped. "The Creator is weak, sparing me and knowing I could return one day."

"You will not win."

"Look at your now, war-ravaged land and tell me that I have not already won."

"I will not give you the crystals. I would see these creatures released rather than fall into your hands. They deserve freedom."

"And yet you and your people have drained their power for your own use of magic. Borrowing what doesn't belong to you is considered a reason to die in my eyes."

"Die I shall, but you will never have the crystals."

"What are you doing?" Sebastian asked as Alphira walked toward the window. He used what little magic he had left to close the window. The latch on it locked in place.

Alphira turned around and used some magic of her own, knocking him against a wall. She threw the window open and climbed up upon the sill as Sebastian managed to get back up. "They were scattered from you once, Baelin, and now they shall be scattered once more!" At those words she leaped from the window and used one last spell to scatter the crystals, sewn into her dress, throughout the world.

"No!" Sebastian cried out as he ran to the window. He saw the remains of Alphira lying on the ground below.

***

Mianya, gasped, sitting up in her bed. "She's dead!" she said. Her heart beat fast and she could not stop her hands from trembling. She hung her feet over the side of the bed. Drops of sweat had formed on her brow. *How can this be?* She thought.

Her dove had spied upon the fair Queen of Shalya, giving Mianya vision of the events. Now seeing the true nature of Sebastian for herself, she knew that another council of the Elves must be called together.

"Guards!" Mianya yelled. Two Elven guards entered the room. They knelt before Mianya and looked at her with intent. "I need you to go to my mother and explain that an emergency council must be called upon." They both saluted and quickly stood up and exited the room.

She looked at herself in the mirror and flashed back to when she used to serve Baelin. She touched her pale skin and could see the ghost-white color her hair used to be. Her eyes were blood red and blue veins protruded from under her eyes. She looked like death itself.

"Please," Mianya said as she scanned her face with her hands. "I don't want to go back."

Beloved, fear not.

"Creator, I do not understand why you show grace," she said. "But if you didn't, I wouldn't be here today. Thank you!"

The loud sound of a horn blew. The council had agreed

to meet. Mianya dressed quickly and headed from her room to the council's antechamber. She entered a great white room where chairs were placed in a half-circle. The sun shone brightly into the magnificent room through the high arching windows. Splotches of light reflected to the ceiling off the golden chairs like stars in the heavens. Green satin cloth was draped around the doorways and windows along with vines that grew up against the white stone walls.

The Melyarian advisors were already sitting in the room and Mianya quickly took her seat amongst them. Soon the A'esaiah advisors to Thulian came through the white doors and sat down. Finally, in walked Thulian and Thalandria, deep in unpleasant conversation. Upon entering the room, they abruptly stopped speaking and took their seats in front of the forty Elves that sat waiting for the news.

"Mianya," Thalandria said from her seat. "Please enlighten us on this emergency council."

Mianya looked at her mother who nodded. She stood up and looked into the faces of the council who were at the time calm and serene. "Alphira is dead."

They all spoke among themselves and the room was filled with murmurings. She saw the distress on some of their faces. Thalandria had no expression but pursed her lips. "How did you acquire this information, if I may ask?"

"I feared so I sent my dove to check out the Shalyan lands." Mianya had no emotion in what she had just said for fear of her mother's disapproval.

"What did I tell you dear sister," Thulian spoke up. "We now need to retreat because we are in danger of being perceived as a threat."

"Hold your tongue brother." Thalandria raised her hand. "Tell me what you saw." Her eyes were intently fixated upon Mianya.

"Alphira had a woman play her faux but Sebastian suspected and killed her. After that he went to the tower in the northern hills and found Alphira hiding in the upper chambers. He killed all her guards and approached her. She was frightened when he admitted to being Baelin. He was after the crystals that contained the Creatures of Old. She threw herself off the tower and scattered the crystals like the Heavenly Knight did two thousand years ago. We must find and release the creatures before he acquires them. It is my understanding that he is weak after being in that crystal and is attempting to drain the crystals of their power."

"We must stop him at all costs." Thalandria stated.

"No sister, we must warn and take refuge in the ice caves of Norya."

"Have you no faith in the Creator? He is on our side."

"He abandoned us, sister! He allowed Baelin to return. Do you honestly believe He has our best interests in mind?"

"Do you see that pendant you are wearing? If you don't believe, take off our covenant."

"You know I cannot do that lest I die."

"Your lack of faith has made you dead already."

"Mother," Mianya interjected, "the task at hand still needs to be discussed."

"Very well." Thalandria stood and faced her council. "All in favor of fighting with the Creator, stand please and extend your right palm."

Ten Elves stood and did this. Mianya was not one of them. Thalandria looked at her daughter and then to Thulian who sat with a smirk on his face. "Very well, we shall hide in Norya. May King Hendor have more success in persuading you than I have."

"We have no means to destroy him, sister, so do not be distraught," Thulian said.

"There is a way," Mianya spoke up.

"Please enlighten us," Thulian said.

"When the Heavenly Knight was leaving the battle, I ran to him and kissed his neck and thanked Him for saving me. He handed me a white crystal. Much like the ones that Baelin had trapped the Creatures of Old within. He whispered in my ear that it was the key to glory."

"You mean the sword?" Thalandria asked.

"Correct. He told me that with this key and the light within, the wielder of glory, would be able to destroy Baelin."

"And where is this key you speak of?" Thulian asked.

"I do not have it any longer. I lost it when I attempted to destroy Baelin's castle."

"You are a fool!" Thulian stood up, pointing his finger at Mianya. "How could you be given something so vital and let it disappear?"

"Thulian!" Thalandria said, "You are out of line!"

"I have failed on multiple occasions mother." Mianya sat down. "He has every right to call me a fool." She showed her mother her scar on her ankle. "I received this from something within the castle. If Baelin has escaped, he has the key within his grasps."

"Our races are doomed dear sister. We must leave immediately." Thulian stood and exited the room. Following after him was the rest of the council except Thalandria and Mianya.

"I am terribly sorry mother." Mianya avoided her mother's looks.

"Do not worry, my daughter. We are victorious with the Creator on our side. If He is powerful enough to make you whole again, He is powerful enough to save this earth. I do not doubt his working power."

"Your faith is stronger than mine."

"I will meet you at the docks. I will discuss our plan of attack with King Hendor. Thulian will be wise soon and reason."

Thalandria exited the room, leaving Mianya sitting in her chair. *I know what I must do*, she thought. Taking a deep breath and letting it out with a sigh, she stood and exited the room to prepare for her quest.

CHAPTER FIVE

To Deny Oneself

Carter walked outside to split wood. The air was still cool but the snow had completely melted. Spring was just around the corner and Carter was looking forward to the new fresh start nature would have. The beautiful lilac fields were where Karen spent most of her time and Carter could not wait to share those times with her.

Another royal courier approached Carter and handed him a letter. He put his duties aside to deliver the letter to Father Isaac. He went to the study and knocked on the door. "Come in!" Isaac said.

"A letter came from the King just now." Carter said, handing over the letter. "I will go do my chores now."

Father Isaac held up his hand. "Wait." He opened the letter and read it. He set the letter down and looked at Carter. "I wanted to give you something to read. In it there are mental exercises that I want you to practice in your free time." He handed Carter the book that was lying on his desk.

"All Right," Carter said. "What was the letter if I may ask?"

"We are at war with Shalya. War taxes are raised slightly."

"I was led to believe that Shalya is a peaceful nation.

Isn't the queen King Phillip's cousin?"

"This is what concerns me. It is time that we focus more on the specifics of your training. Right now I was testing your obedience through tasks that you didn't understand. There are many things the Creator requires of us that we don't understand but we must remain obedient."

"My faith must be weak then."

"Do not fret Carter Lockwood. You are still young and have so much to learn. It is a process."

"I have a problem that has been bothering me for some time."

"Hmmm?"

"Karen was here looking for a book a few weeks ago. She was telling me that the Elves left the King's coronation. She seems to think that Sebastian has some evil spirit within him."

"And you don't?"

"Hearing about Allear going to war with one of our allies is very disconcerting. Do you think that maybe the King is being negatively influenced by Sebastian?"

"It is highly possible. Shalya is rumored to contain great treasures of magic. Baelin craved power so it would make sense that he would strike them first. Let us hope the Elves are wise and become aware of this event."

"I must go speak with Karen and apologize." Carter stood up and ran out of the room.

"Carter!" Isaac called after him.

***

"Hand me some foxtail oil." Eleanor said as she was stirring one of her pots of perfume.

Karen looked through the vials and found it. She handed it to her mother who put one drop in and handed it back to Karen. Eleanor reversed her stirring to counter clockwise. Purple foam was coming to the surface along with a sweet scent.

"How do you know all these techniques?" Karen asked.

"Practice and experimentation," Eleanor said.

The door opened and Susan popped her head inside. "Karen," she said, "Carter is here."

What does he want? She thought.

"You are going to have to talk to him eventually." Eleanor said. "It's all right. I don't need you right now."

Karen took off her apron and hung it on the wall. Before she opened the door, she ran her fingers through her hair. Carter was standing there with a smile on his face. She stopped trying to stand her ground but found herself running to him and wrapped her arms around his waist, burying her face into his strong chest. "I can't resist you Carter!" she said.

He wrapped his arms around her. "I came to say I am sorry," he said.

She looked up at him and frowned. "What did you say?"

"That I am sorry for not listening to you. I love you and when you need me, I need to be there for you."

"Thank you. I love you too." She let go of Carter and walked over to the window. "Did you hear we are at war? Phillip will not listen to me. He is adamant that Sebastian is wiser than all of his father's advisors combined."

"So it was Sebastian's idea. Father Isaac seems to believe you."

"And you don't still?" she asked.

"I believe something serious is happening but I can't say what is or isn't until I see the facts myself. I don't go and do or say things off of hunches."

"One of the advisors has been rumored to have died by accidental causes. I do not think that this is just coincidence. I do remember something strange about Sebastian. After—."

"Karen," Carter interrupted.

"Just listen to me please. After Phillip's birthday, I saw them a week later and Sebastian showed signs of hostility. I remember Phillip saying that they went to Death Mountain to explore. Maybe something happened on Death Mountain that Phillip could tell me about."

"Karen, I don't want you to go see Phillip anymore. It is too dangerous."

"He needs me more than ever. I can't abandon him!"

"For one, it's not healthy for him to see you so often. And second, if Sebastian is actually dangerous, I fear for your safety around him. I will not let him hurt you."

"Do not worry about me. My father will protect me. I also don't think that Phillip would let Sebastian hurt me either.

"I need to go finish my chores for Father Isaac and I will see you soon. I am glad that we had this talk."

"Goodbye, my love."

***

"Carter," Father Isaac said as Carter was splitting wood.

"I didn't expect to see you out here, Father," Carter said as he took another swing at the log, splitting it in two.

"There is something important that I was meaning to tell you before you rushed off to find Karen."

"Yes?"

"This is going to be hard for you to hear and accept but it is what must be done if you are serious about being a Holy Warrior."

"Whatever it is, I accept. The will of the Creator is greater than my own."

"You must not pursue Miss Proudmoore any longer. You must remain celibate and focus on your tasks given to you by the Creator."

"What?" Carter dropped the axe and looked at Isaac.

"Please tell me that this is a test. I thought I had to give up certain foods or something like that but my soul mate? How can I give up the most precious thing that I have."

"It is not best for you with the plans that the Creator has. I know exactly how you feel. It is difficult but it is what must be done."

"How could you know exactly how I feel?" Carter's hands balled up into fists. "You can't tell me I can't have Karen when you don't even understand. You have never had a woman love you the way Karen loves me. And I love her."

"Her name was Irene."

"Who?"

"The woman I was to marry. I was like you, young and in love. My mentor warned me of the same thing. He allowed me to pursue Irene but strongly advised against it. She held my focus day in and day out. I was consumed by her beauty and her charm. She watched me train and get stronger as a Holy Warrior. A lot of my motivation was for her and not the Creator. She got in the way, and I was blinded by love so he took her away from me."

"What? What do you mean? Why would he take her away?" Carter was beginning to worry. He thought about his dream and what the celestial being told him about Karen being taken.

"One night the village nearby the monastery where I was training was being ravaged by a bear. I went with the other men training with me and I noticed the bear had clawed its way into Irene's home. That is when I heard the screams. I ran as fast as I could but it was too late. I cut up the bear into as many pieces as I could because I was enraged and furious. I thought, *how could this happen to me?* I loved the Creator and wanted to serve him. Why would he take the one thing that I cherished? Those next few years were dark for me. I almost took my life a couple times but my mentor stopped me. He warned me that this would happen. My duty was not just to Irene but to everyone. I was so focused on her and myself that I lost sight of my true calling.

"I know that the Creator has great plans for you Carter Lockwood. You are destined for much more than I was ever able to accomplish. Don't allow yourself any opportunity to lose sight of your path. I believe that the Creator wants to use you to destroy Baelin."

"I'm sorry Father but I don't think that I could live a life without Karen. I will do my best to not lose sight of my calling but Karen is a part of me. I strongly feel that the Creator gave her to me. She reminds me of the good things the Creator has made."

"I cannot stop you but I know you will be disappointed if you do not end this now."

"I will never give up on Karen." Carter picked up the axe and continued to split wood. He now was distraught.

CHAPTER SIX

Counter Plan

Mianya found her way to shore after days of rowing in the boat she took from the ship. She wished she could have shared her plan but she knew that her mother would have persuaded her to stay with them. Stopping Baelin the best way she knew how was the only thing that was on her mind. She had almost reached the northern Coast of Allear but her first destination was going to be closer to where Sebastian resided.

Mianya had sensed some power radiating from Death Mountain to the east of the Faerie Forest and knew Sebastian would head there first. If she wanted to stop him, she had to be one step ahead and she hastened on foot because she had not brought enough gold to purchase a steed. She headed down the main road south toward Firestone. On her way she saw a small haven of trees that contained some great power within. The power was calling to her to be released but she had more pressing crystals to attend to.

She made her way up the path from the base of the mountain. Trees stretched far and wide, separating her from Phoenix Castle which protruded in the distance. She saw a flock of birds fly from the forest into the open sky. Sensing their fear she could only imagine that Sebastian was on pursuit.

The power's pulse was very strong and Mianya could sense it nearby. She continued to climb up the steep side of the mountain and finally managed to reach a nest. She looked around to see if the mother eagle was nearby but there was no sign. The eggs hadn't hatched yet so she needed to be cautious not to disturb them. On the side of the nest she saw a shining white crystal.

She jumped inside the massive nest and quickly retrieved it. Taking her pendant from around her neck, she held out the crystal and cracked it with the sharp end of the pendant. A bright white light flashed and the cry of some creature echoed through the air.

Her ears perked as she heard quick movement. She hastened from the nest and found a large boulder to hide behind, watching the nest intently, and moments later she saw Sebastian crawl into the nest. The crystal was reduced to a pile of dust on the bottom of the nest.

Mianya watched Sebastian's body tense as he gripped his hand around the sword. Drawing it from its sheath he began stabbing the giant eggs until the remains of the beasts oozed out. A loud screech could be heard from the east. Mianya looked up and saw a great eagle fly over her head and straight for Sebastian.

Its claws were extended as it went for Sebastian; he dove and rolled out of the way. Keeping his sword up, he swung, keeping the eagle at bay. One more dive, Sebastian was disarmed and his sword was lying a few feet away. He ran for it but the bird had grabbed him by the shoulders and pinned him down.

Sebastian was moving his head trying to avoid the pecking of the bird. Mianya saw Sebastian moving his foot around trying to grip the sword. He managed to slide the hilt toward him and attempt to lift it up with his feet. He positioned the sword, all the while trying to avoid the vicious attacks of the head. He thrust the sword up into the bird.

The bird screeched out and released Sebastian's shoulders. It flapped its wings and fell into the side of the nest. Sebastian grabbed his sword and swung at the eagle, cutting off its claw. Blood was covering the nest as the bird flapped around and finally fell off the edge and onto the cliff below. Sebastian struggled to hold the sword as his arms were now covered with his blood.

Mianya saw him look in her direction and quickly hid herself behind the rock. In haste, she sprinted and jumped down from the cliffs below her and made her way to the mountain path. She continued east toward the town of Kakaran.

***

Mianya had bested Sebastian at releasing the crystals before he could drain them of their power. Days went by and she could see the frustration on his face each time he found the dust of the crystal on the ground.

She found herself staying on higher ground to avoid him but as they reached the eastern coast, the trees were few and far between. She knew that she had to be more cautious now so that Sebastian couldn't intercept her.

She camped out on the beach and knew she was miles ahead of him. She watched the stars above and marveled at their beauty. "Creator, you are powerful enough to make all of these stars and this earth. Why not just destroy Baelin and rid the world of his presence."

Do not fret with such things child.

"But I am weary of this pain. This burden is too great for me."

My grace is sufficient.

She laid her head down on the sand and rested her eyes. She woke up to the burning sensation of her ankle again. She knew Sebastian was on the move so Mianya stood up and ran into the ocean to find the crystal within the depths. The sea was glimmering with the sunrise over the waters.

She swam endlessly until she reached the point where she had to dive to retrieve the crystal. She spotted the faint light it emitted and snatched it up so she could quickly return to the surface. She gasped when she broke through the surface and quickly grabbed her pendant. She had no idea if Sebastian was nearby because she could not sense him. She shattered the crystal, emitting a blue flash. With haste she swam toward the shore.

On the beach was Sebastian's horse unattended along with his satchel of supplies. Mianya scanned the area and the waters but saw no sign of him anywhere. She quickly made her way to shore and searched through the satchel and discarded it in the sand. Mounting the steed, she headed north to find the next crystal, hoping to slow Sebastian down.

She reached a small forest and felt a strong power emitting from the area. She searched for hours but could not find it. She noticed a cliff with cracks within it and began searching through them and finally saw the light of the crystal. She couldn't reach it with her hand after stretching it as far as she could. She took off her pendant and tried swinging it and hoping it would knock the crystal. She heard a small clink and there was a red flash of light.

She put on her pendant and headed back toward the small meadow where she left the steed tied up. She saw it grazing and started toward it. The silhouette of a man came from a tree above and she quickly did a back flip to avoid his clutches.

"I knew it was you who has been besting my attempts Mianya," Sebastian said.

"Sebastian," she replied, taking a few steps back. "Or should I say Baelin." She could not help but admire his beautiful face and pale skin. He drew her in like he had years ago but he also struck fear into her soul.

"I wonder how you recognized me so easily. I am guessing my gentle touch brings back pleasant memories." He laughed.

"Your touch is poison!"

"Allear will be mine to control and then the rest of the world. I will not fail like last time. I shall receive all praise and glory as the ruler of the earth!"

"The light will prevail! It has conquered you once and it can do it again."

"Fool! The Creator left his weapon on earth if I have heard correctly. How can I be destroyed otherwise? I already have alternatives for power if these crystals do not aid my quest."

What does he mean? She thought. "You lie." She stepped back once more as he began moving slowly to the right.

"Am I? Mysery." She cringed at hearing that name. "You remember your sisters do you not? Payne and Phayde?"

What is he saying? There is no way he is doing what I think he is planning. That is dark ancient magic.

"Yes, I plan to find a virgin with no hope left in her and bring back my daughters of turmoil. I am sure they would be glad to see you alive and well. Your beauty and soul restored."

"You are mad!"

"Do you feel threatened by me?"

"Never, I know that the Creator will always prevail. He is your creator as well. He will crush you like the serpent you are!"

"I love the fire within your soul. I will quickly extinguish it." Sebastian lunged forward.

Mianya sprinted westward through the trees. She continued as fast as she could, weaving in and out of the forest, ducking under branches and leaping over logs that had fallen. She heard hooves behind her. Looking back briefly, she saw Sebastian quickly advancing upon her. Sebastian rode up beside her and attempted to grab her, but she ducked and darted eastward.

Still the pursuit did not stop, and through the trees Mianya saw the shadow of Sebastian actively pursuing her. She leaped over a fallen tree trunk and kept up her fast pace. Sebastian gradually got closer and closer to Mianya until they were finally side by side. He made another attempt to grab her but she was too quick for him.

Mianya continued to run through the wood until her path dead-ended at the cliff. She turned around to face Sebastian as he slowed to a stop. "Enough!" Sebastian yelled, slowing to a trot. "I am done with your pathetic games! The Creator saved you once but this time he cannot!"

Sebastian started for her with his sword in hand. Mianya grabbed her pendant and closed her eyes. She wished that she could evade his hands somehow and Sebastian stopped as Mianya disappeared out of sight.

Mianya watched him through the trees and sighed in relief that she had evaded him with the divine help. "The light is the key," she whispered to herself. Sebastian looked furious and turned his head in every which direction. He finally looked in her direction. So she took that as her cue to sprint away and find the stronger crystals in Allear.

CHAPTER SEVEN

Abduction

"Karen, please tell me that you're not still upset with me," Carter said. "Karen?"

"What?" She said, snapping out of her thoughts. "What did you say?"

"I asked if you were still upset," he said. He began stroking her arm.

"No, I am still thinking."

"About Sebastian? Do not worry too hard about all this or you will make yourself sick."

She leaned back against Carter and let him run his fingers through her hair. She could smell his scent permeate the air. In his arms only she felt safe. "I don't want to worry but I can't help but be concerned. Another advisor of Phillip's has just disappeared and what if Phillip is next."

"Why do you care so much about Phillip?" Carter asked.

Karen sat up and turned to look at him. Her eyes became heavy. "Are you jealous?" she asked. "Phillip is not a threat, Carter. He doesn't have anyone to take care of him and show him love."

"But is it really healthy for you to give him false hope that he can be with you?"

"I don't see it that way. He doesn't believe in the light.

This is a dangerous position to be in. I want him to know truth but right now his head is filled with lies."

"I can't stop you from caring about him." Carter said and he frowned.

"What is it?"

"Saying that made me think of what Father Isaac told me."

"What did he tell you?" She crawled close and wrapped her arms around him. "You can tell me."

"He told me that you and I cannot be together. He said you will distract me from my mission."

"And what do you think? Do you feel there is truth in that statement? I love you so much and if I was stopping you from doing great things then I would step aside with a bittersweet spirit."

"Never Karen, you are my everything and soon to be my helper once you become my bride. You show me things that I lack in my own life. I have never met anyone who is as caring and compassionate towards others as you are. I also love your feisty attitude."

Karen smiled and smacked him on the arm. She leaned up and kissed him, wrapping her arms around his neck and began stroking his jaw.

"This is my favorite place," he said as she let go of him and went back to lying in his arms. He reached over and plucked a lilac and placed it within her hair.

"I just remembered!" Karen sat up straight. "My mother was going to help me plan for the wedding! She finally has time. I am so sorry but I must leave you." She turned to him and kissed him. "I love—" she kissed him again, "You!" She didn't want to let go of him.

"Did you want me to walk with you? It's beginning to get dark." He stood up and helped her stand.

"No, I should be fine." She picked up her basket full of lilacs and sprinted toward Firestone. She turned to wave and continued home.

Karen was sitting at the table talking with her mother, Eleanor, and her sister, Susan, about her wedding plans. "I want lilacs, mother," Karen said.

"What is with you and lilacs?" Susan asked.

"Don't judge me Susan!" She sighed and smiled. "Lilacs are just special to me. I guess it's because it makes me think of Carter. I first saw him in the lilac fields. Did I tell you that?"

"You know, Karen, some people are allergic to lilacs," replied Susan.

"Be quiet Susan. This is my wedding, not yours. You should go find a man for yourself instead of desiring mine," Karen said. She was attempting to make Susan uncomfortable.

"What are you saying?" Susan asked as she stood up.

"Now, now, no arguments," Eleanor said, grabbing Susan by the arm.

Susan sat and scowled at Karen. Karen just smiled and continued writing on the parchments. Out of the corner of her eye she saw Susan smile.

"Can I please French-braid your hair for the wedding?"

"Now you are just being annoying. I want my hair down. Mother, would you please tell Susan that she can do what she wants on her own wedding day. In fact, make her leave. She's obviously not understanding I make the decisions. I am already stressed about wanting everything to be perfect because Carter is worth it all."

Eleanor slouched back in her chair with a long sigh and began fanning herself with one of the pieces of parchment lying on the table. "Do you want me to help you Karen?" Eleanor asked. "You are making this experience unbearable."

Thomas ran into the room with a doll in his hand. Marie came in right after him, ran over to her mother, and began to cry. "Mother! He's hurting my Penelope!"

Eleanor sighed and sat up in her chair. "All right!" Eleanor yelled. "I have had—"

Peter Proudmoore walked into the room. "Thomas," he said in a stern voice, "Do I need to remind you to be kind to your sister? Please, give her back her doll. Marie, do not whine or I will take Penelope."

Thomas hunched over and slowly walked over to Marie and handed Penelope back to her. Marie stuck her tongue out at him when he made a face of disgust. Thomas ran into the other room and Marie followed after him.

Karen stood up and saw that her father had her dress in his hands. She got up from her chair and ran over, taking the dress from her father so that she could try it on. She held it against her and twirled around. "This is going to look so wonderful on me!" She ran into the other room and tried it on. When she returned her mother gasped.

"Oh, you look lovely!" Eleanor said as she started to tear up. "My baby is going to be married."

"Mother, don't be sad. I won't be far from here. I know you wished that you could have stayed near your parents after you were married to father."

"I am just overwhelmed with joy."

"I love you, mother, and you too, father." She took up her parents' hands and leaned in to kiss them both on the cheek. "In just five days I shall be wed and live happily ever after."

"Fairy tales..." Susan muttered to herself.

Karen just sighed at Susan's comment and continued beaming happily.

There was a crash as the front door flew open. Four castle guards and Sebastian walked into the room. "There she is!" Sebastian said, pointing to Karen. Two of the four guards seized her while the other two restrained her parents and sister.

"No!" screamed Karen. "What are you doing?! Get

your hands off of me!" She tried to get her hands free from their grasp but it was no use.

"Hello there, Karen," Sebastian said. He walked over to her and ran his fingers through her hair, plucking out the lilac Carter had placed there. "It is a pleasure to see you again. What a beautiful flower." He walked over to the fireplace and threw it among the flames.

"What do you want, Sebastian?" She asked.

"So hostile." He continued to smile. "I love it. Let us cut to the chase. Phillip has requested that you become his wife and I have come to fulfill that request."

"What?" Karen stopped struggling. Her eyes were wide as she couldn't believe what he was saying. "You lie! Phillip would never force me to do anything!"

"Take her away." He said and turned to walk out.

"Please!" screamed Eleanor, "You cannot do this!" She stood up and started towards the guards. "Leave her alone!" Sebastian slapped her across the face, knocking her to the floor. Eleanor looked up at him from the floor and held her throbbing cheek.

Karen tried to flail her arms, but it was no use. The men had a firm grip on her and started to drag her out of the house. Her legs were kicking violently in the air.

Karen's father ran to the corner of the room, grabbed his sword, and charged the soldiers. Sebastian drew his sword and in one quick movement thrust it into Karen's father. As the bloody blade was ripped out of him, Karen's father stepped back and fell to the floor as blood stained his tunic. Sebastian wiped the blood off his sword with one of Eleanor's curtains and put it back in his sheath.

"No!" screamed Karen, "Father!" She began to cry uncontrollably. "Father!"

Eleanor wailed and ran to her husband. "No! Peter!" she started to sob, "Please, don't die!" She tried to mop up the blood with her dress. "Please, stay with me! Please!" she screamed. "How could you!" She looked up at

Sebastian with her red, dismal face.

Peter lay on the floor and moaned as he tried to breathe. She tried to put pressure on the wound to stop the bleeding.

"Take her away!" Sebastian said to the guards as Karen was dragged out of the house. "You should have been wiser old man." Sebastian exited the house after the guards, leaving the rest of the Proudmoore family weeping behind him.

***

Sebastian dragged Karen into the throne room by her arm and threw her to the floor. Her hair was matted across her face and she stared at the red carpet beneath her. The image of her father lying on the floor, bleeding to death mortified her. She began shaking.

"Welcome my new Queen!" Phillip said.

"Answer him!" Sebastian said as he tugged on her hair.

"How could you—"she whispered. "How could you!?" She screamed as she got to her feet. She headed toward Phillip with her hands balled into fists. Her eyes were narrow with hatred as she screamed, "I hate you!"

Sebastian grabbed Karen by her neck and threw her to the floor. She tried to get up but he put his foot on her back. Every time she moved he put more pressure on her back.

"Stop!" Phillip said. "Let go of her!" He ran to Karen and Sebastian lifted his foot. Brushing the hair from her face, Phillip looked at her tear-stained cheeks and puffy red eyes.

She looked at him and slapped him across the face. He stood up and looked at her with a blank expression. Sebastian grabbed her by the hair and pulled her up. "How dare you touch your King!"

"It's not like you won't eventually kill him yourself!" she screamed.

He gripped her hair and smacked her across the face.

"You little tramp!" He threw her to the floor and kicked her.

"Sebastian!" Phillip yelled. "Don't touch her!"

"You are going to let her behave this way?" Sebastian asked.

Karen looked up and with trembling hands, wiped the blood from her face. She saw compassion on Phillip's face. "How could you do this to me?" She asked.

"I love you, Karen. I want to be with you."

"If you loved me, you would want me to be happy. Now my father is dead." She began weeping again.

"What do you mean?" Phillip looked at Sebastian. "What did you do Sebastian?"

"I was defending myself." Sebastian stated. "He came at me with a sword."

"You're a liar!" Karen screamed. "You murdered my father!"

"Karen, I had no idea. I know what it is like to lose my father. I am so sorry."

"Phillip," Sebastian said. "Talk with me." He ushered Phillip over toward the throne. He spoke softly. "Do not become weak. Do you not see that she is trying to manipulate you with her emotions? How can you rule when you are easily swayed? You said you wanted her and the people will respect you with a Queen at your side. Now I must urge you to give her a few days to let this sink in. I will lock her away while I go on my journey and when I return she should be ready and understanding of her new role as Queen. Do you understand? I do not wish you to do anything drastic with me absent."

"I understand. I just love her so much."

"She loves you but she needs time." Sebastian turned and yelled, "Guards!"

Two guards walked into the room and stopped, waiting for their orders. "Take Miss Proudmoore to her chambers and see to it that she does not leave." They both nodded and seized her.

"Phillip!" she screamed, "Please don't let him do this to me! Phillip!" She continued to scream as they dragged her out of the room. Phillip did not look at her once as she pleaded for him to help her.

CHAPTER EIGHT

To Be a Holy Warrior

This is going to be too easy, Carter thought. He watched Father Isaac intently as he stood just a few feet away with just a staff in hand. He didn't want to hurt the old man but at the same time he was being trained. "Are you sure you want go through with sparring against me?" Carter asked.

"You call yourself a Holy Warrior and you are afraid to take on an old man?" Isaac replied.

Carter charged at Isaac and swung his sword, which Isaac deflected with his staff. Carter was baffled that Father Isaac could move that fast. He watched as the old man showed no expression of success. Carter ran at Father Isaac once more with his sword and was going to attempt to disarm him. Instead, Father Isaac spun out of the way and knocked the back of Carter's calves with his staff, knocking him to the ground. The next thing Carter knew, he was on the ground and Isaac's staff was pinned against his chest.

"You shouldn't use brute strength alone, Carter," Isaac said, "You need to use your mind. Find where the opponent would be weakest and attack."

"What good are these muscles if I can't use them to my advantage?" Carter asked.

"You can do a lot of damage, Carter, but technique is what you need. You are smart enough Carter but it takes time and that is why I am here to help you. Creator won't take me now." Isaac laughed. "It looks like we have company."

Carter looked up and saw Eleanor come from the forest. She looked exhausted and tears stained her cheeks. She saw Carter lying on the ground and ran to him. She got down on her knees and grabbed his hand. "Please help me," she said.

"Eleanor what happened?" Carter asked. He had never seen Eleanor show the slightest emotion over anything since he had known her. Could something have happened to Karen?

"Peter—" she sobbed.

Carter sighed with relief when she didn't say Karen, but he was still worried.

"And... Karen." She said. Wiping her nose with her sleeve, she wrapped her arms around Carter.

"Let's go inside my dear," Isaac said. He put his hands on her shoulders and helped her up. He led her inside with Carter following behind. "Eliza!"

"Yes?" Eliza said as she emerged from the kitchen. "Is everything all right?"

"Please make some tea for Mrs. Proudmoore," he said, "Please have a seat." He pulled out a chair from the table. Eleanor sat down and put her face into her palms. "Take your time my dear."

Eleanor took a deep breath and looked at Carter, then at Isaac. "Karen was trying on her dress for the wedding when Sebastian barged in. He seized Karen and told us that the King had demanded that she become his Queen. When they tried to take her away, Peter tried to stop them and he..." she began to cry.

"Sebastian..." Carter said, "killed him?" Eleanor nodded. Carter shot up from his chair and pounded the table, causing Eleanor to jump slightly.

"Carter, don't go and do what I think you are planning," Isaac stated.

"He took Karen and killed her father!" Carter said. "I should have listened to her when she told me. I should have protected her. How do I kill Sebastian or Baelin? Whoever he is!"

"Carter, I warned you that this could happen and that you must not lose sight of your calling," Isaac said. "If you attempt to fight Sebastian and rescue Karen, you will die. One man cannot go against a whole fleet of guards. Sebastian is also in high standings with the King."

"Then I will kill the King!" Carter's fists were balled so tight that the veins in his arms were protruding.

"Sit down!" Isaac said.

Eliza walked into the room and looked at Carter first. She placed the tea in front of Eleanor and walked back into the kitchen. Eleanor picked up the tea and her hands trembled as she tried to take a sip.

"Careful dear," Isaac said, "You don't want to burn your tongue."

"I can't just sit and be idle while my love is taken to be another man's wife!" Carter didn't sit down but paced back and forth. *What can I do?* He thought.

"Carter—" Eleanor said, "Father Isaac is right. You can't attempt to rescue Karen. She would be heartbroken if anything happened to you on her behalf. Maybe no harm will come to her."

"How do we know?" Carter asked.

Eleanor shrugged her shoulders and looked down at her tea. Isaac just patted Eleanor's hands and looked at Carter with a stern expression. "You must obey the Creator first above all else. Even above your own desires."

"I can't think," Carter said. "I need to go out."

"Carter—" Eleanor said.

"Yes?" He replied.

"Promise me you won't do anything about this. At least for now."

How could she ask this of me? He thought. *Doesn't she*

want justice also? Is this part of my training? Do I really want to be a Holy Warrior? He stood there for a moment and looked down at the ground. When he looked into her eyes he couldn't say no. "I promise."

CHAPTER NINE

Sebastian's Plan

Karen stared out her window and saw the shadow of a rider returning to the castle. She knew it could only be Sebastian because she had been trapped in the tower for days and no one had attempted to see her except the maid with provisions and to change the urn given to her.

She looked around her prison and it was an elegant room. A beautiful armoire in the corner of the room was where she had placed her wedding dress that her father had made. She dared not look at it for fear of losing herself to another breakdown.

She made her way over to the beautiful vanity table and grabbed the gem-studded brush and began to brush her hair with long strokes. She admired how beautiful she was with her outfit but knew they were only gifts from Phillip to attempt to woo her. She had already decided she would refuse to marry Phillip because she didn't love him.

As Karen continued to brush her hair, Sebastian entered the room. She made eye contact with him through the mirror and she couldn't breathe as cold chills ran down her spine. She averted her eyes to the table where the perfumes and powders were neatly organized. A vase filled with lilacs sat next to them. She heard the footsteps come closer.

"My, my," Sebastian said. "You are breathtaking. You

will make a fine Queen." He took some of her hair and ran his fingers through it, dropping strand by strand. "Well, it looks as if someone is speechless in my presence. Will you not say something pleasant?"

Karen continued to brush her hair and avoid looking at him. "I have nothing to say to you." she said. She attempted to get up but Sebastian grabbed her wrist and squeezed. She fell to the floor and cringed in pain.

"You will speak when I speak to you!" Sebastian said.

"You're hurting me!" Karen said as she tried to fight the pain.

Sebastian pulled Karen up by the wrist and threw her against the wall. She looked up at him as he walked toward her again. She held her hands up and closed her eyes, thinking that he was going to hit or kick her. He knelt down and began stroking her hair. "As long as you co-operate my pet, no harm will come to you." he said.

"Why are you doing this?" She couldn't look at him but kept her eyes closed.

"You serve a purpose in my plan."

"What do you want from me?"

"Your virginity."

Karen opened her eyes and looked at him. She wanted to get up and run but fear paralyzed her. *This cannot be happening to me,* she thought. Sebastian's face had a sinister smile on it. "Please don't do this." Her voice was almost inaudible.

"I could make you my Queen once I control the world."

"I don't want any part in your world. The Creator is always victorious."

"Ah, another delusional servant of the great Creator. I will break your will and you will be hopeless with no one to love. One by one I will kill everything you love until you have nothing left to live for."

Karen's felt the blood rush down her body as her heart sank into the pit of her stomach. She felt sick with the thought of Sebastian killing everyone she loved. She wanted to cry but she couldn't in front of Sebastian. She had to stay strong and not let him get to her. But how could she warn her family?

"Now," Sebastian said, "what should be my reason to have your family executed?" He stood up and walked toward the window. "I have just the thing my pet. I will tell Phillip that your mother has been keeping the traitor Mianya within her home."

"Phillip would never believe you!" Karen said.

"Dear Karen," Sebastian said, "do you not see that I control Phillip?"

Karen wished she had acted sooner but what could she have done to stop Sebastian. She was sitting in front of a powerful ancient demon, who could kill her instantly if he wanted. She watched as Sebastian walked out of the room, leaving her alone and helpless in the room. The door shut and the latch echoed in her mind, crushing all hope of saving her mother and siblings.

A tap caught Karen's attention to the window. There was a white dove fluttering outside the window and it looked like it wanted to get in. *Maybe this dove will help me*, Karen thought. *But that's crazy. It's just a bird but what other options do I have.*

Karen got up and opened the window. The dove flew in and perched upon the frame of the mirror of the vanity table. She found a quill and parchment in the drawer and began writing furiously. She rolled up the parchment and put it in front of the bird. It reached out, taking the letter in its beak, and flew out of the window.

Karen ran to the window to watch it fly down toward the town. *How strange*, she thought. *It's like the bird knew I needed help.* In the distance there were thunder clouds flashing with lightning. Karen could only hope for her family's escape.

CHAPTER TEN

Escape

"Momma! Look!" Marie said, pointing to the window. The dove was fluttering against the window. "It has something in its mouth."

"What are you talking about Marie?" Eleanor asked. She walked over from the fireplace to get a closer look, and saw that the dove indeed had something. When she opened the window, it flew inside and dropped the letter on the table and flew out. Eleanor closed the window and latched it.

"How strange," Susan said, "I wonder who sent it."

Adam walked over to the table and picked up the parchment. He unrolled it and his eyes scanned the page. "Mother," he said. "You want to read this. It's from Karen."

Eleanor took the letter and when she read it, she dropped it. She looked out the window and scanned the street. No one was in the street. She turned to Adam and Susan, trembling. "We must go quickly!" she said, "Where is Thomas?"

"In the other room," Susan said. "Why?"

"Adam, go get Thomas!"

Adam ran into the other room and Thomas followed after. Eleanor began snuffing out the candles. "Adam and

Susan, take your brother and sister outside."

"What is happening?" Susan asked.

Eleanor ran and cupped her face and said, "Just trust me. We need to leave this instant! Now take your sister outside!"

"Penelope!" Marie screamed.

Susan ran into the bedroom and came out with a doll. She handed it to Marie and picked her up, following after Adam and Thomas.

Dark clouds covered the night sky as the Proudmoores used the cover of darkness to escape the city. Eleanor saw only one guard at the gate and he was talking to one of the barmaids before her shift. She waited in the shadows with her hand over Marie's mouth. All she could hear was their breathing. At the opportune time, they swiftly escaped before the allotted time that the gate be locked that night.

It began to thunder as the rain came down. The Proudmoores made their way through the farmland outside the walls of Firestone. Avoiding the roads, they went directly east, over Faerie Hill. The rain poured down as they made their way up the slippery and muddy terrain.

Marie was walking and slipped in the mud, dropping her doll. Susan picked Marie up and they continued up the slope. When they reached the top, they could see their home was on fire in the distance but was going out from the rain.

They finally reached the edge of the forest and the wind was blowing the branches of the trees violently. They could hear among all the noise the faint sound of the city bells being rung. Eleanor made out the shadows of men on horses riding up the great hill.

"We must hurry! They know we have gone!" Eleanor said.

Through the trees they could finally see the light of the monastery. Safety was just in arms reach when Eleanor looked around and noticed that Thomas was missing.

"Where is Thomas?" she said. Both Adam and Susan looked at her and then at each other. "Take Marie!"

As the three children headed toward the monastery, Eleanor headed west to search for Thomas. She heard a scream in the distance and began running toward the sound. She fell short of the clearing and hid behind a fallen tree trunk. She saw four men as well as Sebastian.

"Please!" Thomas screamed, "Let me go!"

"Where are they?" Sebastian asked.

"I don't know! Please let me go!"

Sebastian smacked Thomas across the face. Eleanor's heart sank. *Go save your son*, she thought. She saw Sebastian and she froze. No muscle in her body would move.

"Very well," Sebastian said, "we shall take him to the dungeon. I have plans for him." Sebastian looked east in the direction of the monastery. "Tomorrow we will search the monastery."

Eleanor watched them as they took Thomas and rode away back to Firestone. "No…" she said. On her hands and knees she crawled to the spot where Thomas was. They had stripped his tunic from him. She grasped the tunic in her bosom and went into fetal position, letting the rain fall on her. She had abandoned her son.

She thought that she had been lying there for hours when a gentle hand touched her. She looked up and saw Carter standing above her. "Eleanor," he said, "I am so glad I found you." She stared up at his face and found peace in his calm gentle expression.

"They…,"she said, "they took Thomas."

Carter helped her up and walked her back to the monastery. She was soaked and covered in mud. As they entered the threshold of the monastery, Eliza was there with a blanket. She walked over and wrapped it around Eleanor and led her into the kitchen. "Let's get you a nice hot bath," Eliza said.

"Father," Carter said to Isaac, "She said that they captured Thomas. Why is Sebastian doing all of this?"

"One can only guess for now Carter," Isaac said. "I do believe that if you seek answers, it is best to look for the one who knows him best."

"And who is that?"

"The one that used to serve him, Mianya."

"You mean the Elf Princess? The one that Karen was obsessing about?"

"Correct."

Eliza entered the room. "She is taking a bath and I will take her to her bed," Eliza said, "She mentioned that Sebastian was coming here tomorrow."

"We must use the hidden rooms," Isaac said, "There the Proudmoores and Carter can hide."

"Why do I need to hide?" Carter asked.

"Sebastian knows that you were to be married to Karen. He must have a reason that he is trying to get her family. You're destined to do great things and we must keep you safe."

"I can fight him!" Carter said.

"You have much to learn. Part of your commitment as a Holy Warrior is obeying my requests."

"Very well."

***

Carter peered through the tiny hole that gave access to the Narthex. He saw the door open as Sebastian stood there with his guards. "Search the place," Sebastian said. The guards went from room to room, turning over tables and searching anything that could conceal a person.

Carter looked back at the Proudmoore family huddled in a corner. Eleanor had Marie in her arms while Adam and Susan sat on either side of her. There were two monks in the room with them as requested by Isaac.

"Where are the Proudmoores?" Sebastian asked.

"This is a holy place," Isaac replied.

Sebastian grabbed Isaac by the collar. "If you have been hiding them," Sebastian said, "I will kill you and everyone in this place." He threw Isaac to the floor.

"Stop," Eliza said, "You have no right to come in here."

Sebastian walked over to Eliza and smacked her across the face. She fell and looked up at Sebastian. Isaac walked over and helped Eliza up. "Now, you have no right to hurt a lady! We want no trouble from you," Isaac said.

A guard emerged from one of the back rooms. "My Lord, there is no one," he said.

Sebastian drew his sword and stuck it into Father Isaac. As he pushed the blade further in, he said, "You have crossed me for the last time old man." Eliza screamed as Sebastian pulled out the sword from Isaac's body.

Carter turned and headed toward the door. The monks in the building stood in his way. "Move," Carter whispered.

"I am sorry, but Father Isaac gave us specific orders," the monk said.

Eliza took her hand and put it over the wound on Father Isaac's stomach. Sebastian walked toward the door. "Mark my words that I will be back," Sebastian said, "and next time this place will burn to the ground." Sebastian exited followed by his men.

Carter ran into the room. He had his sword in hand and ran toward the door. "Carter, you can't!" Eliza screamed, "Please help me!"

"Carter..." Isaac said.

Carter stopped and turned around. The sword dropped from his hand as he walked over to Father Isaac. He took up the frail old man's hand. "Please don't go."

"You will still be trained...," Isaac said, grunting as he attempted to move. His breathing was getting softer. "I was just the vessel..."

"Father, try not to move." Carter said.

"The Creator will train you…." He took his hand and pointed to the ceiling. "Look to him…. for guidance…." His hand dropped and his cold dead eyes stared into Carter's.

"No!" Carter said. He put his face in his bloody hands and wept.

CHAPTER ELEVEN

Hostage

Karen looked at herself in the mirror as the maid began tightening the corset. She looked down at her hand and observed the diamond that complimented her delicate hands. Phillip's mother's ring really did look lovely but she wished she wasn't forced to marry him. Suddenly she could not breathe as the corset was being pulled tighter to her waist. "Is that too tight, my lady?" the maid asked.

"A… little…" Karen breathed out. She could feel the veins in her face tighten as the blood was being constricted.

"You will look lovely in this dress. The king had the best seamstress in the land make it special for you."

In the corner of the room was mounted a beautiful white wedding dress. The train was long and elegant with diamonds sewn into the delicate fabric. The diamonds sparkled brilliantly as the rays of the sun coming from the window hit them.

Karen started to tear up as she wished and hoped that this day would never come. Thoughts of Carter flooded her mind. She wished that he would come save her and protect her purity. Her dignity would soon be stripped away and she would never feel the touch of Carter's warm lips against hers. "Why…" she whispered to herself.

"Something the matter, my lady?" asked the maid with

concern.

"Oh, I am fine. I am just besieged at all of this."

"I completely agree. It is so wonderful to be young and in love. You will make a beautiful queen."

"Queen..." she repeated to herself. The very idea still seemed very foreign to her.

A light breeze blew through the window and brought the sweet scent of lilacs to Karen's nostrils. She inhaled deeply and then let out a sigh as she remembered how she had happiness once upon a time. This comfort quickly left her as the smell left the room. Everything that had happened in the past few months seemed like a nightmare to her. There was still a small ray of hope that gave her peace.

"I will be back shortly. Do not move," the maid said as she made her exit.

Sebastian walked through the door as the maid left and grinned. Karen saw him and she felt like someone had tightened the corset more but no one was near her. He walked swiftly across the room and came up behind her. He ran his fingers through her hair and whispered, "You will make a lovely queen." Her fear petrified her as she stared straight ahead. "You will be mine when I have no more use for Phillip."

"You're mad!" She spoke boldly when he threatened Phillip. She knew that Sebastian would hurt Phillip and she feared for that day. "How could you do this to Phillip?"

Sebastian grabbed her and threw her to the floor and said, "I am no friend to Phillip, that was Sebastian but now his body is mine." Sebastian pulled out the parchment that Karen had sent her family. "I do not know how you managed to pull off this little stunt but your attempt has been in vain."

Karen turned white as she looked at him. He looked so arrogant but she had no way to know if he was lying or not. "You will still never win!" she said.

"I think that I will," he said. He walked toward the door. "Put on a smile now, my Queen. This is your time to shine."

"I found them. The king's mother loved these combs," the maid said as she entered the room with two diamond studded golden combs. She saw Karen on the floor with tears in her eyes. She dropped the combs and ran to Karen to help her up. "My lady! Are you all right?"

"Yes, yes, I am fine," Karen replied. "I just fell over. These corsets bind my ribs too tight and I got light-headed."

"I am sure we could loosen them some more."

The maid loosened the corset and helped Karen put on her dress. She started doing Karen's hair and gently placed the golden combs in her hair. "You look lovely, my dear," the maid said as she pulled out a handkerchief and dabbed at her own wet eyes. As time got closer to the hour, Karen began to tremble. She felt like her heart was protruding from her chest.

The maid grabbed Karen's hand and led her out of the room. Carefully she walked down the stone steps as the train of her dress followed behind her. Once inside the main hall, Karen approached the large wooden doors and wished she could turn and run. She forced a pleasant smile, knowing there was no turning back now.

The doors opened and she walked with even steps toward the spot where Phillip was standing. He smiled as Karen stood beside him. The elderly man, standing right in front of them, began to speak, "Hail those who are in attendance on this happy occasion. We are gathered here to join this man and this woman in holy matrimony." The man looked at Sebastian. His lip quivered as he stopped for a second from his speech. "Do you take Karen as your Queen, my King?"

"I do." Phillip said.

The old man turned to Karen and said, "And you, my

lady?"

Karen's thoughts raced through her mind. She hesitated as Carter's face penetrated her mind. She wanted to run and find her true beloved. She thought of his muscular arms embracing her and protecting her from everything. She was fearful and thought that love was never this complicated. She then thought of Phillip and how Sebastian planned to hurt him if she didn't cooperate. She wanted to warn Phillip of his clueless state, but Sebastian was too manipulative.

"My lady?" the man repeated as he glanced at Sebastian and then shifted his eyes back to her. Beads of sweat were forming on the man's brow.

"I..." she said as she looked back at Sebastian standing in the back of the room glaring at Karen. She quickly looked forward and choked out the words, "I do..."

"You may kiss the bride." The man let out a quiet sigh as he looked at Sebastian once more.

Karen closed her eyes firmly to hold back the tears that were beginning to form. Phillip's shaking lips met Karen's and quickly left them. It was dry and cold. Phillip's kiss could not compare with Carter's.

"I am so happy," Phillip whispered in her ear.

Karen bit her lip and nodded with her eyes still tightly closed.

***

Karen walked into the bedroom, which was covered with lilacs, but the sight and smell of them didn't bring her comfort this time. Standing near the gold-draped bed was Phillip. He twiddled his thumbs nervously as he looked at his new bride. Dressed in her nightgown, she slowly walked over to the bed and tried to avoid eye contact. She knew what Phillip wanted and it made her sick to her stomach. They both slipped into the covers and Phillip glanced over at her.

He laid his hand on her knee and leaned over to her. She felt violated. He slowly brought his face closer to hers and began to kiss her gentle lips. The longer he did this the more confident he became. Tears coursed down Karen's face as she felt him get more confident. "Please…" she whispered through her closed lips that were occupied by Phillip's.

Phillip backed away and looked at her teary blue eyes. He asked, "Are you all right?"

"Please…" she replied. "I am so weary…"

Phillip did nothing more but stare at Karen. She desperately hoped for the best and laid her head on the pillow. Closing her eyes, she could sense his eyes watching her. Her unstable emotions exhausted her and her mind became very calm. She thought of Carter holding her gently in his arms and drifted off into pleasant memories.

Phillip leaned over, gently caressed her cheek, and said, "Sleep well, my love."

Karen woke up the next morning with the bed to herself. Staring at the ceiling, she wondered how she got out of that situation. She remembered that Sebastian had told her that he needed her virginity. She vowed that she would remain a virgin for the rest of her life if Carter did not save her. *He will and must save me*, she thought. She would kill herself before she would let Sebastian use her.

Karen got out of bed and walked to the window. She looked at the beautiful clear day and began humming. She gracefully walked over to her vanity table and began brushing her hair with long strokes. She changed into a baby blue dress and walked out to the castle garden.

Karen walked to the pond and watched the swans gracefully glide across the water. The lush, green grass welcomed her as she gently lay upon it. She had a book full of Carter's deepest affection. Her mother managed to smuggle it to her before she was forced to flee for her life. She flipped through the pages and sighed as she read the words written.

Suddenly she heard barking and Karen looked back to see Phillip's dog running towards her. The dog pounced on Karen and began licking her frantically. Karen giggled and said, "It is good to see you as well Mitzi."

Karen was playing fetch when Mitzi stopped and looked toward the castle and began to growl. Sebastian appeared from the castle and approached Karen. Mitzi began barking frantically at Sebastian. Sebastian glared at her and growled angrily, sending Mitzi running away in fear.

"Stupid mutt," Sebastian said as he looked at Karen's innocent face. "How are you, my queen?"

Karen sat silently and stared at the ground. She did not want to talk to him and wished that he would leave her.

"Answer me when I address you!" Sebastian said.

"I am staying pure," she said, "What more do you want from me?"

"What is this?" Sebastian picked up the book full of Carter's sweet words to Karen. "My, my. This is a very affectionate book you have here." With a flick of his wrist he threw it in the water.

She watched as the book began sinking and knew that those words were now lost forever, even if she were to somehow retrieve it later. She wanted to run but there was nowhere to run. All she had now was the hope that the light gave her and the memories.

"I wish you to come with me."

Karen followed Sebastian into the castle and they arrived at a door she had never seen before. He opened it and a musty smell crept into her nostrils. She wanted to throw up. She followed him down a set of stairs and into a dark room with faint lighting. Karen realized that she must be in the dungeon, but why?

As Karen walked past the cells of the other prisoners, the men in them called out to her. "Save us! Please have mercy on us!" Karen could not bear to be down here. All her pleasantness and joy felt like it was stripped away in a moment of time. At the end of the dark hall was a man guarding a door. As Sebastian approached, the guards quickly unlocked the door. Karen followed Sebastian through the threshold and found herself in the presence of her youngest brother.

Chained to the wall was Thomas. He was lying on the floor in a ball and across his arms were burn marks. With sad eyes, Thomas looked up slowly to see who had come into the room. Karen darted forward and caught up Thomas in her arms and they began to weep. "Thomas! Oh, Thomas!" she cried. She wanted to protect him from anything that Sebastian could do to him.

"Karen..." Thomas replied. He started to cry as he latched onto his older sister.

"What have they done to you?" Karen asked

"Please make them stop... I am frightened."

Sebastian walked forward to pull Karen back. He grabbed a handful of her hair and began dragging her backwards. With arms stretched out, Thomas cried out, "Karen! Please!" Karen laid there on the floor with dirt and water staining her dress. She wanted to take care of her brother and hated what Sebastian was doing.

Sebastian snapped his fingers and a large man came in with a metal rod that was red hot at the tip. "No, No! Please!" Thomas cried as the man approached him. Thomas squirmed to get away from the large man but he knew it was no use. "Tell me—where did your family go?" Sebastian ordered.

"I have no idea..." Thomas replied.

"Wrong answer!"

The large man lifted and placed the red hot metal against his skin. Thomas screamed and flailed his body as his flesh was burned.

"Thomas!" Karen screamed as she tried to run forward

and stop the man, but Sebastian had a firm grasp on her. "Please stop hurting him!" Karen wanted to embrace her brother, to protect him. Anger and sorrow flooded her mind. She saw no hope in this place. This place was full of torture and death and she couldn't bear it.

Sebastian was keeping his hold on her back and watched her as she struggled to get loose. The man took the metal away from Thomas's skin and left the room. Exhausted from her struggling, Karen fell to the floor and placed her face on the cold, hard stones. She wept because she could not reach her brother in time. She could hear his groaning and tears.

Another man walked into the room and said, "Lord Sebastian."

"What information do you have?" he replied.

"There is still no sign of the other Proudmoores or even Carter Lockwood."

Karen feared for the rest of her family when she heard these words.

"Send men to watch the monastery intently. Kill anyone who is protecting them."

"Yes, my lord." The guard left.

Karen heard Sebastian growl, "Mianya..." He turned to Karen and picked her up by the arm. "I love you, Thomas!" She called to him, "Stay strong!" Sebastian escorted Karen out of the prison and told the guards to take her out of this place and ordered that she not be allowed to visit her brother under any circumstances.

Sebastian turned to look at Thomas sprawled out on the floor. He walked over and knelt down. Grabbing a handful of hair, Sebastian forced Thomas to look him in the face. "Your will is strong. It will benefit me greatly." He let go of Thomas and walked out of the prison.

***

Karen looked out her window and saw Sebastian ride off. She was not sure what he was up to but knew it must be evil. A great peace fell upon her in his absence. She felt as if shackles had been removed from her hands and feet. One thing still weighed heavily on her, though. She needed to care for her brother, but did not know how to slip past the guards.

Karen thought of two ideas. She debated with herself whether it would be better to seduce a guard or Phillip. She knew seducing Phillip could lead to something she would regret. The guards, however, would not be able to do anything to her without showing dishonor to the king.

Karen dressed into a fitting purple dress and went to brush her hair. She soon gave up after barely brushing it without hurting her tender scalp. She pulled out a glass perfume bottle and sprayed herself with the scent of lilacs. She looked herself over to make sure she had made herself presentable. "Thomas, I am coming for you," she said to herself. Phillip walked into the room and stopped to look at Karen.

"You look breathtaking, my Queen."

"Thank you," she replied as she got up from the chair to leave. She started to walk past him, but he grabbed her arm.

"What is it, Phillip?" she asked.

"I want to know you better. We are married now, but you seem so distant."

"Phillip, can we please talk about this later?"

"No. You are my wife and you will submit to me."

Karen stopped and stood motionless. She was at a loss for words and could only think of the physical pain Sebastian would inflict on her later. She closed her eyes and nodded slowly. Phillip gently placed his hands on the small of her back and put his face to her tender skin. "You smell amazing," he said as he started to kiss her passionately.

Karen refused to return the kiss and tried to make

Phillip uncomfortable. She made no movement and began to cry again. She felt violated and wanted to hide herself from the world. She wished that something would give Phillip reason to stop.

"Why won't you love me, Karen?" he asked.

"I cannot love someone who doesn't love me."

"But I do love you. How could you say something like that?" He got up and looked into her eyes.

"My father. My family. My life." She said, "All of it stripped from me!"

"This is your new and better life. I can give you anything you desire."

"I never wanted to give up my old life! You took my life from me! You would never do that to someone you loved! Your father and mother would be ashamed!"

"How dare you speak to me about my parents! Get out of my sight!"

"Phillip, this isn't you! Sebastian is brainwashing you!"

"Enough! Leave my sight! Sebastian is right; emotions do make me weak."

Karen was shocked. Quickly she seized her moment of freedom and escaped through the door. Behind her she heard the sound of glass breaking as she walked down the hallway. She bowed her head. "Phillip… my friend… please reason." Now she could hear weeping coming from the room. She wanted to go back inside and comfort Phillip, but she could not lead him on. She reverted to her original plan and continued on her way to the dungeon.

Upon arriving at the dungeon, she took a deep breath and opened the door. She gagged as the musty smell clouded the air, and pulled out her handkerchief to cover her nose and mouth. She walked forward through the men reaching out to her and calling for help.

The faces of the men were filled with sorrow and pain. She thought of how many lives Sebastian had destroyed. She wanted to free these men but had no way to do it.

"Karen! Please, Karen!" called out a familiar voice.

"Jaseph?" Karen asked as she looked at the ragged, dirty man standing behind the bars of the nearest cell. He was one of Phillip's friends before he met Sebastian.

"Please convince Phillip to free me. He has already had Garret and Braden murdered."

"Why are you captured?"

"I feel that it is an act of revenge for how we treated Phillip. We were young and immature, and now my actions have come back to haunt me." Jaseph began to sob.

"I am sorry he has done this, Jaseph. Sadly, I am a prisoner myself. Sebastian is the cause behind Phillip's actions. Forgive Phillip. He does not see reality clearly anymore. I know personally that Phillip admired you three. He was gentle and kind once."

"I do not—"

"Think about it for a while. I know you have a heart to forgive. I must hurry and tend to my brother. I am sorry. If I can, I will try to come down more often."

"Thank you." Jaseph held out his hand. Karen's gentle hands grabbed it and she kissed it softly. She walked towards Thomas' cell.

The guard in front of Thomas's cell saw Karen and looked perplexed. "What are you doing here, my lady?" he asked.

"I have come to see my brother."

"I am not permitted to let you enter. I am sorry, but you must leave now."

"Oh, but I have also come to see you. You are such a strong man," she said as she batted her eyelashes. She hated what she was doing, but she had to see her brother.

She moved delicately over to the guard and stroked his cheek. She let her hand lay on his face and looked deeply into his eyes. "Won't you let me have a moment with my brother?" she asked.

"Well…" he replied, looking around.

"I assure you that Sebastian would never find out."

"I am not too sure about this, my lady."

She leaned forward and began to kiss him passionately. He said nothing when she removed her lips from his. He looked at her face, took out his key, and unlocked the door. Karen hugged him. "Thank you so much!" After the guard turned around, she wiped her mouth in disgust.

She walked lightly inside the cell. "Thomas!" she called. Thomas beamed when he saw Karen alone. Karen ran to him and embraced him. He winced as she touched his tender burn marks. "Sorry," she said.

"How did you get here?" Thomas asked her.

"I found a way," she said.

"Oh, I am so happy to see you."

"How are you doing?"

"I'm cold and hungry." His voice began to shake. "I hope mother and everyone are safe from him."

"I love you so much. Do not fear. I am sure mother and the others are fine and safe. Carter should be with them now and he won't let anything happen to any of them."

"Is he going to kill me?"

"I will not let anything happen to you. You have my word. I would die to protect you."

"What does he want from me, then?"

"I don't know. All I know is that he wants me. You are just being used to make me miserable."

"I love you so much, Karen." Thomas began crying as Karen cuddled him and stroked his head.

"I love you, too, Thomas. I will try to get a blanket down here and some fresh bread and water."

"What is this?" said Phillip's voice from behind them.

Karen looked back, surprised to see Phillip standing in the doorway. She got up and walked over to Phillip to plead with him. "Please let Thomas have some food and a warm blanket."

"She seduced me, my King," the guard interjected and

quickly looked away from Karen, his eyes darting nervously.

"Shut up!" Phillip said. "Why don't you obey when Sebastian is absent? Guards!" Two men walked into the room and grabbed Karen up by the arms. "Take her and lock her in her old room and if any of you touch her the way this fool did, I will have Sebastian deal with you."

As they dragged Karen out of the room, she looked back at Thomas and cried out, "I love you!" Phillip looked at Thomas and then exited. The door slammed shut, and Thomas was again alone in the dark, cold prison.

CHAPTER TWELVE

Unicorns

Carter knocked once on the door and heard no reply. He cracked the door opened and saw Eleanor, lying in bed. "I brought some food for you," he said. He walked over and set down a tray with fresh hot eggs and warm bread. Eleanor didn't look at him or even move an inch as she stared up toward the window. "Please, eat something."

Her eyes averted from the window toward Carter. Her lips were dry and chapped. "I…" she said.

"Your children need you," Carter said, sitting on the edge of the bed. "You need to regain your strength."

"I have already failed them," Eleanor said.

"No you haven't!" Carter stood up. "Marie has been asking to see you all day."

"I just laid there and watched them take my son away." She looked toward the window again. "He is as good as dead."

"There is always hope but don't let fear and regret hold you down. Think about your children."

"I can't. I need to leave."

"Please think, Eleanor!"

She sat up and looked into his eyes. "I cannot protect my children! I will leave in the morning. You must keep them safe. I need some time to think."

Carter ran his hands through his hair and walked around the room. Carter walked toward the door and turned his head to look at her. "What would I tell them if you leave?"

"Think of something." She looked back toward the window as Carter slammed the door closed behind him.

***

Carter woke up to a door being opened and then shut. He sat up and looked outside as the full moon brightened the sky. He then heard soft footsteps walking down the hall. They sounded too small for a grown woman.

Walking outside, he saw Eleanor, covered in a cloak, standing with Marie. Her face looked solemn as she stared at her child's face.

"Momma," Marie said, "where are you going?"

"Go inside Marie."

"Take me with you, Momma!" Marie walked over to Eleanor and hugged her leg. Tears were streaming down her cheeks now.

Eleanor looked up and saw Carter standing just a few feet away. She pulled Marie off her leg and stood there, looking at Carter. "I can't, I'm sorry," Eleanor said.

"No!" Marie screamed, "Take me with you!"

Carter walked over and knelt down beside Marie and wrapped his arms around her body. He could feel her heart beating fast as her muscles tensed against his touch. Eleanor looked down at him and turned north toward the forest. "Be good my child," Eleanor said as she walked into the shadow of the trees.

"Momma!" Marie screamed as she wrestled in Carter's strong arms. After one minute her body became limp and she laid her head against Carter's chest.

"I'm sorry Marie," Carter said. Picking her up into his arms, he walked towards the monastery and when inside, placed her in her bed. He knelt beside her bed and began stroking her hair. He began to whisper so to not wake up the twins. "Your mother loves you very much." He said, "She just needed to go away for a while but she will be back."

Marie breathed in short breaths after crying, with her chest rising and falling violently. "And I love you too Marie," Carter said, trying not to cry. "You are so innocent and sweet just like your older sister. I will protect you with my life."

Once inside, Marie curled up into a ball and wrapped the covers tightly around her small body as she turned to face the wall. Carter continued to run his hand through her hair until she fell asleep.

***

Carter was sitting on his bed, reading one of Father Isaac's books from his study, when Adam threw open the door and stomped toward Carter. His jaw was flexed and his hands in fists as he pushed into Carter and attempted to punch him. "How could you!" Adam said.

Carter put the book down and stood up, grabbing Adam's flailing arms. Susan had run into the room. "Adam! Stop!" she said.

"No!" Adam said. "He let mother go and now Marie won't talk! You should have warned us!"

"Mother probably had a good reason for leaving us with Carter," Susan said as she looked at Carter.

Carter picked up Adam and pinned him against the wall until he stopped trying to move. "I'm sorry," Carter said, "Your mother didn't give me a reason for leaving. But I assured her that I would keep you three safe."

Adam spit at Carter when he was released and ran out of the room. Susan started after Adam and then stopped in the threshold of the doorway. She turned around and said, "It's all right Carter. We trust you and thank you for keeping us safe." She ran out of the room.

It was dusk when the children came into the kitchen. Carter was sitting at a table as Eliza was pulling fresh bread from the oven. It had the aroma of garlic and salt. Adam saw Carter and stopped, glaring at him.

"Carter!" a monk said. He ran into the kitchen and panted. "There was a strange flash outside! I do not know if it is Sebastian!"

The monk led the children to the secret room and Carter walked into the other room to look out the window. He saw nothing among the forest. Out of the thickets the head of a white horse appeared with a silver horn upon its head. Carter was in shock seeing that a Unicorn stood before his eyes. A few dozen flashes filled the air but the Unicorn was not startled.

"Strange," Carter said. He ran through the secret door and motioned for the Proudmoore children.

He led them outside and then held out his arm to stop them from stepping any closer. There were now five Unicorns grazing in the distance.

"Are those…?" Susan asked.

"Yes," Carter said, "Unicorns."

"I have read about them," Susan said, her eyes glazed over. Her heart was beating fast and she took one step closer. The Unicorns lifted their heads and stared. "I thought that they were encased in crystals by Baelin."

"Are you serious?" Adam said, "Someone probably put those horns on horses. You know that no one in their right mind believes in those stories."

"It's history!" Susan said. "It is as real as you and I are standing here."

"Father just told us those stories to give us some comfort at night." Adam said.

"No he didn't!" Susan replied. "Are you saying that Father lied to us? I know he believed in the Creator. Carter?" She looked at Carter.

"What does he know?" Adam said as he turned toward the monastery. "He is as foolish as dad was! And now look where father is! Dead!"

"Adam!" Susan shrieked. "How could you?" By then Adam was already walking toward the monastery.

"Forgive him Susan," Carter said, "I believe he is still grieving over many losses."

Susan looked at him with red, puffy eyes and smiled. "Thank you," she said.

***

"Carter," said a monk. "Your brother has urgent news."

Carter made his way to the Narthex where Christian was waiting. He was draped in a dark hood covering his face.

"What brings you here Christian?" Carter asked.

"A scout spotted you and the Proudmoore children in the forest yesterday," Christian said, "He has already made his way to Phoenix Castle. You must flee over the mountain to Kakaran before Sebastian's men seize you."

"What about the monastery?"

"The monks will be fine. I will tell them what to say and then find a safe place to hide."

"Surely Sebastian will have the place burned."

"Then I suggest you make yourselves known for fleeing and create a false trail."

CHAPTER THIRTEEN

Death Mountain

The Proudmoores were waiting out front of the monastery as Carter headed for the door. "I am coming with you." Eliza said.

"Eliza, what are you doing?" Carter said, holding his hand up to stop her. "You can't come with us. They need you here and if Eleanor returns she needs to know that her children are safe."

"I told you already. I will follow you anywhere," she said.

"Eliza, I thought that I made myself clear when I told you I was to marry Karen."

"But," she said, as she fiddled with a ring on her finger. "I love you."

"No you don't," Carter replied, "You can't because it will never be. If you do care about me like you say, please let me go and do not follow me."

He put his hood over his head and walked outside. The four of them headed east into the forest. Carter headed north for about a mile to set down a fire, hoping to lure the soldiers north and then met back with the children to continue east.

It was dark in the heart of the forest with the tall trees towering over them. They eventually grew tired and slowed their pace. Marie slouched and panted. "Can we stop yet?" she asked.

"Where are you taking us?" Adam asked.

"You have been really quiet this whole time Carter," Susan interjected.

Carter stopped walking, turned around, and said, "Far away from Sebastian." He knew his priority was to keep the Proudmoores safe.

"That's a wonderful idea," Adam said, clapping his hands together and then rolled his eyes.

"I have had enough of your attitude, Adam." Carter said.

"I'm not so fond of you myself."

"Adam, grow up," Susan said. "I am sure Carter knows exactly what he is doing."

"Really now? If he loved Karen so much why didn't he rescue her? Why didn't he stop mother from leaving? He is pathetic."

"Adam, what are you saying?" Susan said. "Mother knows what is best for her. As for Karen, would you love knowing that she is safe and happy because she knows we are alive, or would prefer she be safe and miserable because she knows we are all dead?" Susan responded.

Adam crossed his arms and wrinkled his brow. He sat down on the forest floor and leaned against a tree.

"We should find a place to rest," Carter said.

"Finally!" Marie said.

"We cannot make a fire and draw attention to ourselves. I have brought blankets and we will keep each other warm. That hollow tree should be a good place to rest. It will allow us to be out of sight from anyone who can hurt us." Carter walked over to the tree and began pulling three wool blankets from his bag.

"I am not sharing the same tree with him!" Adam said. "I'll sleep over here." Adam walked over to a collection of bushes, crawled inside, and fell asleep.

They covered themselves with the blankets and fell asleep quickly in spite of the ground being cold and hard. Carter woke up during the night. He took his extra blanket and went to the bushes where Adam was, and gently laid the blanket over Adam. He walked back to the hollow tree and fell back asleep.

***

Susan woke up the next morning and looked up at rays of light shining through the green canopy overshadowing the forest floor. She looked at Marie, who was asleep, and the empty blanket where Carter had slept. Her stomach began to growl, so she got up and looked through the sack that Carter had brought along. She found a delicious looking apple and grabbed it. She stood up and, taking a bite of the apple, proceeded through the trees. She soon found Carter walking towards her. "Good morning," she said.

"Good morning, Susan!" he replied.

"Is there anything to eat?" Susan asked.

"I saw a few rabbits, but I think it best not to cook anything until we have reached the base of the mountain." Carter walked with Susan back to where Adam and Marie were. They were eating the other two apples Carter had packed. "We should head out again," he said.

It was early in the evening as they arrived at the base of Death Mountain. "Are we going to climb that?" Marie said as she looked up at the high cliffs.

"No, not here," Carter replied. "There is a safer path somewhere south of here."

They walked south and the smell of roasting chicken permeated in the air. Carter stopped and squinted through the trees. He saw a small hut with smoke coming from the vent of the pipe in the roof. He walked over to the hut with the Proudmoores following behind him. Carter walked up to the door and knocked. The door cracked open slightly and a man said, "Who's there?"

"My name is Carter Lockwood and we are tired and hungry."

"What business have you? Who sent you?" the man asked

"Sir, we are attempting a journey over the mountain here and request a place to stay the night. I live at the monastery."

The door swung open and an old man quickly walked past Carter and headed to a small shack. Carter watched the man and shrugged his shoulders when he looked at the children. The man walked into the shack and brought out a skinned deer. "I suppose that I should prepare this then," the man said, smiling.

At the table, they all crowded around while the man placed the food on the table. "Does anyone wish to bless the meal?" the old man said.

"Do what to the food?" Marie asked.

"He wants us to pray to the Creator and thank Him for our provisions," Carter said to her. He was smiling because the man was a believer in the Creator.

They all bowed their heads as the old man prayed, "Heavenly Knight sent by the great Creator, thank you for the peace of the world and I pray that the peace may sustain through time. Thank you for always providing protection even when we do not always see it."

Adam looked at the old man and muttered to himself, "Fairytales. Foolishness."

That night, as the children slept, Carter and the old man were deep in conversation. "So you said you saw unicorns, huh?" asked the old man.

"There were five of them," Carter replied. "Do you know what this means?"

"Well, I saw a white flash a while ago up there on the top of the mountain. I believe the Creatures of Old are returning to this world."

"So, all of this is happening for a reason."

"I know all things happen for a greater purpose in life than you or I are able to understand. I do not know for sure, but I think that something big is coming."

"I remember hearing stories about Creatures of Old merging their souls and giving their powers to humans," Carter said.

"Yes, but unfortunately those few who obtained such power are not alive to confirm what most people call a tall tale. You mentioned that a man named Sebastian is chasing you?"

"Yes. He is the King's right hand. They have been friends since childhood."

"Two years ago, I was up on the mountain and I felt the ground shake. I heard the sound of a young man yelling and I followed the sound. I found myself face to face with King Phillip, Prince Phillip at the time. He told me that his friend, who I am guessing is Sebastian, had been caved in. About half an hour later from digging, I heard the voice of another young man behind me. The young man that Prince Phillip was looking for was standing in the mouth of the cave. He gave me chills when I looked into his eyes. I believe that Phillip called him Sebastian."

"You mean Phillip and Sebastian were at this mountain?"

"He told the Prince that he had found another way out. Prince Phillip asked him why he was acting so strange and replied to the prince with very harsh words. That cave always gave me discomfort when I would pass by it. You might want to take a look for yourself, if you are interested."

"I might just do that."

***

The next morning Carter, Adam, Susan and Marie started off to find the safest path over Death Mountain. About half an hour up the mountain, Marie slowed down. "I'm tired," she said, "Can we rest?"

"We must make some decent ground before we stop for the night," Carter replied. "Did you want me to carry you?" He picked up Marie and carried her quite a ways and then let her walk once the path became less steep.

They reached a nice area to stop and rest but the smell of rotting flesh filled the air. "Gross!" Susan said. "What is that horrible smell?" They looked around and saw a rotting giant eagle carcass on a ledge in the distance. They picked up their pace until the smell was no longer in the air. "We will set up camp here," Carter said, pointing to a flat rock surface.

"Finally…" Marie said. She plumped herself down on the ground and huffed and wheezed.

Carter unpacked a small tent and blankets. "Adam, would you please go find some wood so we can make a fire?" Carter asked. Adam grunted and walked off. After Carter had assembled the tent for the girls to use, he said, "I am going to look around. Susan, would you mind cooking the deer meat when Adam comes back with that wood?"

Carter walked east and started to look for any caves with strange markings written on the walls. He came across a few, but they were only a few feet deep. The sun started to set as he came across the last cave he was going to check. He had brought a torch and proceeded inside and found the cave he had been looking for. He walked in a few feet deeper but was stopped by huge rocks that blocked the rest of the cave. He thought that there must have been another way in. He walked outside and up on a ledge he saw a small opening. He climbed up to it and crawled inside.

The passage got wider and wider as Carter went deeper

inside. He soon found himself in a place with scattered clothes lying in front of an old looking door. The door was locked. He thought that it might be weak from age and would open if he used enough force. He rammed into the door and it flew open, causing dust to fly through the air. He found himself in a dark room. He almost gagged at the foul smell but he couldn't decide what it was. He was inside a bedroom and in the corner was an open lockbox. Lying below the box was a small doll. The room looked like it had been ransacked. There were papers all over the floor and odd contraptions placed aimlessly throughout the room. He saw nothing of interest and decided to go through the other door in the room. It led to a descending staircase.

Carter walked down the stone stairs and walked through a red curtain. There he found a large, dark room with a high ceiling. To his left was another door. He walked over to it and opened it, revealing a room with lots of books. He walked inside the room. All the books looked old and worn. A bright red book lying on a table caught his attention. He picked up the book and observed the outside. The great Elven family seal, similar to the book Isaac gave him, was engraved in gold and underneath it was the letter *M*.

Karen was looking for information on the Elves, Carter thought. *Maybe this has some information that could prove beneficial.* He decided to keep the book and view it later.

He looked at the room again and saw that this place was probably filled with books full of dark magic. Walking to the bookcase Carter took his torch and lit the old books on fire. Shrieks came from the flames that made the hairs on the back of his neck stand up. Carter ran from the room, past the curtain in the large room and lit it on fire as well. As he made his way into the bedroom, he lit the papers scattered on the floor on fire and escaped through the door he had entered. There was a loud crash that came from within and a thick smoke quickly followed after him.

As Carter crawled out of the opening in the mountain

he heard Susan calling, "Carter!"

"Up here!" he yelled. Carter climbed down and met Susan on the ledge below.

"Where have you been? We have been worried. You have been gone a long time."

"I'm sorry. I found a cave and inside was a door that led to an underground castle."

"Why is there smoke coming from that cave?" Susan asked.

"It may sound crazy but I believe that it was an ancient castle that belonged to Baelin. I saved this book before I destroyed the place. It looks promising."

"Wait, slow down." Susan said. "Is that screaming that I hear?"

"Yes. I can't explain what is going on but pieces are fitting together in my mind." Carter said. He coughed from the smoke. ""Karen was right. She suspected that Sebastian was different and I think it was because he fell into that castle and something must have possessed him."

"How did you know where it was?"

"The old man told me that two years ago he helped King Phillip find Sebastian when Sebastian was trapped in a blocked cave. I was curious when the old man told me that Sebastian found another way out, so I looked for the other opening."

The smoke was billowing forth from the cave now and rose high into the sky. "I am sure someone will see this smoke if it continues on into the morning," Susan said.

"You're right. We should go back to sleep while we can."

They walked back to the campsite and Adam stood up when he saw Carter. "You fool!" he said. "Were you just going to leave us like everyone else?"

"Adam, stop it!" Susan said. "You are acting foolish!"

"No! He is irresponsible! He walks off and fails to tell us anything! I am an adult, you know! I deserve answers!"

"You sure are not acting like an adult right now," Carter said.

"Please, let us just get some sleep and make haste to wherever Carter is taking us," Susan said.

Adam stomped off and came back after fifteen minutes. They all fell asleep, the girls in the tent and Adam and Carter outside under the stars. During the early morning, Marie woke up and cried. Carter got up and looked in the tent, finding Marie sitting up and Susan fast asleep. "Carter, I had a bad dream," Marie said with tears flowing down her face as she crawled out of the tent.

"Tell me about it," he said with his arms wide open.

She crawled into his arms and laid her head down as he embraced her in a hug. "I want momma. She left and I was standing there but I was not able to follow after her. She told me goodbye forever."

"Your mother will come back, Marie. Do not fear. Your mother loves you very much and just went away for a while. My brother Christian and Eliza will tell her where we are when she goes back to the monastery."

The sky was becoming brighter as the sun began to rise. The smoke was still in the air but almost depleted. Carter heard the sound of men shouting and horses galloping. "Get up!" he said as he got up to shake Adam and Susan awake. "They are coming. Get out of here!"

Adam rubbed his eyes. "I am staying and fighting with you!" he said.

"No, you are not. I told your mother I would not let anything happen to you."

Susan grabbed Adam's arm and pulled him with her as they headed east up the mountain path. Carter found his sword lying on the ground and quickly picked it up. He waited for the Allearian men to ride closer.

Ten Allearian soldiers rode up the mountain on horses. They saw Carter standing there with his sword in hand. The man in charge was not Sebastian and held up his hand as the riders slowly came to a halt. "Who are you?"

"I am Carter Lockwood and you will not harm those children!"

"We have our orders."

"They are just children," Carter said as the men started to ride towards Carter with swords drawn. Carter feared for the children and knew that the chances of him surviving against ten soldiers were slim.

A great roar echoed through the mountains, causing Carter to refocus from his desires to his duties. The soldiers' horses were startled and stood on their hind legs, knocking the soldiers off the saddles. The soldiers stood up and picked up their swords as another roar reverberated through the mountains, causing the earth to shake.

Out of the clouds flew a great white dragon with a long, slender head and a massive body. On the dragon's head were tiny wings, which were its ears. It had huge white teeth and its eyes were golden. Its tail was long and had fins at the tip.

The dragon swooped down and grabbed five of the soldiers in its massive claws and threw them to their death below. The remaining five attempted to run, but the dragon grabbed four more and devoured them. The dragon landed on the mountain surface, causing the ground to tremble once again. Its large tail swiped at the last soldier and knocked him off the mountain's edge.

Carter stood before the fearsome creature and tried to swallow a lump in his throat. His heart beat fast as the adrenaline kicked in. The great dragon looked into Carter's eyes and warmth, not fear, filled Carter's soul. He felt an odd peace in the dragon's presence. The dragon flew up into the sky and disappeared beyond the clouds.

Carter's legs shook but he couldn't move them. He had never seen a real dragon before but all the pictures of dragons he had seen looked nothing like this one. *Where did this dragon come from?* He thought.

He remembered the children and ran to the camp, grabbed his bag, and followed them. "Adam!" he called out. "Susan! Marie!"

Carter reached the highest point of the mountain path and looked down. At the base he saw his small home village of Kakaran. Down the path were Susan, Adam and Marie resting against a large boulder on the mountain. "Susan!" he called out. Susan looked up and smiled. Marie stood up and started to run towards Carter.

A harpy flew down and snatched Marie into the air. Her screams echoed through the air. Susan and Adam ran up to Carter as Carter watched to see where the harpy would take her. High in the cliffs, Carter could hear Marie scream again as the harpy laughed in its high pitched squeal.

"Carter!" Susan said as she approached him, "We have to save her!"

"We must hurry!" Carter said quickly as he led them up the rocky terrain.

They reached the cliff where the harpy nests lay. Five harpies flew around and saw Carter and the twins. Carter drew his sword and said, "Fight me, foul birds."

"How insulting!" replied one of the harpies. "We are not foul and we are not birds."

The harpies flew down and began to scratch at Carter with their claws. Carter cut off one of the harpies' feet and she screamed in pain. The other four harpies swooped down and tried to gouge out his eyes. He covered his head as they scratched at his forearm with their claws.

Susan looked around and stopped to think for a moment. She opened Carter's bag and took out the red tome with the Elven family seal. When she opened it, a giant shadowed hand came out of the pages and grabbed one of the harpies by the feet. The harpy screamed as it was being dragged into the pages. She snapped the book shut after it consumed her, standing with wide eyes as the rest of the harpies flew away in fear saying, "Dark magic! Dark magic! Get away!"

"What was that?" Adam said.

"I have no idea...." she said, as she stared at the book. She fumbled with the latch as she turned it to lock.

"Marie!" called Carter.

"Up here!" Marie said.

Carter climbed up a tree that a harpy nest hung from. Inside was Marie crouching in fear. "I am here," Carter said as he held out his hand. He pulled her out and Susan sighed. "I am going to drop you and Adam will catch you. All right?"

"All right," she replied.

Carter let go of Marie and Adam caught her in his arms. As Carter climbed down, Susan ran to Marie and embraced her in a hug. "I was so worried!" Susan said.

"The harpy cut my arm with her claws," Marie replied, holding out her arm. She stared at the minor scratch and then smiled. "It doesn't hurt too bad."

They sat down and cleaned Marie's wound. Once they were done, they climbed down from the cliffs. "What happened to the Allearian Soldiers?" Susan asked.

"A great white dragon came and killed them," said Carter.

"That is impossible. The only dragons left are the Noryan dragons," Susan replied. "Maybe a Creature of Old saved you."

"This was not just any dragon." Carter said. "All the dragons I have seen in paintings looked nothing like this one. It was a Creature of Old, though, I am sure."

"It saved you and didn't harm you at all?"

"Yes, it stared straight at me and flew away after it killed the soldiers."

"It was like a guardian!" Susan said.

"It would be best if we move before the harpies return," Adam said.

"Yes, my home village of Kakaran is about half a day's

journey." Carter was relieved that the journey was almost over. He had been anticipating seeing his family again after many years.

When night fell, they camped out on the side of the mountain path. They had eaten most of their food and had only bread left. They ate that and rested through the night.

Carter woke up the next morning and saw the strange red tome that Susan had opened. He looked at the markings on the cover again. *Who did this book belong to? The Elves did not use dark magic. They never use any magic because their powers came internally*, he thought to himself. He quickly put the book in his bag and starting packing up as the Proudmoore children woke up from their sleep.

They traveled down the mountain and reached the base. "Yippee!" cried Marie. "I hated that mountain. Please, I don't ever want to do that again."

Kakaran was a small peaceful village. The cottages were small, but beautiful. Flowers bordered the homes and were hung gaily in the village square. It smelled wonderful and brought back pleasant memories of Carter's childhood. A breeze blew and brought the scent of lilacs to his nostrils. Carter sighed and his heart hurt, thinking about Karen.

Carter and the Proudmoore children walked until they reached the eastern edge of the village. At the end of the road they found a beautiful cottage. Carter's eyes brightened as he thought of his parents and sister greeting him.

CHAPTER FOURTEEN

The Forest Haven

Rain clouds formed the next day and it began to pour, making it difficult to travel through the fields past Faerie Forrest. Eleanor attempted to cover herself, but it was no use. The road started to get muddy and there was no cover around except a small eastern forest in the distance. She could not continue long in this weather and tried to find shelter among the trees.

She was pleased to see that little rain made it through the thick coverings of the tree tops. The forest was filled with multicolored plants and had a mysterious aura about it. She heard the voice of a woman singing and decided to follow the beautiful voice.

She stopped when she reached a tiny, strangely lit, but beautiful meadow. The rain had stopped, and rays of sunlight peeked through the clouds and caused the wet grass to sparkle like a diamond mine. Sitting on the grass next to a small pond was a beautiful woman. The maiden had long blonde hair and her skin was delicate and smooth. She was washing her feet with the clear, pure water.

As she inched forward, Eleanor stepped on a twig and snapped it. The woman looked up, her sapphire eyes peering into Eleanor's own. Eleanor realized that this woman was not human, but an Elf. She wondered why an

Elf, such as this one, would be out here alone.

The Elf, Mianya, stood up, walked forward, and began singing again. Eleanor's eyes suddenly felt very heavy. She laid her head down on the lush grass and was soon asleep.

Mianya walked over to Eleanor, picked up her frail body, and moved her to the middle of the meadow. She looked at Eleanor and watched over her as she slept through the night.

The next morning, Mianya walked over to the pond and peered deep into the water. She reached into the water and pulled out five small, colorful crystals. She crushed them all together and flashes of colorful light shone through the forest. Mianya looked once more at Eleanor and then darted east through the trees.

Giggles could be heard throughout the forest and five flying lights darted about. "Free!" yelled five little voices. They belonged to the pixies that had been freed from their prisons. They flew into the meadow and began dancing along the water. The pixie with green light beaming from her stopped and saw Eleanor asleep on the grass.

"Oh! A human!" she said. "Ruby, Amethyst, Topaz, Azure! Come look!"

"What should we do with her, Jade?" they replied in their girlish tones.

"She is so peaceful, "said Amethyst.

Eleanor's eyes opened slowly and stared at the five little lights hovering over her body. She thought she was in some bizarre dream again. "Oh no! She has seen us!" said Ruby.

"Quick, let us dispose of her," replied Topaz.

"Please have mercy on me, little ones," Eleanor said quickly. She could not believe that this was real, but if it was, she did not want them to dispose of her.

Azure pulled out her splinter-sized dagger and landed on Eleanor's body. She walked lightly over to her head and pointed it at her nose. "Why should we not?" The prick from the dagger definitely proved that this was not a dream.

"I will not harm you. I will not let anyone know you exist," Eleanor said.

"What is your name?" Amethyst asked.

"Eleanor Proudmoore."

"Sisters, do you hear that?" Topaz spoke up.

"Oh I do! I do!" Ruby said as she danced through the air and giggled, covering her mouth with her hands.

Suddenly, Jade fell onto the grass. Her sisters gasped and flew to her. "Her life is depleting," Azure said. "Her power must have been drained too much to survive."

"What should we do?" Amethyst asked as she clasped her hands over her mouth.

"I know!" Ruby said happily.

They all looked at Ruby. "How could you be so joyful during such a time?" asked Topaz. Eleanor looked at the pixies with deep pity and bewilderment.

"The child," Ruby whispered to her sisters.

"Oh!" they all replied.

The pixies flew to Eleanor and fluttered around her head. "Please, will you help us?" Amethyst asked. "We won't dispose of you. We are sorry for mentioning such a wicked deed."

"What do you mean by 'help you'?" Eleanor asked.

"Your child and our sister are dying."

"I am with child!?" Eleanor asked. She had no idea that she was pregnant. She was so shocked when her husband was murdered that she did not pay much attention to anything. Unbeknownst to Eleanor, her anxiety was killing her child.

"You didn't know that you were with child?" Topaz asked. Eleanor shook her head and Ruby giggled.

"Well," Amethyst said, "We know how to save them both."

"All right, how?" Eleanor replied. She was nervous at what they were going to say, but they seemed supernatural, so maybe something supernatural would happen.

"We must have your child take on my sister's spirit." Amethyst said.

"What do you mean?"

"We are Creatures of Old. We are able to merge our souls with humans' souls and give them special powers, but it depends on the willingness of the creature."

"How will this work?" She wanted to try anything to save one of her children.

"Please just remain completely still."

The pixies flew to their sister Jade and picked her up. They placed her limp body on Eleanor's stomach. Suddenly Jade dissolved into Eleanor's skin and Eleanor's belly began to glow bright green. Eleanor looked at her stomach and then the pixies. She could not believe this just happened. *What would I give birth to? Would it be human?*

"Is it done?" Eleanor asked finally.

"Yes! Yes! Yes!" Ruby said as she bounced around the meadow.

"I can feel them both regaining strength," Azure said.

A smile came to each of the pixies faces as they danced around Eleanor with joy.

"What will you name her?" Topaz asked curiously.

"I do believe her name should be Jade since your sister gave her strength," Eleanor replied happily.

"I do! Do! Do! Love that name." Ruby said excitedly and giggled.

Eleanor slowly got up and looked at the forest around her. It was bright and festive with colorful leaves. "This place is beautiful," Eleanor said.

"We love it too," replied Azure.

"What do you call it?"

"We are the pixies of the sun shrine. That is what this place is."

"What is the sun shrine?"

"Oh, we cannot speak of it to a human. I am sorry."

"That is all right. I should be leaving now anyways."

"What do you mean? Where are you headed?" asked Topaz. "How can you leave when you have just arrived?"

"To a small village called Harte."

"What is there?" Azure spoke up.

"My parents live there."

"Shall we accompany you?" Ruby asked.

"No, sisters," replied Amethyst. "We cannot leave our safe haven. We must protect ourselves from what we cannot speak of."

"But Jade…" said Topaz.

"She will be fine," Amethyst said.

"Oh, all right," Topaz said with her head down.

Eleanor walked away and waved goodbye to her new friends. "Goodbye," they called after her. "Come visit us with Jade sometime." Eleanor returned to the field and found the path she had been traveling previously.

CHAPTER FIFTEEN
Kakaran

Adam crossed his arms as he followed Carter and his sisters to the small home, covered in flowers. As they approached they could hear barking coming from behind the door. Carter knocked on the door and a woman's voice could be heard, "Shush!" The door swung open and Adam's jaw dropped when he saw her.

"Carter!" the girl said as she leaped onto him and wrapped her arms around his neck.

Carter laughed. "Good to see you Lia," he said. He pulled her off of him and pushed her to a distance. "You have grown so much!"

"You look bigger yourself," Lia said as she poked at his muscles. "Is Christian here also?" She looked around.

"No," Carter replied, "Sadly it's just me. But I have brought guests! Lia, this is Karen's brother and two sisters; Adam, Susan and Marie."

"Nice to meet you," Lia said as she extended her hand out. When she shook Adam's hand, she became flushed.

What is her problem? Adam thought. He let go of her hand and looked away. He felt the blood rush to his face and his palms began to sweat.

"This is my sister Lia," Carter said to the Proudmoores.

"Please come inside," Lia said, stepping aside and

letting them pass. "I was just about to make some tea. Mother and Father went out to the lake for a walk. They should be back shortly. Just be prepared Carter, mother might cry when she sees you."

"I wouldn't expect anything else." Carter laughed as he sat down at the table.

"Lia," Susan said, "How old are you?"

"I am sixteen," she said. She poured the tea into four cups and distributed them. When she handed the first one to Adam, she fumbled when his hands touched hers and the cup fell to the floor, spilling hot tea all over. "Oh no!"

"Here let me go grab a rag," Carter said, getting up and leaving the room.

"He doesn't know where mother moved them," she said. "Excuse me." Lia followed after him.

Susan elbowed Adam and he looked at her. "What?" he asked.

"Why are you acting so funny?" Susan asked. Marie giggled.

"What are you talking about?" Adam crossed his arms again.

"I didn't know you were so sensitive." Susan poked at Adam and he brushed her hand away.

"Shut up!" he said.

Carter and Lia entered the room with a handful of rags. "We didn't need this many," Lia said. Adam stood up and walked out of the room. His face was flushed and he had a pallor complexion.

"What's wrong with Adam?" Lia asked.

"More than you want to know," Susan replied as she laughed with Marie.

***

Adam walked down a dirt path north. He began kicking a rock and kicked it all the way until he reached a lake. He kicked the rock right into the water. "Stupid Susan," he said to himself. Of course he thought that Lia was beautiful but he knew after his recent behavior with Carter, there would be no chance. *Maybe if I apologize to Carter?* He thought. *But then he will suspect something. I don't know what to do.*

"Adam!" Lia called out. "Oh there you are!" She ran up to him. She bent over and put her hands on her knees and panted. "Carter…" She held up one finger. "Carter was going to come after you but I said that I would."

"Why?" Adam asked. *Why would Carter come after me? I can take care of myself.*

"He was worried that you would get lost. My parents have returned and my mother is preparing mutton."

Adam nodded and walked with Lia back to the house. The whole time she talked about her favorite spots to go where she could be alone. She tried to ask Adam questions but he would give one word answers or shrug and say, "I don't know."

Adam and Lia entered the house and salted meat permeated the air. "This is Adam," Carter said to his mother. "He is Susan's twin."

"It is very nice to meet you," Mrs. Lockwood said, "The food should be done soon."

Adam sat down as Susan stood up. "Lia, were you going to show me your dresses?" Susan asked.

"Are you sure you want to see them?" Lia asked, "They aren't very good."

"Are you kidding? I am sure they are lovely."

"All right," Lia said as she began walking out with Susan following her. "So tell me about your journey over the mountain?" Marie trailed behind the both of them.

"Adam," Carter said, "I was going to go out and meet my father because he wanted to show me something. Did you want to go?"

"No," Adam said. "I'll stay here."

"He can help me taste the food before I serve it," Mrs. Lockwood said as she was cutting up a loaf of bread she had baked. "Bring your father back soon because I don't want to hear him complain about cold meat." Carter nodded and kissed his mother before exiting.

***

The next few days, Carter helped his dad cut down trees for the next winter. Lia was teaching Susan and Marie some techniques her mother had shown her for sewing. Being around Mrs. Lockwood was making Adam miss his mother.

Adam decided to go to the lake for a swim before the weather got too cold. He undressed on the dock and jumped in. He wanted to see how far the bottom was and dove down. Out of the corner of his eye, the sunlight caught an object in the water and sparkled in the water. Adam reached for it and noticed it was a green crystal. He could feel the pressure of the water upon his body and quickly he returned to the surface before he drowned.

Adam was about to jump up on the dock to observe the crystal when he spotted Lia tip-toeing away with his clothes. "What are you doing?" Adam asked.

"Oh!" Lia said. Her face was red as she turned around to look at Adam. "I was just going to take your clothes and make you panic. I was going to give them back… eventually."

"I think I will take them back now if you don't mind." *Why would she think taking my clothes is funny?* he thought.

"I guess I have an odd sense of humor," Lia said. She walked towards him.

Adam nodded and then saw an Elf walking down the dock. Lia looked back and saw her and stopped in place, staring. Mianya reached the edge and knelt down and held out her hand. "Please," she said. Adam slowly handed her the crystal. Her sapphire blue eyes seemed to be peering into his soul. She was the same Elf he remembered from the castle during the coronation of the King.

Mianya stood up and nodded at Lia. She began sprinting from the dock and made her way into the forest.

"That was strange," Lia said, staring into the woods. "What did you give her?"

"It looked like a crystal," Adam replied. "I found it when I dove to the bottom."

"I wonder what she wanted with it."

"Lia?" Adam asked.

"What?" Lia looked down at Adam who was still wading in the water. "Oh sorry!" She handed him the cloth and dropped his clothes.

"Well, are you going to turn away?"

She blushed and turned to look the other way. "Who swims naked?"

"I didn't think that anyone was going to be around." Adam got out of the water and dried off, quickly putting on his clothes. He began to tie his tunic when a green flash came from the forest. "What was that?"

"I don't know! Are you decent?"

"Yes." Adam wanted to see what was in that forest. It was like the same flash that happened outside the monastery, when the unicorns appeared.

"I actually came here because Susan wanted me to get you and try on something that we had sewn together." She covered her mouth and laughed.

"Do you mind if I hang out here for a little while?" He was going to determine to find out what that flash was. "I will catch up with you shortly."

"Okay...," Lia said as her brow wrinkled.

Adam headed towards the forest once Lia left. He looked around to find anything out of the ordinary but he saw nothing. There was no sign of the Elf either. As he went deeper into the forest the trees began to thicken and the roots were coming up from the earth.

With the sound of crunching leaves beneath his every step, Adam thought he heard a faint hiss. He looked back and still saw nothing. When he turned, he saw a snake tail slither behind a tree. His heart began to beat and he swallowed a hard lump in his throat. Slowly walking forward he saw the head of a massive snake lift its head from behind the tree trunk.

"Please," the snake said softly. It opened its mouth, showing giant fangs and it lunged forward.

Adam dove out of the way and rolled into a protruding root. He grabbed his head and rubbed it seeing the snake slither by. He got up and began running south toward Kakaran. He looked back and didn't see the snake pursuing him. He turned his head and fell straight to the floor as he smacked into the scaly body. He couldn't see the head.

When he stood up, the snake lunged forward again and wrapped its body around Adam. Slowly it squeezed Adam and with each breath he attempted to take, the space for his lungs to expand became less.

"If you do not run," the snake said, "I will release you."

Adam could feel the pressure build in all of his veins as they felt they would burst if he was bound any tighter. His face was hot as he attempted to nod. He felt the blood freely move once more through his body as the snake released him. He took deep breaths, lying on the forest floor.

"I need your assistance young warrior," the snake said, "My name is Yua."

"How are you able to talk?" Adam sat up.

"I am an ancient being. I have recently been released."

So that is what she was doing, Adam thought. He closed his eyes and pinched himself but when he opened his eyes, he saw the snake still there.

"We must hurry." Yua said.

"What do you want from me?"

"My powers have been drained too great and I need to merge my soul with yours. Only the soul of a human can keep me alive now."

"What?" Adam asked. *Is this thing crazy? There is no way this is real.*

"If you do not help me I will be forced to devour you. Then I will have strength to find a proper host."

"How can you be real? You are what we call a Creature of Old, but I thought those were just myths."

"We are very real. Touch me if you do not believe. Baelin trapped all of us creatures in crystal prisons when we banded together to stop him. We failed."

"So Baelin is back?" Adam asked, standing up now that he could feel his legs.

"I believe so. You must make a decision young warrior."

"What will happen to me if I agree to this?"

"I will release my energy into a potion that you must drink. You will be quick and nimble, able to strike quickly with deadly force. Your mind will be sharpened and you will be cunning."

"Are you sure I won't die?"

"If you want to die, that can be arranged." Yua raised his head back into striking position.

"Wait!" Adam held up his hand. "I'll do it!"

Yua lowered his head and said, "Very well." He began to glow green. The brighter he became, Adam had to shield his eyes.

When Adam uncovered his eyes, he saw a small vial lying on the ground. He reached down and picked it up and looked intently at it. *Maybe I can save my siblings with this power,* he thought. He pulled out the cork and closed his eyes, emptying the liquid in one gulp.

He gagged, grabbing his throat. His eyes were wide open and the veins were protruding from his neck. He fell to the floor and began foaming at the mouth. Suddenly he stopped moving.

***

"Adam!" Lia called out.

Adam opened his eyes and the forest was close to dark. He heard footsteps and a voice call out, "Adam, where are you!"

"Over here," he said in a hoarse voice. He could smell her coming closer. It was the strangest feeling.

"I was looking for you!" she said while running and kneeling down beside him. "I thought you were right behind me. We must move or else we both will be lost this deep in the forest."

They both got up and Lia looked at him and brushed off the leaves. When he looked at her she dropped her jaw. "Adam, your eyes."

"What do you mean?" he asked.

"They are like a yellowish-green color. And they glow sort of."

"It must be the effect of the moon." He closed his eyes and rubbed them. When he opened them she was still staring at him. "Let's go shall we?"

They made their way to the forest edge and saw the cottage in the distance. Carter pulled Adam aside when they entered and said, "Where have you been? I was getting worried that Sebastian's men had found you."

"I'm here aren't I?" Adam said as he walked past Carter.

"I have seen the way you look at Lia," Carter said. "You have a lot of growing up to do if you are thinking about pursuing her."

Adam stopped and looked back at Carter and wanted to reply with an apology but his pride kept him. He turned and continued walking.

That night Adam couldn't go to sleep. When Carter came into the room Adam finally decided to show a little appreciation. "Carter," he said.

"You are still awake?" Carter asked as he climbed into his bed.

"I couldn't sleep because I have been feeling guilty about how I have been acting. I don't even know where this is coming from but I truly mean it."

"You don't need to worry. All is forgiven. I only want your best interest in mind."

"There was something that happened to me today that I wanted to talk to you about. I don't know how to explain it. Have you noticed my eyes?"

"What?"

"It started with that Elf that I saw at the coronation. She was the same one, breathtaking, and took this crystal that I found at the bottom of the lake. I went into the forest after her and found this massive snake and it spoke to me. I think it was a Creature of Old."

"You saw the Elf princess Mianya? Which way did she go?"

"North I believe but I am not sure. Lia saw her also. This is the crazy part though. He asked to merge his soul with mine and turned into this vial. I drank it and woke up with these strange senses and I feel a little stronger too."

"I have heard of that. I must find this Elf and ask her why she is looking for the crystals and get some answers. Maybe her people can help me rescue Karen and stop Phillip and Sebastian."

"I want to rescue my sister and brother. I am stronger now with this new power."

"You are still young and could easily get hurt. Once your mother arrives I will set off to search for Mianya."

CHAPTER SIXTEEN
The Huntress

Mianya admired the smooth yellow crystal within her palm. The energy was too great she had no idea how she had missed it earlier. The pulse coming from it made her fear however because the more dangerous creatures had the most power. She looked at the small scratch on her forearm from the previous creature she had released. It must have been wild and scared which made it unpredictable.

She noticed that the creatures released were unpredictable. Some appearing where she had released them and others, appearing somewhere entirely different, unbeknownst to her.

She knew Sebastian would be in pursuit of her once more so she quickly grabbed her pendant and smashed it onto the crystal. It cracked as bright yellow light flashed in the air. Now was her time to move, she sprinted north through the forest. She could hear the creature giggle and shielded herself among the foliage, as the beautiful fairy flew past her and disappeared among the trees.

Mianya had exhausted herself in Allear, and decided it was time to move west. South of her people's dwelling was an island known for its miscreants of men. The depravity of man was evident there as everyone did what was right in his own eyes.

She scanned the area as she attempted to move. She sprinted off north until she reached Harte, a small fishing village. She had quite a few gold coins from when she last encountered Sebastian absent from his goods.

As she reached the docks, she spotted a beautiful ship. It was made of fine gopher wood and the design was impeccable. She boarded it and ran her fingers along the railing. The mast was thick and sturdy, able to brave a fierce storm.

"Can I help you?" A man's voice asked.

She turned around and saw a short little bald man with a fuzzy brown beard. He looked aged with a few grey strands of hair and wrinkles around his eyes.

"I was looking to acquire a boat for a journey." Mianya said.

"Where were you headed?" he asked, walking by her and picking up some rope.

"The Isle of Thieves." She said.

The man dropped the rope and looked at her. "Are you crazy?" He asked. "What would a beautiful, innocent creature like you want with a place like that?"

"I am on a quest. I require passage to that island however. I will pay a handsome price for your boat."

"Well if you insist. Let me go down below and get my boys up. We can leave as soon as they set up."

"O no! You are not planning some crazy trip!" A lady said, coming up from below. "I won't allow it!"

"Darling," the man said to his wife, "It will be a safe journey."

"Safe?" she scoffed. "You call traveling to a place like that safe?"

"I assure you madam," Mianya said. "I will not take your husband into any danger."

"Well you won't catch me on this ship headed to that cursed place!" she said.

"Please don't be like this," the sailor replied.

"I will give you one month and if you don't return, do not expect me to be here."

"What about our boys?"

"Take them," she threw up her hands, "I can't stop you. Now I need a drink!"

Mianya watched as the plump lady walked off the boat and onto the dock. The man shrugged his shoulders and went down below. Mianya began preparing the ship for its journey. She had spent some time on ships that she knew a thing or two.

The men came up the deck and began working. In record time they got everything up and began heading off out to sea. Mianya knew it was a matter of time before the wife came running out. Pubs in Allear had her face on a wanted poster.

Like clockwork she saw the plump lady running out with a parchment in her hand. She was waving her hands violently in the air. When she reached the dock, she attempted to jump up while waving her hands, which was a mistake because she ended up falling in the water.

Mianya just smiled and said, "You know your wife has nothing to fear."

"Why is that?" the sailor said.

"I am only requesting you to bring me in sight of the island. I will swim the rest of the way."

"My lady, the water is freezing. Not to mention strange things lurk in these waters as of late."

Mianya laughed. "I will be fine," she said, "You are too kind to worry but if death hasn't taken me yet, I do not fear it anytime soon. Here is your payment." She handed him thirty gold coins.

"My lady!" His eyes widened. "I cannot accept such a generous payment."

"Take it." She yawned. "I must rest. It has been days since I slept anywhere but the ground." She headed down to the bottom of the ship and fell asleep to the gentle rocking.

***

They arrived in safe distance to the island shore.
Mianya could hear the loud music and laughter coming
from the town in the distance. She observed the moon's
reflection over the dark waters.

"Are you sure you want to swim?" the sailor asked.

"I thank you for your concern but I must be off. I
appreciate your willingness to take me this far." She leaned
over and kissed his bald head. She couldn't see but
assumed he was blushing as he smiled widely.

She said goodbye to the sailor's sons and climbed up on
the railing of the ship. She dove into the ice-cold waters
and began swimming to shore.

When she surfaced from the ocean, she could smell the
garbage and feces on the streets. She walked carefully over
drunken men, who were unshaven, some lying in vomit.

She slipped into the pub to find shelter for the night and
dry off. The innkeeper smiled at her, showing missing
teeth.

"Hey you cheated!" a large man said.

"At least my wife isn't a whore!" the other said.

The man stood up and flipped the table and threw a
punch. Men began throwing chairs and fighting amongst
themselves.

"I would like one room please," Mianya said, handing
him a gold coin. The innkeeper ducked at an incoming
glass bottle. He grabbed a key and handed it to Mianya.
She retreated upstairs and locked herself in the room,
hearing the commotion from below.

She was attempting to dry off when an eerie feeling
came over her. Mianya's heart began to race as she
attempted to listen for any sound of movement. She turned
the key slowly and unlocked it. Tiptoeing to the end of the

hall, she peered down the stairs.

Sebastian was standing at the counter with a sword to the innkeeper's throat. "Where is the Elf?" he asked. With trembling hands, the innkeeper pointed up the stairs.

Mianya gasped, running as quietly as she could, down to her room. She closed the door and locked it. Running over to the window, she attempted to open it but it was stuck. She managed to crack it open far enough to squeeze through. She could hear the handle of the door being turned. She managed to slip out the window and made her way onto the roof. The door was being pounded violently.

Climbing down some barrels piled up against the side of the pub, she saw Sebastian poke his head out of the window and look around. She leaned against the wall, concealed by the shadows. When his head went back inside, she moved as quickly as she could east.

The forest was heavy with moss and dead-looking trees. The ground was sticky and wet. Mianya knew she needed to move quicker and attempted to tree hop but the branches were too weak. She attempted to run through some sticky mud but it slowed her down too much. She finally reached a hollow tree and hid inside.

She was panting, peering out occasionally to see if Sebastian was still in pursuit. Her eyes caught something red and shiny in the distance. It was wedged within a hollow part of a tree but it was a ways off. Her face was hot as her heart pounded in her chest.

It was now or never. She sprinted from her hiding place and reached the other side. She stuck her hand inside and grabbed the crystal. A dagger flew past her head and stuck deep into the blackened bark. She whipped her head back to see Sebastian standing there with a grimace look.

He sprinted toward her and she climbed the tree as quick as she could. She began hopping from branch to branch as he pursued her from below. She headed east, looking down she found that he was still in serious pursuit.

As she turned her head, she took a blow to the face, making contact with a branch. Down she fell, hitting branches until she hit the ground with force. She could see bright flashes of light, floating around her.

Sebastian walked over and placed his foot on her chest and pointed his sword at her neck. "There is no escaping me this time," Sebastian said. "You have evaded me for the last time. I will however spare you if you will join me once more. Dear sweet Mysery, your tortured spirit smells so pleasant."

"I will never join you!" Mianya said. "The Light will keep me safe. I will never go back to your ways. If you do not remember, the knight has victory over you and your curse."

"Very well," he said, pointing the sword closer. "Hand me the crystal!" He held out his free hand.

Mianya clutched the crystal within her hand. Slowly she raised it and placed it in his palm. She let her hand fall to the ground. She was sore but was able to move again.

Sebastian admired the crystal and began draining it. A dagger flew through the air and landed in his wrist. He dropped the crystal and looked to his left. Standing there was a dirty looking woman with scraps for clothes. She was running towards him with her unkempt fiery red hair flowing behind her. She threw another dagger and it landed in his thigh. Sebastian clenched his teeth as he looked at the knife sticking out of his leg. He grunted as he attempted to pull it out.

"Give me crystal!" the woman said.

Mianya reached up quickly and turned the knife, causing Sebastian to cry out in pain. She kicked his feet from under him and grabbed the crystal when she got up. She looked at the wild woman who now had two small swords wielded.

Sebastian picked up his sword and deflected the woman's blows. She attacked him with pure rage and no skill. She did a back-flip as Sebastian pushed her back with his own strength. They began to duel. The woman was now on the defensive side, occasionally taking a jab at him.

Mianya was now running north from her current location while the both of them were distracted. She continued until she reached the edge of the forest. To her left was barren wasteland but knew that some sort of shelter was best until she knew Sebastian wasn't near. She found a small cave on a beach to the north, and before she entered, she took out the crystal. Sebastian hadn't drained it much at all thankfully so she cracked it with her pendant and ran inside the cave to take shelter.

Although she was freezing, she slept without a fire, fearing that it would signal unwanted company. Mianya opened her eyes at dawn and saw the wild woman standing in the mouth of the cave. She ran toward Mianya with her daggers raised. She had a large gash on her forearm. Mianya kicked her feet up and flipped the woman over her. She sat up in a crouching position ready to fight. She took a dagger from the side of her thigh and held it ready to fight. The woman got up from the sand and screamed as she charged at Mianya. Mianya began to deflect the attacks with one dagger but with one false move she lost her footing. Falling to the floor, Mianya had the woman over her with her daggers against Mianya's neck.

"Where is crystal?" the woman said, there was a fierceness in her eyes.

"I released it," Mianya replied.

The woman's eyes softened a bit when she said this. Her brow rose as she said, "You? How?"

"I am trying to stop that man you were fighting from killing the creatures within the crystals."

The woman removed the daggers from Mianya's throat and stood up, holding out her filthy hand. Mianya looked at her for a moment and then took it as she was helped up. "Tiandra," the woman said, beating her chest.

"I am Mianya, princess of the Elves." Mianya said.

"How you release crystal?"

"With this." Mianya held up her pendant. She watched as Tiandra's eyes widened. "Why are you after the crystals?"

"Tiandra fought creature for food. It spoke and tell Tiandra that it needs help. It went inside of me. I feel strong now."

"So it chose you as its host body. I could use a companion to help me protect the crystals from Sebastian."

Tiandra grunted and held her forearm. Mianya grabbed her arm and said, "Here let's clean and wrap this up." She poured some of her drinking water to clear the sand out of the wound and then wrapped it in some linen.

"Tiandra thank. How Mianya release Chimera?"

"So that is what creature you have merged in your being. I have noticed that some creatures appear in random area around the world. Some however appear where you release them. I got this scar from one of them." She showed Tiandra the small scar on her left shoulder.

"What evil man's name?"

"He goes by Sebastian but his true name is Baelin. He is trying to gain power to rule the world. He wants to kill everything good and pure until nothing but destruction comes to all. The only way I know how to stop him is find the Heavenly Knight's sword."

"Sword?"

"Two thousand years ago when the Creatures of Old and Sebastian were trapped in crystal prisons, the knight created a white crystal which was the key that would gain access to the sword that would ultimately stop Baelin. I do not know however where this key is currently or what creature would come out of it."

"We search for crystals now?"

"Yes, we shall go. I sense there are many crystals on this island; but the more I release, the weaker my senses get."

"I will help." Tiandra took out her bag and dumped out four crystals. "You release now?"

Mianya picked up the crystals and one by one she shattered them, causing multiple colors to shine through the air. Mianya motioned for Tiandra to follow and they headed east toward the barren part of the Island.

CHAPTER SEVENTEEN

Finding the Elf Princess

Lia clapped as Adam disarmed Carter. Carter picked up his sword from the snow and looked at his sister. "I thought you were rooting for me?" Carter asked.

"Can I not cheer for both?" Lia said, winking at Adam.

"Again," Adam said, getting into stance.

Carter sighed and got into stance as well. In the distance he saw two women approaching. He lowered his sword and noticed that it was Eliza and Eleanor. *What is Eliza doing here?* Carter thought. He was excited to see Eleanor and noticed that she was carrying something in her arms.

"Mother!" Adam said. He dropped his sword and ran to his mother with arms wide open. She held her hand up and pointed to a sleeping baby in her arms.

"Who is she? She has a strange presence about her," Adam said.

"This is your baby sister Jade." Eleanor said.

"Congratulations," Carter said as he approached Eleanor. "You never told us that you were pregnant before your husband died."

"I had no idea myself. I was so distraught that I thought my mood was due to the tragedy."

"Momma?" said Marie who was walking toward them

through the snow. She started crying and ran saying, "Momma! Momma!"

"Oh Marie! My sweet child." Eleanor handed Jade over to Eliza. She scooped up Marie into her arms and kissed her over and over. "I am back now and I will never leave you again! I love you so much!"

"Please promise."

"I promise."

Eleanor grabbed the crystal hanging around Marie's neck. "What a beautiful blue crystal," She said, "Where did you get it?"

"I found it in the water," Marie replied, "The water lady gave it to me."

"On her birthday she snuck out and almost drowned in the lake," Adam said.

"It was amazing," Carter said, "he could sense that she was missing after his encounter with a Creature of Old."

"Creature of Old?" Eleanor asked.

"Yes," Adam said, "It was released by Mianya."

"I encountered Mianya also on my journey to Harte," Eleanor said.

"Do you believe that she could be in that northern area of Allear?" Carter asked.

"It has been months since that encounter. The creatures she released were pixies. One of them merged their soul with Jade here and saved her life."

"I was wondering why I had some strange connection with her," Adam said. "She sure is cute."

"Do you all mind heading inside?" Carter asked. "I would like to speak to Eleanor alone."

Adam and Lia looked at him and nodded. Adam took Marie from Eleanor's arms and the three of them headed towards the house. Carter looked at Eliza who didn't move at first but finally she realized that he wanted her to leave as well and she followed after them.

"What did you want to talk about?" Eleanor asked.

"I think I need to leave," Carter said, "I believe that Mianya has answers that I need. She must know something because she is trying to release these creatures. Maybe she can tell me the way to save Karen and Thomas as well as stop Sebastian."

"This is all so new to me," Eleanor said, "I didn't realize that any of this could be real until I really saw. I was blinded by logic but it takes some faith now I know. I trust your decision but please be careful. Karen needs you and it would devastate her if something were to happen to you."

"I promise I will return with news once I find Mianya. Maybe her people will be able to help us take back Allear from Sebastian."

"One can only hope. I just hope Thomas is all right as well." Eleanor wrapped her arms around Carter and hugged him tight. She released him and they walked back to the cottage together to rest for the evening.

***

Carter packed some warm blankets and enough provisions as he could manage. Sitting next to his bed he saw the strange red book. He grabbed it and packed it away, hoping to get some answers soon. Not knowing if Mianya was still in the northwestern part of Allear, he grabbed his bag and headed for the door.

As he reached for the handle to open it quietly, he felt a small touch on his right shoulder. Turning around, he saw Eliza standing there with wide eyes. He wanted to ignore her and just turn and leave but he knew she would try to follow him if he didn't tell her to go back to sleep. He knew she was only here just to see him. With any excuse she could, she always took the opportunity.

"Eliza," Carter said, trying to keep his voice down. "Go back to bed."

"Take me with you," She said. She started to take a few

steps forward but he put his hand up.

"You need to stop pursuing me. I know how you feel and you have made it clear. I don't want to see you hurt yourself trying to win my love when you know my heart will never be yours."

"That is why I love you so much. You do care about me."

"You are kind to others and I know you want to help people but it is not healthy for you to be around me."

"I don't care if you hurt me. I would gladly be in pain knowing I can't have you as long as I can be in your presence."

"My answer will always be no." Carter wished that she would stop hurting herself but he could do nothing more. "Goodbye Eliza. Please do not follow me again. Find someone who will love you the way you deserve."

Eliza was trembling. She started walking towards Carter again and tried to push his hand away so she could get closer. Carter grabbed her shoulders and pushed her away. She fell backwards and looked up at him from the floor as tears formed in her eyes.

"I'm sorry," Carter said. "Please do not try to touch me. You are only making this worse for yourself. May the Creator heal your affliction."

Carter went outside and began heading north toward Harte on the east side of Death Mountain. He occasionally looked back to see that Eliza was not following him. He could not believe that Eliza would attempt to throw herself upon him the way she did. He worried for her safety because he didn't want her to harm herself. Now realizing that he was a temptation to most women, he thought of how he could turn off most women to his natural charm.

He made his way north close to the mountainside. The snow in the area was getting deep as winter was coming on strong this year. He found a cave in the side of the mountain that he was going to use for shelter.

During the night something had triggered a small avalanche and the mouth of the cave was covered in snow. Carter woke up to darkness and his fire that he spent hours making had been snuffed out. He felt with his hands and found where the cave's mouth was and began to panic as he attempted to dig himself out.

"Creator, please don't let me die here. I want to save Karen and others from Sebastian." He continued to dig until he couldn't feel his fingers anymore. It was no use. He found where he laid his blankets and attempted to curl up in them to warm himself. He couldn't sleep and his heart was beating fast.

A small beam of light peered into the cave as the sound of crunching snow got Carter's attention. Someone was digging him out and he wondered how whoever was outside, knew that he was trapped. A small frail hand poked through the snow. Eliza must have followed him and saw that he was trapped.

"I will get you out!" yelled a voice from outside.

Carter couldn't make out whether it was a male or female because it could have been both. He helped dig from within and when he saw who was on the other side, he thought it was Eliza but it was a young boy.

"Are you all right?" the boy asked.

"I am fine!" Carter said, panting as he placed his hands on his knees. "How did you know where to find me?"

"I... uh..." the boy said. "I..."

"It doesn't matter," Carter said, "I owe you my life."

The boy looked at Carter and then looked away. Carter went to the back of the cave and grabbed his stuff. When he came out he found the boy standing there with his arms crossed and shivering.

"My name is Carter Lockwood," Carter said as he extended his hand out.

The boy extended his hand out and Carter noticed how clammy his hands were. He could feel the fast pulse racing from the boy. "Neil!" the boy said. He cleared his throat. "Neil Harper."

"Thank you for rescuing me but I must be off." Carter nodded.

"Where are you headed?" Neil asked. "If you wouldn't mind sharing." His eyes shifted again.

"I am headed north toward Harte," Carter said, "I am looking for someone."

"I was wondering if I would be able to join you." Neil said.

Why would he want to come with me? Carter thought. *This boy is very strange to be all the way out here in the middle of nowhere. He looks like someone that I know but it can't be.* "If you would like," Carter said.

"Excellent!" Neil said, picking up his bag from the snow and swinging it over his shoulder.

As they were walking Carter made an effort to be polite with conversation because he sensed Neil was a little uncomfortable. "What brought you all the way out here?" Carter asked.

"I was actually looking for adventure." Neil said.

"This time of year is an odd time to start an adventure. Wouldn't you rather do it with better weather conditions?"

"My family thought that I couldn't amount to anything and I wanted to prove them wrong."

"You didn't want to try something a little closer to home?"

"Um…" Neil replied.

"It's all right. I'll stop asking you questions if you would like."

"No!" Neil said. "I mean, I like you asking me questions. It gives us something to talk about."

As Carter and Neil continued to travel north, they found the path. They reached a forest edge that was covered in thick trees. Little light entered through the canopy of leaves. "What forest is this?" Neil asked.

"I believe this is the Yellow Forest," Carter said.

"It looks pretty dark in there," Neil said as he stopped walking.

"You don't have to come with me if you don't want to. I am sure your family misses you."

"I have come too far to turn back now! Are you good with a sword?"

"I am decent but I haven't perfected my skills yet. I was training to be a Holy Warrior before my mentor was murdered."

Neil began to tear up and Carter stopped to look at him. Neil quickly wiped his eyes and took a deep breath. "Sorry," he said.

Why is he crying? Carter thought. "Did I say something to upset you?"

"I just don't like death," Neil said, "We should go. I trust you can protect us if anything happens."

"I can teach you how to protect yourself if you would like."

"Sometimes I like being vulnerable."

"What?"

"Never mind." Neil started walking towards the forest and disappeared among the shadows.

Carter followed after and when they were a few miles inside they heard faint giggling echoing through the trees. Neil gasped and picked up a stick, holding it high in the air. He looked around in all directions and then toward Carter.

"It's most likely the wind. If we were really threatened, I would have my sword out."

"Then draw your sword!" Neil said. He gasped again and swung the stick up higher looking up into the trees. "I heard something come from over there!"

"Calm down," Carter said, "You are driving me mad." Carter turned and saw a flash of yellow light. He quickly drew his sword and held it up.

A root burst from the ground. It grabbed Carter by the

wrist and flew him against a tree. He dropped his sword and winced from the pain. Neil was spinning and swinging the branch he was holding. Roots sprung from the group and wrapped around him and constricted.

"Ouch!" Neil screamed.

"Who dares enter my forest?" A girl's voice said among the trees.

Carter managed to get up from the ground and tried to run for his sword once more. A root came up and tripped him as it wrapped around his ankle. He grabbed his chest and he attempted to gasp for breath after getting the wind knocked out of him. More roots came up and wrapped around his other foot and wrists, holding him on the ground.

"Please!" Neil said. "Let us go! Whoever you are!"

"I am the watcher of these Woods!" the girly voice said.

"Please don't kill us!" Neil said.

"Quiet!" Carter said. He had managed finally to catch his breath. "Whoever you are, you must let us go. We are on a quest to stop a great evil!"

"I do not like liars!" the voice said. "You shall fear the wrath of Thenia!" A beautiful faerie appeared, seated on a branch with her legs crossed. She had a fair face with beautiful blonde hair. She emitted a yellow glow around her. "The most beautiful Faerie in all the land!" She covered her mouth and giggled.

"What do you want from us?" Carter asked.

"I want to know what you are doing in my forest." Thenia asked, as she jumped down from the branch and fluttered over to Carter. "My, my. You are a handsome human! Maybe I should just keep you!"

"I am on a quest to find the Elf Princess."

"Which one? There are three." Thenia scoffed.

"Mianya is the only Elf princess that I know of." Carter said.

"I wouldn't know this as I have been trapped for many years."

"So you are a Creature of Old that Mianya has been releasing."

"Why would that demon release us when she helped trap us in the first place?"

"She is no longer a demon. I am trying to find answers from her. I believe that Baelin has returned."

The roots tightened around Carter and he grunted. "What do you take me for?" Thenia said as she placed a foot on his chest. "Do I look like a fool to you?"

"I speak the truth my lady."

"Flattery will not save you!"

"Please go look in my bag over there. Inside there is a red book with the Elves crest on the cover."

Thenia walked over and rummaged through the bag. She threw the bag when she saw the red book. "Icky!" she said. "That smells of demon taint! There is an evil inside of it. It is definitely Mianya's."

"I beg of you to release us. I must find out more. If I can find Glory then I can stop Baelin."

Thenia stopped and looked at Carter. "What did you just say?" she asked.

"I am trying to stop Baelin. It is part of my calling from the Creator."

"Hm, I do sense the hope of the light within your soul now." Her face softened. "How do you know that you can stop Baelin?"

"I had a dream. There was a terrible dragon—" Carter said.

"All right!" Thenia interrupted. "Don't go into detail about that demon. I know all about him and I fear to be reminded of his terror. I will release you. Promise me you will destroy Baelin and bring peace once more."

The roots went back into the earth and Carter and Neil stood up and brushed themselves off. "Please forgive my hasty attacks. I have been on edge ever since I was released."

"How long have you been released?"

"Not long at all. Maybe a few days time?" Thenia flew up to the branch she appeared on. "I am a little disoriented still. I am sorry that I cannot be much help."

"That information is most helpful. Thank you." Carter turned to Neil who was resting against a tree. "Let's go Neil if you still want an adventure."

"I will give you safe passage through my forest." Thenia giggled and then disappeared.

"That was very strange," Neil said, "What was she? And who is Baelin?"

"She was a Creature of Old. I don't know what Baelin wants but he is an ancient demon that possesses the body of a man named Sebastian. We must make haste; however, I can tell you more on the way." Carter started north down the path once more with Neil following behind.

CHAPTER EIGHTEEN

The Isle of Thieves

The cool ocean air was blowing inland. Neil's teeth were chattering as he attempted to warm his arms with his hands by rubbing them violently.

"You need to bulk up and maybe you won't be so cold," Carter said.

"I have always been small like this," Neil replied. "I guess you could say I was a runt."

Carter laughed. "Being a runt isn't always a bad thing. Most things we think are bad often turn out to be one of our strengths. You seem very caring and compassionate and I need to work on being more caring. I am not gentle when I should be in some encounters with people. So, I am sorry if I was too harsh on you in the forest."

"O don't be sorry. I am used to it." Neil smiled at Carter.

"Good, we are almost there. I can smell the salt from the ocean."

"I have never been to the sea before."

"I remember it vaguely when I was a young lad."

"It smells quite pleasant."

"They have a thing called a beach along the coasts. There's tons of sand as numerous as the stars in the sky."

"Sounds wonderful! Look, I think I see the ocean! I

wish I could put my feet into the water."

"You might catch cold during this time of year. We don't have time to be sightseeing. We are looking for the Elf princess."

"Where do you think that we could find her?"

"My first option is to always go to an inn. They usually have a pub below where travelers exchange information."

They continued down the path. The wind was quite strong, almost knocking Neil down. "Why is it so windy?" Neil said as Carter laughed. They made it inside and struggled to pull the door shut. It was silent as all eyes were on the two of them. The soft hum of men and women chattering continued and gradually grew louder each time the wind howled.

"Well, that was weird," Neil said.

"Take a look at this," Carter said, "I believe that this is Mianya." Carter ripped a wanted poster off the wall filled with fliers and wanted signs.

In the picture was a simple drawing of the Elf. The reward was quite high and sealed with the royal insignia. Carter stared at the poster intently. Neil shoved another wanted poster in Carters face. "Isn't this one for you?" Neil whispered.

"They have one for us?" Carter whispered. He couldn't believe that he was a wanted man. He looked around and noticed that everyone had now ignored them and returned to their conversations. He saw his name along with the Proudmoores at an even higher price than Mianya's bounty. He casually slipped the paper into his tunic and looked at Neil who was still watching the boisterous men, drinking to their hearts content.

"What do you want to do with this one?" Neil asked.

"We need to find her." Carter walked over to the counter where a burly man was cleaning glasses. "Excuse me!"

"What can I get for ye?" The man asked.

"Have you seen this Elf?" Carter asked.

The man laughed. "Eh, I wish. I could use a bit o' coin for me purse."

"Thank you for your time. I would like a room." Carter placed a few coins on the counter.

"Thank ye kindly," the man said, "I shall return with your key." He disappeared behind the door.

"I have seen that Elf. She mesmerized my husband and tricked him into giving her passage to the Isle of Thieves." A plump woman said.

The Innkeeper came back in and handed a key to Carter. "It will be the first room on the right when ye head up the stairs," He said. The plump woman took a long swig from her mug and set it down on the counter. "Give me another!" she said.

"Ye better watch out. Ye might become a drunk." The man laughed. He gave her another mug and returned to cleaning the other glasses.

"Do you know when they left?" Carter sat next to her.

"Just yesterday." She belched.

"Is there a ship that can take us? I need to find her."

"There would be no shipmasters stupid enough to travel near that cursed island."

"Please." Carter handed her a gold coin. "It is of high importance that I speak with Mianya."

The woman sighed. "I have a cousin west of here in the town of Viktor. His name is Luc and mention that Mary sent you."

"Thank you for your help." Carter grabbed her hand and shook it. He grabbed a coin from his purse and laid it on the counter for the barkeeper. "Another drink for the lady after she is done."

Carter and Neil headed up the stairs. The room was well worn but comfortable. "We need to find a quick way to reach Viktor," Carter said. He began to take off his tunic as he prepared for bed. "Are you doing well Neil? You look a little pale."

"I'm fine," Neil said. His eyes shifted to the window.

"Do you want the bed? I can sleep on the floor."

"No… um… you can have the bed. I am fine sleeping on the floor."

Carter threw a pillow and a blanket on the floor. "If you want to trade places, just let me know. Good night."

"Night!"

What's wrong with him? Carter thought. *He has been jumpy since we came into the room.*

"Carter, are you still awake?" Neil asked.

"Yes," Carter said.

"I just wanted to let you know that I do think you are gentle and compassionate."

"What?"

"We were talking about it earlier. You said you weren't but I see differently."

"Thanks."

"So you never told me more about Sebastian and Baelin."

"What do you want to know?"

"What is motivating you to find this Mianya? You want to stop Sebastian, but why?"

"He has taken someone I care about. She means the world to me. The more I learn about who Sebastian is, I realize he must be stopped. Mianya knows the most about Baelin and I need to find out as much as I can. The world is in danger with him loose."

"Is this a lover that he stole from you?"

"Well I wouldn't call her that because we aren't intimate. Marriage is a sacred thing and it would be a vile thing to corrupt it beforehand. She is however the woman I am to marry. Her name is Karen Proudmoore."

"She sounds lovely."

"She is a wonderful woman. My heart aches for her family because they are being pursued by Sebastian as well.

No one is safe anymore."

"Have you not been in contact since she was abducted?"

Carter's eyebrows raised and he sat up to look at Neil. "Did I say something wrong?" Neil asked.

"Nothing, you seem interested in Karen. I wasn't expecting that because I thought you wanted to know more about Sebastian and Baelin."

"I enjoy hearing stories about love because I believe love is a powerful thing."

"Well, love is an action not a feeling. It is stronger when one chooses to love. There is then a stronger foundation for that love. Feelings change but a choice to love will always stay constant."

"You seem very wise beyond your years. I have never heard of anyone describe love like that."

"It is the will and knowledge of the Creator. I am not wise when it comes to these values. The world today thinks that values have no absolutes and that ethics are subjective based on one's personal views but that is a misconception. There are absolutes in the world but people turn a blind eye because they find it offensive."

"That's very interesting. I would like to hear more."

"I would love to tell you more. Unfortunately it is late and we must rise early to get to Viktor. We can talk more tomorrow." Carter laid his head down again and began to reminisce about Karen and the wonderful times they had spent together. He clutched the pillow close to his chest and fell asleep.

***

"Neil!" Carter said as he pulled the pillow from under Neil's head.

"What!?" Neil said as he sat up.

"We have to get moving. The earlier we reach Viktor,

the sooner we can be on our way to the Isle of Thieves." Carter opened the door and grabbed the pitcher, sitting on the floor. He poured it out and began to wash his hands and face. "Hurry and wash up."

Neil rolled out of the covers and stood up, stretching his arms. He let out a big yawn and looked out the window. Carter began loosening his tunic and slipped it off and began to run the rag across his torso. He cleared his throat and held the cloth out towards Neil. He noticed the wide eyes and gaping mouth of Neil when he saw him.

"Is something wrong?" Carter asked.

"I...," Neil's voice cracked.

"Not used to washing up around others?"

Neil looked toward the floor as his cheeks became red.

"Don't worry. I will give you your privacy." Carter tied up his tunic after placing it on. "I will meet you downstairs. Don't take too long."

There was a frail lady at the bar with a pleasant smile on her face. She must be the wife, Carter thought. He bowed his head when she greeted him. "Could I interest ye in some breakfast? Fresh eggs right from the chickens."

"No thank you," Carter said, "We will be on our way." He placed the room key on the counter and she thanked him.

Not too long had passed and Neil came down the steps. He saw the lady at the bar and exchanged good mornings. "What smells so good?" Neil asked.

"Would you like some eggs and bacon?" The lady asked.

"I would love some!" Neil sat at the bar.

"We must really be on our way," Carter said pulling Neil off the stool by the arm.

"But this is fresh food," Neil replied.

"We have delicious traveling rations." Carter smiled as Neil wrinkled his nose. "Thank you again for the room. Have a lovely day."

They went outside and walked down the road that was headed west out of town. It was the ocean to the right of them and the yellow forest to their left. Neil continually watched the woods.

"I thought I heard giggling," Neil said.

"Don't be so paranoid," Carter said as he laughed.

"How many of those creepy creatures are out there?"

"What makes them creepy?"

"The fact that they are randomly appearing out of nowhere scares me."

"I thought I saw something long and serpent-like emerge from the water below us!"

"And you want to go on the ocean now?" Neil began to hasten his steps.

"Lighten up!" Carter was laughing harder now. "There is nothing. You are really paranoid. I guess it's good you are traveling with me now isn't it. We are going to make a man out of you."

"I don't appreciate being mocked."

"I think I see Viktor."

"Or being ignored...." His voice trailed off.

They reached the docks and found many ships being prepared for voyages. Carter asked around and was pointed in the direction of Luc's ship. It was a strong burley man with black curly hair. He had his left ear pierced and his right eye was swollen. Carter walked up to him but Neil slowed his steps. "Excuse me," Carter asked, getting the man's attention. "Would you happen to be Luc?"

"Yer, that is I." Luc replied.

"Your cousin Mary said that you would possibly give us safe passage on your ship."

"And may I beseech where ye would be headin'?"

"To the Isle of Thieves."

The man let out a raspy laugh. "Normally I be chargin' ya double but Mary must know my love fer adventure! I be chargin' ten gold pieces."

"That is really expensive," Neil said from behind Carter.

"Travelin' ain't cheap young master." The man snorted and spit on the deck. "Land lover." He laughed again when Neil rolled his eyes.

Carter took out his coin purse and handed Luc ten gold pieces.

"Aye, let's be settin' sail in the next hour. What are ye lookin' for at a place like the Isle?

"The Elf Princess Mianya," Carter said.

"I think I saw a wanted poster for an Elf in the bar. A very high price if I be correct."

"She is no criminal," Carter said as he began picking up rope and hauling it over toward the ship mast.

"O a man of politics." Luc began to prepare the mast with the help of Carter while Neil sat on the steps and watched. "If ye wanting work, there is a mop and bucket below." Luc spit again.

Within the hour they had set sail.   Carter noticed that Neil looked a little green. Neil's arms were clutched around the railing of the ship. "Why do I feel so terrible?" Neil said.

"Don't feel bad Luc," Carter said, "He needs to be toughed up."

"I have a few choice words for you…," Neil replied, "Oh…." He leaned over and vomited.

"Why don't ye head below deck," Luc said. "Rest always helps."

Neil went below and fell asleep in one of the hammocks hung between two of the beams. He tossed and turned, staring at the ceiling and finally fell asleep.

***

Neil woke up in a cold sweat and looked around. He saw Carter in the Hammock above him and sighed. The ship was still rocking and Neil had some color back to his face. It had been a few days and he remained below for the remainder of the trip. A faint roar echoed outside. Neil rolled out of the hammock and lost his balance. He fell on his face and groaned as he attempted to get back up. The ship rocked hard and he knocked into one of the beams.

When he reached the deck, he saw something giant flying towards the ship. He grabbed his stomach and stumbled toward the railing of the ship to hold onto. Another roar filled the air and Carter ran up this time.

"What was that?" Carter asked.

Neil moaned and pointed toward the direction of where he saw the flying beast. He then leaned over and vomited again. "I thought I was getting better," he said.

"Neil, do you know what that is?" Carter asked.

"No," he replied.

"It's a dragon!" Carter couldn't believe his eyes. It wasn't the same as the dragon he encountered but another. This one was much bulkier compared to the slender white dragon that he had encountered on the peak of Death Mountain. The reddish hue to its scales reflected the moon's beam giving it the effect that it was on fire. "How majestic," Carter said.

"What is a dragon? Is it another one of those creatures?"

"Yes, and it is magnificent. Do you see the way the moonlight reflects off the scales?"

"It is quite stunning." Neil moaned again. "It is getting closer!"

"It might not even see us. Some dragons I read about are blind and go off other senses."

"So it might smell how delicious we taste and eat us?"

"Don't be ridiculous." Carter's thoughts went back to the white dragon. He guessed that it would protect him again if anything happened. He looked around for the white dragon but saw no sign. The red dragon flew overhead and he felt no sense of fear.

"I thought it was going to breathe fire on us!" Neil said, now lying on the deck.

"It probably thought we didn't taste good enough." Carter laughed and went down below the deck.

Neil rolled his eyes and crawled slowly toward the door to head below. He was moaning until he reached his hammock.

"Still feeling ill?" Carter asked. "Get some sleep. I feel we are close. Luc will wake us when we get there."

***

"Land ho!" Luc cried out from deck.

Carter and Neil emerged from below and saw the port town. It was early morning before the sun had raised into the sky. The town was quiet with little movement. Luc set the anchor down and released a row boat to take them to shore.

"I wish ye the best o' luck," Luc said. He waved them off and rowed back to his ship.

"So now we are stuck on an island where men would kill for a gold coin," Neil said looking around.

The streets smelled like feces and vomit. Men were asleep with bottles in their hands. The wind blew trash through the streets. Neil covered his nose and mouth with his hand as Carter led the way toward the pub.

"Carter," Neil said, grasping his shoulder. "I don't feel so well."

"But we are on land again," Carter said. He felt Neil's hand slide from his shoulder. He looked back and saw Neil on the ground. He had apparently fainted. Grabbing him up into his arms, Carter ran toward the pub and kicked the door open. "I need some water!"

A grungy old hag came out from the back room and saw Neil limp in Carter's arms. She went back and came out with a glass of water. "Looks like dehydration," the hag said.

"How do you know?" Carter asked.

"Has she been vomiting?"

"She? His name is Neil. And yes he has."

"This should do the trick. Lift his head would you honey?"

Carter lifted up Neil and the lady poured some water into his mouth.

"Is he going to be all right?"

"Just give it time and then some more water for the poor dear. Were you on the sea?"

"Yes, how do you know?"

"You aren't passed out drunk like all the other men in this city. Pretty handsome if I do say so myself." She smiled, showing her rotted teeth and gave Carter a wink.

Carter felt the chills run down his spine as she looked at him like that. *I've got to get some answers*, he thought. He forced a smile and nodded. "Do you know where we might find this Elf?" Carter said. He held out the wanted poster he took from the pub in Harte.

"Never seen her before," replied the woman.

"Is there any information at all about something out of the ordinary? A place perhaps we could look for her? I know that she headed here from Allear."

"All the way from Allear, eh?" She scratched her head and lowered her brow. "What brings you all the way to a place like this?"

"I just told you that we are searching for this Elf." He pointed again to the picture. "It is extremely important."

"Well you could ask my husband. He is drunk and passed out at the moment. I do recall there being some sort of odd commotion the other night. I don't know if that is of any importance. Would you like a room while you wait? Your friend is looking better but needs a little bit more rest and some water."

"Do your doors have proper locks on them?"

"This may be the Isle of Thieves honey, but we do show some decency and respect."

Carter took out his coin purse. He handed a gold coin to the lady and she handed him a key. When he put his purse away he made sure to show that he had a sword with him. He grabbed Neil and headed up the stairs.

The room had a moldy smell. This room seemed to have had furniture piled up near the door. The window was open and he walked over to close it. It was stuck despite all his strength. Neil was moaning on the bed.

"Where am I?" Neil asked.

"Are you feeling better?" Carter said, "There is a glass of water next to the bed. Drink up so you can rehydrate yourself. We have to find Mianya as soon as possible."

"This bed smells."

What's wrong with this boy? Carter thought. *He always has to complain or find something wrong about everything. I have to be patient though. Maybe I can help him.*

Neil leaned over and took a sip of the water. "This is good water."

Carter smiled and then turned to look out the window. He saw the sky getting brighter as the sun was rising over the water.

"Thank you for taking care of me," Neil said, "Did you find any information about Mianya?"

"I am waiting for the innkeeper to sober up. Get some rest."

Neil lay back down and fell asleep. It was a few hours before the town began to stir a bit below. Carter took a short nap and was now pacing back and forth. He watched a few men stumble around the streets when he would look out the window. He sped up his pace.

Carter walked downstairs and the lady was at the counter, wiping it down with a rag. She nodded at Carter and walked to the back room. He could hear her yelling,

"Get your lazy…." Carter heard only bits and pieces. A bald man stumbled into the room.

"Eh, what do you want to know?" He said. He yawned and his wife began screaming in the back again. He grabbed his head and closed his eyes. "Lower your voice would ya? My head is killing me!"

"Sorry to bother you but I was wondering if you have seen this Elf." Carter handed him the parchment.

"Yeah," he said, "I'd seen her. She never left through here though. Some man that was bad news walked in here and spooked everyone. And men around these parts don't get spooked."

"Sebastian."

"Is that his name? Well he comes in here and takes a blade to my throat. Asks me if some Elf is here. I pointed up the stairs. Heard some crashing and saw him run down the stairs and out like he was chasing her or something."

"Do you know which way they headed?"

"Beats me. You could try east. That is where the majority of people live. It's called the City of Thieves. Original isn't it. Well you can't miss it with that huge coliseum and such."

"Thank you." Carter handed him a gold coin and began walking back upstairs.

"Best be careful. With a face like yours, a lot of people would try to take advantage of you."

"Thank you," Carter replied, "I think." He hurried upstairs to get Neil for their voyage east. He was close and he could feel Mianya was not too far.

CHAPTER NINETEEN

Trust and Mistrust

Karen looked across the bed and saw Phillip turned over on his side. She slowly lifted the covers off her and slid off the bed. Constantly watching Phillip she tip-toed over to grab her robe. Making her way across the room, she ran her fingers through her hair. The door creaked slightly when she opened it and light shot inside. Phillip moved and she watched as he turned over on the bed. Her heart was pounding and her hands were frozen, trembling on the cold door handle. She closed the door softly behind her and looked down both ways of the hall.

She sighed and made her way to the right. *Maddie please be there*, she thought. She reached a door after going down a few flights of stairs. She looked around again before entering. A candle was lit on the table but there was no fire going. Next to the candle was a loaf of bread and a note that said: *Couldn't wait up for you. Here is your bread. Destroy this note after you have read it.*

Karen grabbed the bread and the note and snuffed out the candle when she reached the door. She set it on a barrel of lard and closed the door to the kitchen. Karen sprinted for the door across the hall. Her heart was still beating at a rapid pace. She slipped through the doorway and closed it softly behind her.

The dripping of water and smell of sewer water instantly made her lightheaded. She slid her hand across the stone walls as she made her way down the stairs. She could hear the cries and moans coming from below. Guards were scarce at night down in the dungeon which made it her opportune moment.

"Karen!" a voice cried out in the darkness.

"Shhh," She replied in a hushed whisper, "Quiet!"

"You have to get me out of here....," the voice said.

"I'm trapped here myself Jaseph. You know that. I am currently trying to convince Phillip that what he is doing is wrong."

"I can't take it anymore down here," Jaseph said, "I am losing my mind. At least you are the Queen. You are lavished with a comfortable bed and some freedom while I rot down here in this prison!"

"I have tried everything I can think of. Please believe me." Karen started to walk down the hall. "I am sorry; I have to go see my brother."

"What is that you have in your hand?"

"Nothing." Karen tried to hide the loaf of bread within her garments.

"Show it to me!"

"Go to sleep. I must hurry to my brother! Be quiet!"

"Show me or I will call for the guards!"

"You wouldn't." She stopped inching forward and stood looking into the shadowed cell.

"I smell the bread. Give it to me and I won't tell the guards you have been coming to the dungeon while the castle slept."

Karen broke off a tiny portion and put her hand in the cell. A hand grabbed her wrist and she jumped. "The bigger portion!" Jaseph said.

She looked at the larger piece and exchanged the loaf for the small portion that she had ripped off. She could hear the bread being torn as she turned to find her brother. A

- 143 -

guard was standing in front of the door and when he saw her he nodded, taking out his keys. He opened Thomas' door and let Karen inside.

"Thank you," Karen said.

In the corner Thomas was curled up into a ball, shivering violently. Karen began to tear up as she reached out to touch her brother. Her gentle hand stroked his arm at which he woke up with a gasp. He crawled backwards against the wall and was breathing heavy.

"Thomas!" Karen whispered, "Thomas, it's me, Karen. Don't be afraid."

"I thought I was going to be burned again." Thomas said.

His voice was almost inaudible. He looked at Karen who now had her arms opened and crawled closer to her. Karen wrapped her arms around her brother and rocked him.

"There, there," She said, "I'm here now." She could hear him whimpering as he was buried in her arms. "I have something for you. It isn't much but I brought what I could." Thomas sat up and looked at her. She took out the small morsel of bread and handed it to him.

"Thank you," Thomas said. He devoured the bread and crawled back into her arms. "Can you sing for me? Please?"

Karen smiled and began singing him the song that always filled her with joy. At first it was hushed but as she began to think of Carter and the happy memories with her family, she began to sing out. At this point she didn't care if she got caught. She wanted to make her brother feel safe and to not lose the hope of the light; a hope that endures beyond all darkness and time.

"I won't leave you," Karen said, "I cannot come for a while because it is too risky but I will try and bring you more food. Stay strong and remember the light will guide you to peace."

"Please, don't leave me!" Thomas cried out as Karen stood up. "I need you! I don't want to be burned anymore!"

Please don't do this to me, Karen thought. *Don't you know that I won't leave you but I cannot stay right now?* She touched his head with her hand and bent down to kiss him on the forehead. "Have faith in me. Have faith in the Creator. Faith will lead you home sweet brother."

She turned from her brother trying to stop her tears but they couldn't be helped. She could hear his crying behind her as she walked out of her brother's prison. Her heart hurt having to leave him in such a condition, because it felt unfair to be treated so well while her brother was like a caged animal.

***

"Karen," Phillip said. "Wake up darling."

Karen opened her eyes and saw Phillip seated beside her as she lay in bed. He was smiling and she didn't know why. She knew that she wasn't caught last night or he would have a different expression on his face.

"I have something for you," He said, still continuing to beam.

"Can you let me sleep longer?" Karen turned over and covered her head with the sheets.

"Oh no you don't!" Phillip grabbed the warm sheets and stripped the bed completely along with the blanket.

"Phillip!" she shrieked. "It's freezing!"

He walked over to where her robe was and held it open for her to wrap herself inside. Karen rolled her eyes and ran into the robe and covered herself, rubbing her hands up and down her arms. She exhaled and could see the vapors of her breath.

"Do you see this?" Karen asked Phillip. "I can see my breath. Imagine how cold it is in the dungeon. My brother—"

"That's enough!" Phillip said. "You are not ruining my surprise with you complaining about your brother."

"He is just a child!"

"Karen! We are not discussing this!" He held out his hand and smiled again. "Now, follow me."

Karen looked at him for a few seconds and finally took his hand. He led her down the hall to the kitchen. She swallowed a hard lump that was lodged in her throat. She didn't know where he was taking her but her heart now began to hasten its pace.

"Are you well?" Phillip asked, "Your palms are beginning to sweat."

"This robe makes me really warm," She said. "Where are you taking me?"

"I told you," Phillip replied, "It's a surprise."

He led her into the door that led to the dungeon. She stopped on the top step and Phillip tried to pull her along but she was frozen to the stone. She looked at him and shook her head as she began to cry. "I can't come with you!" she said.

"What are you afraid of? Don't you trust me?"

"This is some sick game of yours, isn't it?"

"Please trust me. I promise you the surprise would be worth a smile."

"What did you do to my brother? I haven't visited him, I swear!"

"Don't bother lying to me. I know that you have visited him often. Who do you think gave the guard permission for you to get in?"

"What? What are you saying?"

"Please follow me. I love you Karen and I want to make you happy."

He began to lead her down the steps and this time she followed more willingly. She passed by Jaseph's cell and he was standing at the bars, staring at her. She reached the door and her muscles tensed as Phillip commanded that

Thomas' door be opened.

When the door was opened, she saw a small wooden bed in the corner of the cell. Thomas was asleep beneath the many thin layers of cloth given to him. He was not shivering as Karen had seen him before. There was an empty bowl lying below his bed.

"Why are you doing this?" Karen asked Phillip. "Why did you speak so harshly to me?"

"I'm sorry my Queen." Phillip pulled her close to him. "I had to throw you off the trail to the surprise. We have been married for a year and I wanted to give you something special."

"If you want to give me something, give me freedom."

"You know I cannot allow that. We can discuss this later. Go to your brother." Phillip kissed Karen on the forehead and left the prison.

Karen walked over and sat at the edge of the bed that Thomas had received. She noticed that he had recently received a bath, she reached out and stroked his soft golden hair. Thomas opened his eyes and smiled at Karen when he saw her.

"Do you see what they brought me?" Thomas asked. "How did you do it?"

"I don't know. It wasn't my doing. The Creator is watching over you Thomas."

"They brought me eggs with bacon! I only remember bacon once. Didn't dad say that it was expensive?"

Hearing Thomas talk about her father brought a sharp pain to her heart. Without realizing it she found herself crying. Thomas crawled over to her and hugged her.

"I'm sorry." Thomas said. "I miss dad too."

"Don't be sorry. It's my fault he is dead."

"No it's not!"

"You are just a child. You don't understand such things."

"Do too! Mom told me that dad would have died for

any of us if we were in danger. He didn't die for nothing. Please don't say that!" Thomas began crying with Karen.

She was rubbing Thomas' back. "We will get out of here. Carter will find a way. I just know it."

Thomas wiped his eyes. He looked at Karen long and hard and smiled. "Can you tell Phillip thank you for the food and the bed?"

Karen nodded. "I should go find him. I will come back." She stroked Thomas' cheek and exited the prison.

As she exited the dungeon, Karen saw Maggie come out of the kitchen with a basket full of breads. Maggie attempted to close the door behind her and her basket tumbled onto the stone floor. "Oh dear me!" Maggie said as she bent down to pick up her mess.

"Let me help you," Karen said. She knelt down to grab the bread and placed the loaves into the basket. "Have you seen Phillip, Maggie?"

"I do believe so when I was looking out the window a minute ago." She placed the last loaf into the basket and stood up with Karen. "Best be covering yourself well my Queen. The cold will nip you."

"Maggie, I told you to call me Karen."

"O, but I must be respectful as you are the Queen." She smiled and placed her plump hand on Karen's face. "Sweet girl. May the Creator bless you."

"Thank you," Karen said.

Karen turned from Maggie to head up to her room to grab her fur coat. When she found her way outside, she wrapped her arms around her body. It had not snowed this winter and the earth was dead and brown. There was certain mysticism to the air as the fog wisped through the barren trunks of the trees.

What would Phillip be doing out here? Karen thought. *It's so cold.*

She continued to search behind the castle and heard Phillip's voice coming from near his parents' graves. The dead grass beneath her crunched as she made her way toward the hedges surrounding the grave site. Stopping, she listened and continued stepping as lightly as she could when she heard Phillip continue to talk.

"I don't know what to do anymore," Phillip said. His voice was breaking. "Why did you both leave me?"

Karen peered around the hedge to look at Phillip. He was kneeling before his parents' grave stones. His body was trembling with his face buried in his hands. He wiped his face with his sleeve.

"I have given Karen everything and she still doesn't love me. No one wants me anymore and I am not satisfied. Sebastian continues to tell me that I am weak and I need to be strong but I don't know how. I've lost my way and I want to believe Karen but she doesn't understand that Sebastian is my only friend."

Karen's heart ached hearing Phillip. She wanted to go up and comfort him but Phillip was always like a ticking time bomb with his emotions. She turned to leave and snapped a large twig behind her.

"Who's there?" Phillip asked.

Karen sprinted to the door leading into the castle, hoping Phillip didn't see her. She closed the heavy iron-laced door behind her and panted as she leaned against it. The patrolling guard walked by and Karen stood up and smiled. He nodded and continued past her. She sighed and headed back to see her brother after freshening up in her room.

***

Karen was brushing her hair in front of the mirror after her warm bath. She saw Phillip's reflection in the mirror as he entered the room. She turned to him and smiled. He looked miserable. His eyes were red and puffy and he went straight to his dresser to change into his nightgown.

"Thank you," Karen said.

"What?" Phillip replied. "Oh, it was my pleasure."

"My day was wonderful. Thomas wanted me to tell you that he said 'Thank you.'" Karen continued to brush her hair. "How was your day?"

"Why did you follow me?" He asked. His eyes were narrow as he looked at her.

"Excuse me?"

"I know you followed me to my parents' graves. Do you find it amusing to see me tortured?"

"No, Phillip. I—"

"Don't lie to me!"

"Why are you acting like this again? I care about you. I don't want to see you hurting."

"Poor Phillip! Am I right? Is that how people see me? My father and mother did me a disservice by spoiling me."

"Your father loved you! How dare you think they didn't love you! I wish I knew your mother. I am sorry that she died when you were so young, but don't blame your parents! Blame Sebastian!"

"There you go again! Blaming Sebastian for my misfortunes! He didn't kill my father. He was the only friend I had when my father died. Where were you? Gallivanting in the forest with Carter doing who knows what!"

"Excuse me! I have never done anything with Carter! How dare you suggest that I am that kind of woman!"

"You are right. You should be with me but you hate me!"

"I don't hate you. I may be frustrated and angry but I care about you more than anyone." Karen lowered her voice.

"If you love me, then make love to me. Let me know you. Please Karen, all I want is you."

"I am not some object, Phillip. I am your friend and that is all I will ever be."

"I am broken inside." Phillip was crying now as he walked towards Karen. "I thought that giving your brother that bed would make you love me, but I was wrong. So I took it away!" He tensed his jaw as he grabbed Karen up from her chair. He pushed her against the table and began to run his hands down her arm.

"Ouch!" Karen struggled as Phillip pressed his body against hers, trying to kiss her neck. "What are you doing? Stop!" She pushed him back and slapped him across the face.

Phillip stared at the floor. His breathing was uneven as he looked at Karen with a fire in his eyes. Karen slipped past him and ran for the door.

"Don't you leave Karen! You will regret it!"

Karen looked back and tears were dripping down her cheeks. "I'm sorry Phillip but you are sick. You need help and I can't stand by and watch you torture yourself like this."

She opened the door and ran out. She could hear Phillip yelling for the guards behind her. She made her way to the kitchen, hoping Maggie was still there cleaning up. The room was dark when she entered. She lit a candle placed next to the door and found a corner next to a sack of flour. Sliding down next to it, she sobbed into her hands.

I ruined everything for Thomas, Karen thought. *I love Phillip but I can't show him that I do because he will just be confused. Creator please help me forgive him. He is lost and I just want to help him to know You and experience peace. I have to find a way to stop him from Sebastian's manipulation.*

"I see a light on!" A voice yelled from outside the kitchen door. The door opened and a shadow of a guard walked inside. "Here she is!" Two guards walked toward her and picked her up. Karen made no attempt to struggle. Phillip walked in and the look on his face was no longer soft and compassionate but cold and unforgiving.

"Take her to the dungeon and do not let her leave," Phillip said, "I will let Sebastian deal with her when he returns."

Fear was the only thing Karen felt as she heard Phillip's last words. She watched him as she was dragged out of the room.

CHAPTER TWENTY

The Coliseum

After Carter and Neil left the Pub, they headed east. The streets were not active and not many people showed a liking to the strangers to their town.

"That man over there is making me nervous," Neil said.

"He is just gutting fish," Carter replied.

"But does he have to look at us to do it?" Neil said as he walked to the other side of Carter.

"We are strangers," Carter said, "Wouldn't you be curious if some strange travelers came to your town. This isn't a well-visited place you know."

"And good thing it isn't."

"Be gracious. They are lost in their own way of doing things. More people with knowledge of how to live moral lives should visit and help these people."

"I don't understand your logic. I always was happy when robbers and bad men were sentenced to this isle. Even more excited when they willingly decided to go."

"Let's continue shall we? We must find Mianya sooner than later."

They exited the town and headed east along a narrow path that was depleting fast. Ahead of them was an overgrowth of moss covered trees. The branches of the trees were barren of leaves and a foul odor permeated through the air. Neil covered his nose and mouth but Carter just made a distasteful face.

The ground was wet and muggy. Puddles of mud were scattered all over the area. As they were jumping over a log, Neil landed on a wet spot and sunk knee-deep into the earth.

"It's not funny!" Neil said.

Carter was laughing as he grabbed a branch and pulled Neil out. As Neil was trying to brush off the mud, he pointed to the ground.

"What's that?" Neil asked.

On the ground were scattered small droplets of blood. There were two sets of small footprints in the area. Quite a few deep indentations where there was a struggle. Carter looked around more closely and something caught his eye. He reached down and held up a strand of light golden hair.

"You don't think...," Neil said.

"I see no body," Carter said, "I doubt she would give up so easily. She might be injured. Look, there's another set of footprints."

"I thought you were only looking for one Elf. If one is Mianya's and the others is Sebastian, then whose footprints are those?"

"I have no idea but we must find her."

"The two smaller prints seem to be heading north."

"And those head east. I am not a tracker and I am sure they move fast." *What should I do?* Carter thought. He wanted to head north but he figured that Sebastian might be easier to find. Mianya would most likely try to lay low. "We are heading east," Carter said.

"But why? Mianya's footprints head north."

"I have a feeling that we should head east."

Neil picked up his bag after cleaning the mud off. They continued east through the swamp. When they finally found their way out into the open fields, Neil gave a sigh. Carter looked over, smiled, and continued up the hill that was before them.

When they reached the top, the sun was about to set. Golden blades of grass danced along the hillside as the wind gently brushed against them. There was a deer in the distance grazing near a small brook.

"Wow, what a sight," Neil said.

"I couldn't agree more. I think we should rest. The city can't be too far from us now."

Neil unloaded his backpack on the ground. "If this place wasn't filled with so much trash, I wouldn't mind living here." Neil said.

"Why are you calling these people trash?" Carter asked, "They are no different than you or me."

"They are vile people. You heard how they live and now we are here experiencing it."

"All men are vile. Only the Creator's grace makes a man redeemable. What makes you think that you are better than them?"

"I grew up in Allear."

Carter laughed and sat down. "What are we going to do with you Neil?"

Neil frowned and laid down against his bag after pulling out a blanket. Carter stared up at the sky and watched the stars sparkle in the heavens. He wished Karen could be here to experience the beauty of the night sky. He fell asleep to peaceful memories they shared together.

***

When they reached the sight of the city of thieves, they marveled at the size. Smog covered the air but it was well-occupied. People were crowded in tents outside the city walls. There was a steep path down the side of the hill and Carter began down it.

"Wouldn't you like to find a less steep path?" Neil asked.

"It would probably be a few good miles before we found a place," Carter replied, "There is a path here. We should take it."

They headed down the hill and the Coliseum rose high above the walls. As Carter and Neil got closer, they could hear the hustle and bustle of the citizens going on their daily lives. Screams echoed from those in the Coliseum. Neil slowed his pace.

"What's the matter?" Carter asked, "We are almost there."

"What if we get mugged or killed?" Neil asked, continuing down the rocky path.

"I won't let anything happen to us," Carter smiled at Neil and continued on.

The streets were full of men and women headed to various destinations. Merchants called out with their wares in their hands. Alleyways were filled with sick men curled up in their sad states and some covered in vomit. Carter pointed to a sign that led them to a nearby pub.

Not many men seemed interested in the travelers. The bartender was a short red-haired man. He looked young for his vocation but he was happily cleaning mugs as he whistled.

"Excuse me," Cater asked, "We are inquiring about an Elf. Have you seen her?" Carter held out the parchment with Mianya's face on it.

The man motioned for Carter and Neil to follow. They followed him to a back room. When he opened it, there was a man sitting at a table with a few other men, playing a game of cards. The red-haired man whispered in the plump man's ear and a wide smile appeared on his face. Upon the red-haired man's exit, the fat man stood up and said, "Welcome!"

"We are here of urgent matters. We seek information of an Elf," Carter said.

The man laughed and replied, "Urgent? An Elf?" He

wiped the tears from his eyes and took out a pen and parchment. He scribbled something down and folded it up, handing it out to Carter. "Take this to the guard at the service entrance to the Coliseum. Ivan is the eyes and ears of this fine city."

Carter reached out to take the letter and the fat man seized his wrist. He winked and said, "If you don't find what you are looking for, come back and I may have some uses for you."

Carter nodded but his mind told him to run away as fast as he could. He nodded at Neil and they exited, not looking back. They headed east in the city toward the Coliseum.

Two large men stood at the gate. Leather straps covered their torsos as their fat bellies bulged out. They were laughing amongst themselves when Carter approached. They snarled, holding up their axes, when he stopped before them. Carter calmly handed them the letter. When the one on the left read it, his laughed boomed. "Puny man see boss?" the other asked. They opened the gate and let Carter through.

A tiny man appeared from the shadows. In his high-pitched voice he said, "Follow me. Boss will be excited to have you."

The corridor was dark and musty. Neil shrieked when a rat squeaked and scurried by. Carter rolled his eyes when the man looked back and grinned. The thought of Neil saying or doing something embarrassing worried him. Most of the men in this place sensed fear, like it was a sixth sense.

Another large man was guarding the door and stepped aside when he saw them approach. Light burst into the hall, and the room before then was decorated in gay linens and golden pillars. A man sat on a velvety chair, surrounded by piles of gold laid out before him. A handful of women, dressed provocatively, were petting him and begging at his side like dogs. A few were laid out on the few sofas in the room. A few shirtless men were in the room as well, carrying platters of fresh fruit to the various women. One woman with red hair, who was stroking the man's mustache, perked up when Carter walked in.

"Welcome to my fine coliseum. The most entertaining show you will ever find in existence," said Ivan.

The red-haired woman sat up and whispered something into Ivan's ear. He nodded and she smiled ear to ear. Her eyes never left Carter. Neil looked around the room with his jaw gaping open.

"I was told that you might know where I would find an Elf," Carter said.

He took out his parchment and laid it before Ivan. Ivan leaned over and grasped it with his stubby hands. He looked it over and said, "Hmm." He laid it back down on the table and sat back in his chair, folding his hands together. Each finger had a ring on it of various jewels laded in golden casting. He began twiddling his thumbs and smiled at Carter.

"Before I tell you what you would like to know," Ivan said, "I would like for you to give me something of equal value."

"I have about forty gold pieces on my person," Carter said. He began to reach for his coin purse.

Ivan laughed and sat forward. "You amuse me. What did you say your name was?"

"Carter Lockwood, sir."

"Do you honestly believe I am interested in a few mere pieces of gold? Look around you. Oh no, what I want is you to be my next challenger in my Coliseum."

Somehow I knew that is what he wanted, Carter thought. There was no way he would kill anyone for sport. The very idea sickened him. "I am sorry," Carter replied, "but I will not kill. Let's go Neil."

Carter turned around and began walking towards the door when he heard a snap and two of the large guards shifted in front of the doorway. Neil had not moved from his spot and Ivan was still sitting calmly like he was not worried.

"I don't think you grasp what I just said," Ivan said with a grin on his face. "You will be my next challenger."

"You must kill me then." Carter replied.

"Very well. Guards!"

"Wait!" Neil said, "Let me talk to Carter."

Carter looked at Neil in disbelief of the sudden outburst in time of danger. Neil grabbed Carter's arm and led him to the corner of the room. Carter's eyebrows raised and now he was curious what Neil could possibly have to say.

"You have to fight." Neil whispered. He kept eyeing Ivan.

"What are you saying?" Carter asked.

"Look at his cane," Neil said.

He pointed to the desk and lying against it was a golden cane with a lovely white gem on top. It seemed to absorb and disperse the light in a unique way. A spectrum of colors shone upon the ceiling.

"Didn't you say Mianya was looking for strange crystals?" Neil said.

"Yes," Carter replied.

"Don't you think that the gem on the cane could be a crystal? Think about it this way. We are searching for this Elf princess, Mianya. She must have some way of knowing where these crystals are hiding. If we have one in our possession, she is sure to find us."

"You are brilliant," Carter said. He hugged Neil and lifted him off the ground. Neil blushed. "I still don't think it is wise for me to kill a man just to obtain that crystal."

"Maybe you don't have to kill him," Neil said, "Just give them a good show."

"Ok."

Carter and Neil walked back to the front of the desk. Carter felt more confident now as he was about to state his change in merchandise.

"I will fight, but…." Carter said.

"But?" Ivan replied.

"I would like the gem on your cane instead of information."

"You want this gem?" Ivan looked down at the cane.

"Surely you wouldn't mind parting with such a common gem when you have many fine linens and golden objects at your disposal."

"Oh, such arrogance thinking you would win." Ivan was beaming now. "I will accept your terms. Zekiel will show you to your room."

The short man, who showed them to this room, stood before Carter and bowed. Neil began to follow but was instantly stopped by Ivan's guard.

"This young man will stay here with me and sit in the booth to watch the fight alongside of me."

Neil looked at Carter with wide eyes. Carter gave Neil a reassuring nod and followed Zekiel out of the room and back into the hallway. A few doors down to the left stood one of the guards. He stood aside and opened the door.

The room was lavished with fine linens. A weapon rack was lying in the corner of the room next to a table with various pastries and fruit.

"What is with all the fruit platters?" Carter asked.

"It's boss' signature," Zekiel said, "We don't ask questions."

"Thank you," Carter said, looking around the room.

Zekiel bowed and exited the room. The door closed behind him and Carter heard it lock. *I guess they don't want anyone leaving,* he thought. He walked over to the weapon rack. There were maces, axes, and swords. He looked at his own sheath and drew his magnificent sword from it. He admired the intricate detail on the molding and then returned it to its leather casing.

The bed was rather large with purple silk draped over

the top. He ran his fingers across the material and allowed himself to fall on the bed. He had never experienced such fine quality of a bed and noticed he was dozing off.

When Carter opened his eyes, he felt his tunic was being undone and sat up, almost knocking over the red-haired woman lying next to him. She smirked and reached forward to continue when he grabbed her wrist.

"What are you doing?" Carter asked. He let go of her wrist and slid off the bed, assembling his tunic as he backed away.

"My master said I could help you prepare for your fight in the coliseum," She said.

"Don't come any closer," Carter said. He held up his hand to stop her as she slid off the bed and advanced towards him.

"I have helped many men win their battles," She said as she removed the straps of her dress from her shoulders, allowing the gown to slide down her body.

"Do you not listen?" Carter asked as he ran to the bed to grab a sheet and cover her before she removed anymore of her clothing. His heart was beating fast as he attempted to fight the lust that could easily consume him. "I do not want you!"

She pouted when Carter wrapped the sheet around her and pushed her towards the door. He knocked twice and the window to the door opened. When the door finally opened, he pushed her along so she would leave the room. She looked back at him and had the door shut in her face.

Carter grabbed his forehead and walked over to a chair near the table. He sat down and sat for a while with his head in his hands. *I didn't realize I would be challenged and tempted in every possible way,* Carter thought. *Please help me to deny what is wrong in your eyes. Help that woman find peace as she is searching to please desires that will not satisfy.*

He continued to pray until there was another knock on

the door. He looked up hoping it was someone other than that strange woman. Zekiel walked into the room with a large grin on his face. "Please come with me," he said.

He was led down the hall toward the door to Ivan's chambers, making an immediate left when they reached it. The hall became darker and a gate was before Carter. Inside was a weapon rack with various weapons such as: maces, axes, swords, and spears. Lying on a chair in the corner of the room was a set of clothes.

"Please remove your clothes and put those garments on," Zekiel said, "Master wants to make sure every fight has no tricks."

"Must I expose myself to allow you to know that I have no tricks?" Carter asked.

"Master's orders," Zekiel responded and snapped his fingers.

Carter sighed and began undoing his tunic. He then untied his pants and allowed them to slide down his legs. He kicked them off along with his boots and went to grab the garments lying on the chair.

"Even your undergarments," Zekiel said.

Carter turned around and removed his undergarments, quickly putting on the ones given to him. He geared up in their leather armor which had little protection and put on the boots, binding them as firm as he could because they were too big for him. Carter walked over to the weapon rack and grabbed a very dull sword that had many chips in the blade.

At least this won't be able to kill anyone, Carter thought, swinging the sword a few times. He hoped he didn't have to finish anyone off because this sword would be a slow and painful death.

"I am ready," Carter said.

Zekiel walked over to Carter and quietly said, "If I was you, I would have slept with Alexandra. She is the master's favorite concubine and he views her very highly. I do believe you insulted them both. Be prepared for the worst challenger."

Carter felt the blood leave his face. He looked at the gate before him as it opened slowly. He grasped the sword tightly within his fist and stepped forward. There was no turning back now and he prayed that the Creator would aid him in this battle.

The cry of the people watching was echoing through the air. Carter's heart raced and he could feel the sweat forming on his forehead. The hall seemed endless as he continued down it toward the light at the end. He heard the clanging of the gate behind him as it hit the ground.

He shielded his eyes from the bright sunlight, and realized he must have slept longer than he anticipated when he was in that room. He looked around at the screaming fans and saw a few women faint when he looked at them.

A low drum was being pounded at a slow pace and gradually got faster. There was no one in the arena except Carter. He glanced up and saw the booth where Ivan was residing. Neil was seated in the same booth, fidgeting with the drapes near him.

When the drums stopped, the arena became silent. Not a sound could be heard. Carter stared toward the opening on the other side of the arena for his opponent to emerge.

A giant of a man came forth from the shadows, looking to be about eight feet tall. He stepped into the ring and yelled as his veins protruded from his neck. The crowd went crazy as they screamed even louder. The giant looked at Carter and smiled vindictively.

Carter shifted into his fighting stance, dull blade in hand. He had no intention of killing this man, but neither did he desire to be killed. He looked around at the multitude of people watching and waiting intently for the fight to start, his heart beating even faster than before.

A gong sounded. The giant charged at him and Carter had his sword ready to deflect the blow. Their swords collided and the fight was on. Carter was almost as strong as the giant but not quite strong enough. The protruding veins were evidence of his strength.

"You are a fool to fight me," said the giant man. He bellowed, causing his saliva to land on Carter's face.

The crowd cheered as the two fought vigorously. Their swords deadlocked. The giant quickly threw his head forward into Carter's face. Carter fell down and the giant thrust his blade toward Carter, but Carter rolled away just in time. He could feel the pressure of the blood in his face.

Carter had lost his sword and grabbed his face realizing he had a bloody nose, but he was not going to give up this fight. Winning was his only option. He struggled to evade the giant's blade, and the giant finally caught Carter's armor and pinned him to the ground. The sword stuck in the ground, so the giant began to kick Carter in the ribs.

Carter felt one of his ribs crack and cried out in pain. He had to get free and find an advantage against this massive man.

Carter wrenched himself free and kicked the giant to the ground, causing the ground to tremble. He had torn Carter's armor off and he was no longer protected as he ran to regain his sword. Carter snatched his sword from the ground and ran over to the giant, who was still struggling to get up. Carter kicked the man's sword away from him and put his blade to the giant's throat.

"You're finished," Carter said, breathing heavily. His ribs hurt so bad but he had to fight the pain for now.

The crowd hushed. Breathing heavily, the giant said, "Go ahead and finish me." Carter would not move but remained ready to thrust it into his neck. "Kill him!" the crowd cheered. The words became louder and louder as the crowd chanted for death.

"Do it!" yelled the giant.

"I already won. There's no reason to take your life." Carter removed his blade and walked away. It was the only honorable thing to do.

He heard the crowd cheering instead of jeering. Carter twisted around and saw the giant barreling towards him. Carter tried to dodge but the sharp pain from his side stopped him from moving faster than he would have liked.

The giant grabbed Carter by the neck and lifted him up. He punched him once in the face and threw him to the ground. As Carter slid on the rough ground, he felt the flesh being shredded from his body. He needed a sword which was a few feet away.

He attempted to get up again but the man picked him up again and threw him once more. Carter heard a pop in his left shoulder as he landed on his left arm. He opened his eyes, trying to fight the pain but he wanted to die at this moment.

The giant's sword was a few feet in front him, just in arms reach, but Carter had not the strength to obtain it. The cries of the people became muffled.

"Carter!" cried a voice, "Don't give up. Fight for the Creator! I believe in you."

"Karen?" Carter said.

"Carter the light will prevail! Draw your strength!"

Carter knew the world needed him and slowly got up on his right hand and knees. He saw the giant coming for him again. "For Karen!" Carter yelled, picking up the sword and thrusting it into the man's chest. "And for the Light!" Carter remained on his knees, panting.

Carter looked at the fear-stricken giant. The man coughed blood onto Carter's face. Carter removed the sword and watched the giant fall down to the ground. Carter crawled over to the man and closed his lifeless eyes, saying a prayer. The crowd cheered as the fight was over.

Carter gathered his strength and stood up. He refused to look at any of the people because he was ashamed at what he had just done. He stumbled forward and made his way to the hall that he had come from.

"Carter!" Neil said. He threw himself onto Carter and wrapped his arms around him. "I knew you would do it!"

Carter winced as it hurt to be touched. "Please," Carter said, "I just want to change and leave this place." He grabbed his clothes and handed them to Neil to put in their sack.

"Let me help you," Neil said, putting Carter's right arm over his shoulder. "I was scared you were finished for a moment there. What happened?"

"The light gave me strength," Carter said.

Zekiel clapped in the doorway as Carter and Neil walked toward him. "Very impressive," Zekiel said, "That was master's best fighter. Please, follow me."

Carter and Neil were led into Ivan's chambers. When the red head Alexandra saw Carter shirtless and bruised and bloody, she bit her lip. She bent down and whispered something in Ivan's ear. "No!" he said.

"I think we had a deal," Carter said.

"I don't know about you but I would love to see you fight again and then I will give you what you want," Ivan said with a smile on his face.

"You scum!" Neil said.

"Now now," Ivan said, "I don't want any bloodshed in my chambers. I think it best that you choose your words carefully young traveler."

"It's ok, Neil," Carter said, "We will be leaving then."

"Very well," Ivan said, "Come back soon. I will anticipate it." Ivan laughed and snapped his fingers.

The doors opened and Carter leaned on Neil as they started walking out of the room. Carter felt defeated not getting what he came here for. Mianya was still out there and he was determined to find her. When they reached halfway down the hall, Neil removed himself from under Carter's arm.

"I have something to show you," Neil said in a whisper. He opened his bag and a faint light shone from it.

"Is that?" Carter asked.

"Yeah," Neil said, "I snagged it this morning. I overheard him saying he wasn't going to give it to us. He said he was going to put it with the rest of his jewels. We must hurry before he notices it's missing."

Neil grabbed Carter's arm again. And Carter grasped Neil's arm, holding him back. "Wait!" Carter said, "Someone is coming."

They leaned back into the shadows. The steps got closer when Carter noticed that it was Sebastian. Sebastian stopped and looked in their general direction. His eyes narrowed and he continued down the hall.

Carter mouthed instructions to Neil about when to move and when he said, "Go," they started down the hallway as fast as Carter could move. They were almost to the exit when they heard yelling from behind them. "Faster!" Carter said.

The guards at the gate opened it before they heard the yelling. Carter handed them the parchment. The guards grabbed Neil and Carter when they finally heard the shouting.

Out of the nowhere two hooded people came from behind and knocked out the guards. "Follow us if you want to live," said a woman's voice.

Neil looked back and saw Sebastian among the men running down the hall. The hooded woman closed the gate and led Carter and Neil into a dark alley.

CHAPTER TWENTY ONE

The Red Book

Carter and Neil found themselves in an abandoned house with the two hooded strangers.

"Give us the crystal now!" said Tiandra, pulling down her hood and holding her blade up to Carter's throat.

"No!" Neil said.

"Tiandra, please," Mianya said softly as she raised her hand.

"They have what we want. Why not take it by force?" Tiandra asked.

"Please just give us the crystal," Mianya said quietly. "We would regret hurting you. You have no need for it and it is valuable to us."

"Who are you?" Carter asked. "Show yourself."

Mianya removed her hood and Neil gasped. "Carter, it's Mianya!"

With a swift motion Tiandra grabbed Neil and Mianya grabbed a dagger from her thigh and held it to Carter's throat. "Who are you and how do you know who I am?" Mianya asked.

"You can have the crystal," Carter said, "The only reason I wanted it was to find you."

"What do you mean?" Mianya asked, confused. She held up her blade closer to his neck. "Are you a follower of

Sebastian?"

"That's not the case, dear Mianya. You know things that I need to know," Carter said. "Please, hear me out."

"Hand us the crystal first," Tiandra said.

"The crystal is in that bag," Carter said, pointing to Neil's bag. Mianya released Carter and he grabbed his neck to rub it. "I know Sebastian is dangerous but what does he want with these crystals?"

"You don't need to worry about such things, human," Mianya answered, putting the crystal safely in her bag after Tiandra handed it to her.

She could sense that he had the light within his soul, but wondered how he knew about Sebastian.

"My love, Karen, is captured in his castle and it is necessary for me to know. Sebastian is now pursuing her entire family."

"I apologize for her capture, but you do not need to know about Sebastian."

"Yes, I do, actually. You are the one who is releasing the Creatures of Old."

"You know a lot and you said you have been following me? Who are you?" Mianya asked.

"My name is Carter Lockwood. I am a warrior of the light that trained with the monks who live at the monastery in Faerie Forest."

"Even so, I cannot trust you with my knowledge. You don't have the ability to fight against Sebastian."

"If I have to prove to you that I am capable, I will. In fact, I have something of yours," he said. He walked over to his bag and pulled out the red book with the Elven royal crest on it.

"Where did you get that?" she asked. Her eyes were wide as she had not seen this book since she was a follower of Sebastian.

"I found it," Carter said, "I was escaping with Karen's family over Death Mountain when I stumbled across a strange cave. Inside was what I believe was Baelin's castle."

"No," she said as she finally realized how Baelin escaped. "It all makes sense. It was my fault for not destroying the castle."

"What makes sense?" Carter asked.

"The reason Baelin has returned is because of my foolish mistake," Mianya bowed and shook her head, ashamed.

"So, Sebastian does have the spirit of Baelin inside him?"

"Yes. I don't know whether it was a part of him or one of his demons, but there was something in the castle. In fear, I made it disappear instead of destroying the wretched place and its taint."

"I destroyed it already. I set fire to the place. I could hear the tortured screams of evil beings within the walls of the place."

"It is too late! He is back, and every day he grows stronger. I can only stop him temporarily by releasing the Creatures of Old so he cannot have their power."

"Tell me what this book is," Carter said as he shook it in his hand.

"I don't remember much. It might be my diary. Let me see it."

Carter handed her the mysterious book. She looked at it carefully and tried to remember what she used it for. She unlatched the lock and opened it carefully. A huge shadow flew from the book and went into her. Her body flailed and thrashed on the floor. Suddenly, she became motionless.

***

Mianya woke up and found herself in her bedroom back in Melyaria. The room was filled with gaily colored drapes and had a mysterious aura to it. She looked around and wondered how she got here. Into her room danced her two sisters, Saerwen and Morwen.

She looked at them in disbelief. Her sisters were dead and she knew this must be a trick. But they looked and smelled so real.

"Oh, sisters, his voice is so pleasant!" Saerwen said, "Smooth like honey!" She clasped her hands together and beamed.

"For a human, he is quite handsome!" Morwen added as she grabbed Saerwen's hands to dance.

Saerwen and Morwen danced around the room gleefully. They twirled over to Mianya and included her in their playful dancing. Mianya looked at them as she danced around the room with them. Their skin was soft as she had remembered and gentle.

Mianya realized now where she was. She had experienced this event before. The man that they were referring to was Baelin himself. He did not make himself known until after this took place. The three slowed to a stop and looked at one another.

"Mianya, you must meet him. He speaks gentle words to me in the evening under moonlight," Saerwen said. She sighed and smiled as she danced over to the window to look out at the night's sky.

"Do not meet with him!" Mianya said. Her chest was heaving as she was now furious with her sisters. She clenched her fists so tightly that the color of her hands were now white.

"Dear sister," Saerwen said, "what seems to be the matter?" She raised her eyebrow

"Do not be fooled by his sweet words! He is an evil man! You must listen to me, please! If you allow his false words to penetrate your mind, you will die!"

"Are you well?" Saerwen asked.

"What are you saying? 'Am I well?' You are flirting with death!"

"Dear sister, I do believe you need to lie down. You are speaking madness."

"Shall I go get mother?" Morwen asked.

"You are foolish and are going to ruin the world!" Mianya yelled as she started to leave the room. "I will be the one informing mother!"

Saerwen and Morwen looked at her and then at one another as she made her way to the door. "She has lost it," Morwen whispered. Mianya opened the door and walked swiftly over the threshold.

She was in the forest nearby the haven. The moon shone and fireflies fluttered through the dark trees. Standing with her were her two sisters. The sound of a man's voice, smooth and elegant, filled the forest.

"He is coming, my sisters," Saerwen said with excitement. "You will love him, Mianya. I feel that tonight is the night."

Through the dark trees walked a young man. His dark hair flowed behind his elegant body. He had a beautiful face and Mianya could not look away. He swiftly came to Saerwen and embraced her.

"Sweet maiden," he spoke softly into her ear. "The time has come for you to rule with me. You shall be my queen and there will be no limits to our power."

Saerwen looked intently into his dark eyes and quivered with satisfaction. He gently ran his fingers through her silky, blonde hair. Her breathing became uneven, with her lips parted, as he kissed the nape of her neck seductively.

"I will follow you anywhere, my lord," she whispered back.

Mianya looked horrified. Try as she might, though, she could not look away from Baelin's mesmerizingly attractive face and body. The light within her pendant warmed her spirit and helped her break the trance.

"Stop!" Mianya yelled. Her two sisters and Baelin looked at her with confused faces. "This is wrong, my sisters. He is a demon! Do not believe his lies. Do not give him your souls. You will die because of him!"

"Surely your sister is mad," Baelin laughed. He gently kissed Saerwen on her tender lips. She closed her eyes and he continued to do so.

Mianya could not take any more of this futility. She pulled out a dagger and charged at Baelin. Morwen quickly seized her. "Stop, Mianya!" she cried. "Do not hurt something so beautiful." She then threw Mianya to the ground.

"Some things that are pleasing to the eye can have deadly results," Mianya said. She must inform her mother somehow, and got up to run away. She ran through the trees and saw a bright light ahead. She approached the light and unexpectedly found herself running through the satin curtains covering the doorway to her mother's room. Thalandria sat at her mirror brushing her long beautiful hair and humming a lullaby.

"Mother!" yelled Mianya.

"What is it, my daughters?" Thalandria asked.

Mianya was surprised at her mother's word choice. She was alone—wasn't she? Mianya looked behind her and standing there were her two sisters. Their beauty had faded and their eyes looked cold and tired. Their hair was dull and no longer shone in the light.

"Mother!" spat Saerwen.

"What is wrong with you three? I feel evil from within you," Thalandria said as she looked upon them.

"We deny you and your light, mother!"

"What do you mean? The light is the answer to our life. We are the chosen race."

"We have found a new, stronger power," Saerwen said as she grabbed her pendant from around her neck and threw it to the floor.

Morwen also threw down her pendant. Something inside Mianya wanted to do the same. Her hand slowly reached for her own pendant and began to tremble. She knew that this was wrong and fought every second of it. She looked into her mother's pure, innocent eyes and knew what the right choice was.

"No!" Mianya screamed. The light filled her spirit and her pendant began to glow.

She turned around and slapped Saerwen. Rage filled Saerwen's darkened eyes and she glared at Mianya.

"How dare you!" Saerwen said as she in turn struck Mianya.

Morwen jumped in to grab Mianya. Saerwen started to claw and strike Mianya over and over. "How dare you defy me!" Saerwen screamed. "I will be the new queen of this world! Baelin has promised it!"

Mianya closed her eyes and prayed for this to stop as her flesh was being ripped. She suddenly heard and felt nothing. A deadly stench filled the air. Opening her eyes, she saw a dark room containing her two sisters on either side of Baelin, who was sitting on a throne of skulls.

"Come closer, Mianya, so I can smell your fear better," Baelin ordered.

Mianya felt her legs moving forward. She could not break free of this power. She wanted to cry out, but she had no voice. She came closer and closer to the evil face that was so pleasant to look upon.

"I am so glad you decided to join us," Baelin said pleasantly.

"We are so proud of you, sister," Saerwen said, satisfied.

Saerwen and Morwen looked different. They both had long silver hair and blood-red eyes. Their skin was pale and they looked like they had not slept in ages.

"Silence, Phayde!" Baelin ordered, holding up his hand. "We do not wish to frighten your sister."

Mianya could now smell blood in the air and wanted to gag. The warm pendant resting on her chest pulsed and she felt able to speak.

"Now, throw down your pendant and take on your new, more powerful, form. You will be one of my generals as I conquer this pathetic world, capturing souls and giving me their power," Baelin said with a laugh.

"No!" Mianya shouted. She was not going to give in to the seductive voice of Baelin this time.

"What did you say?" Baelin asked through his teeth. "No one defies me!"

"I will not join you, demon! Go back to hell where you belong!"

"How dare you!" he said as he stood up, slamming his fists on the arms of his chair. His face became somewhat frightening as he glared at her, but somehow it was still captivating.

"You are mad and you will fail. There is no way you will win against the light."

"Just as water extinguishes a flame, I will extinguish your pathetic light. Try to resist my power and not bow before me," he said.

Mianya felt her knees get weak as Baelin was taking control of her body. She started to shake frantically as she was attempting to resist the power. Her body was out of her control and slowly she began kneeling before him. When she went fully into a kneeling position, her two sisters and Baelin laughed.

"Where is your light, Mianya?" he taunted as he walked toward her. "Bow your head and worship me."

"No—" she said.

"Yes!"

Her head started to move as well. She did not want to fight it anymore but she knew that she must. Pain filled her body and she started to breathe uneven breaths.

"YAH! Help me!" she cried out, needing the Creator's intervention.

She gradually became stronger than the force

controlling her body. The light was filling her spirit as she started to get up. Baelin looked at her and there was a fear in his eyes.

"What is this?" he asked.

"You will lose and you will not have me!" Mianya yelled.

Baelin drew his blade and stared at her. Mianya reached up and grabbed hold of her pendant. The warmth became stronger and she could feel the light coursing through her body. A bright light started to shine from the pendant and became stronger and stronger until holy light filled the entire room.

"No!" Baelin screamed as the light consumed the room.

***

"She's starting to come around," said Tiandra.

"Mianya, are you alright?" asked Carter.

Mianya opened her eyes. The room was fuzzy, and she could barely make out the three people crowded around her. The more she blinked the clearer their faces became.

"Can you speak?" Tiandra asked.

"I did it," Mianya whispered. She fought against her memories and conquered them with the light.

"Princess Mianya, are you well?" Carter asked.

"Yes, I am, actually," she said as a smile spread across her face.

"I apologize," Carter started. "I should have warned you about what was inside that book."

"Do not apologize. I am glad that I faced such challenges." Mianya said.

"What do you mean?" Carter asked.

"That was, in fact, my written memories. I faced and conquered them with the light as my guide."

"You mean you relived your memories?" Neil asked.

"Yes—and I defeated them. I thank you for bringing

this book to me. I can now live with a guilt-free conscience. The light is a faithful guide."

"Mianya?" Carter asked.

"Yes, Carter?"

"Is there any way to stop him?"

"As time goes on, he is gradually going to get stronger. The only way he was stopped before was by the sword of the Heavenly Knight."

"The knight is not on earth." Carter said.

"I know, but he left the sword on earth." Mianya said.

"Where is it?" Carter asked.

"It is hidden somewhere. My only guess is the forbidden sea, the sea surrounded by the thickest mist that does not leave."

"That place is a death trap. Why would he want to hide it there? No one would ever find it."

"Exactly. That is why he would most likely have put it there."

"Then how are we to get to it?"

"We will get to it with the key that the Heavenly Knight gave to me before he ascended into the heavens."

"We must get the key and find this sword!" Carter said, standing up and helping Mianya to her feet.

"Unfortunately, Sebastian might have the key." Mianya said. There was no remorse in her voice. She knew that there was a larger plan the Creator had in store.

"Why would he have it?" Carter asked.

"Sebastian is the one, other than you, who found his way into Baelin's old castle, hidden in Death Mountain. That is where I dropped the key."

"You dropped the key?" Carter asked.

"That doesn't matter. What matters is that Sebastian most likely has the key and we need to get it back."

"Well, there's no way that we will get it back with just us," Carter said, "We will need an army."

"Yes, we will need to prepare." Tiandra said.

"Where can we find the opposition?" Carter asked.

"My people have escaped to Norya," Mianya said, "Having combined our forces with the Noryans, we might be able to defeat the Allearian army."

"I will finally be able to see my sweet Karen again," Carter said.

"Let me quickly inform my people of my return." Mianya said, walking over to a boarded window.

Mianya made a small opening in one of the boarded windows and let out a high pitched whistle. A white dove flew into the room and landed on Mianya's finger. She walked over and placed the dove on a worn shelf.

Mianya pulled out parchment and a quill. Her hand moved swiftly but fluidly. She folded the parchment and tied it to the dove's leg. Bending over the dove, she gently gave it a kiss and it flew—directly into the wall. It crashed to the ground, but then flew into the air again and made its way through the small hole.

"Are you positive that it will get to them quickly and safely?" Neil asked.

"I trust her. She is a very good friend." Mianya said with a smile.

"She sure is clumsy." Neil said.

"Neil, please stop talking," Carter requested.

"What are we going to do about the crystals?" Tiandra asked.

"I believe this is the last one in this land that we are able to obtain," Mianya said, "Norya might be a good place to look next."

"Then it is a good thing we are headed there," Carter replied.

CHAPTER TWENTY TWO

What is Love?

Susan stormed into the room and picked up the first thing she could find. There was a spoon lying on the table and when she picked it up, she whacked Adam on the arm.

"Ouch!" Adam yelled, "What was that for?"

"Are you an idiot?" Susan asked, "What is wrong with you?"

"What are you talking about?" Adam asked.

Susan whacked him once more. Adam grabbed the spoon from her hand but that wasn't going to stop her. She was bound to find out why Adam left Lia in tears down by the lake.

"I told Lia that you still love her and to be patient. What did you say to her?"

"She started talking about marriage and starting a family and I didn't know what to say. I am not ready for this responsibility. How would I provide for her? I would like to marry her but I just need some time to sort out how everything would work out if we did get married."

"You need to communicate this better!" Susan said as she smacked him on the arm once more.

"Susan!" Eleanor said as she walked into the room, carrying vials of perfume. "Stop heckling your brother!"

"Mom, he needs this," Susan said.

"Did I ask for an explanation?" Eleanor said, raising her brow.

"No Ma'am."

"Good, now be a good girl and wash up. We are going to the Lockwood's for supper."

"Mother," Adam said, "May I ask you something?"

"Sure," Eleanor said, setting down her vials.

Susan walked slowly toward the door and opened it as slowly as she could so she would be able to hear their conversation. Eleanor cleared her throat and Susan moved a little faster. She closed the door behind her and pressed her ear to the door.

"Now what was all that fuss your sister was making?" Eleanor asked.

"I don't know what to do," Adam said.

Susan could hear the scratching of wood on the ground and knew they were sitting. *This is going to be good*, she thought.

"I love Lia," Adam started again, "I just don't know if I am ready for a commitment to marriage. How would I provide for her?"

"It is good that you are being responsible about this," Eleanor said, "I still don't understand why your sister was antagonizing you."

"Because she is mad."

"Adam!"

"Susan talked to Lia. Lia misunderstood what I meant when I said I needed to think. She brought up the topic of marriage. What should I do?"

"Have you talked to her father?"

"No, I didn't even think of that."

"It would probably be best to make your concerns known to him. He would probably give you great advice. He might even teach you how to be a forester."

"Mom!" Marie said.

The front door slammed shut and Susan tried to listen to

what her mother and Adam were saying.

"Marie," Eleanor said, "Go wash up! You look filthy!"

Marie was running toward the door before Susan realized that she was headed her way. She tried to move toward the basin to act like she was washing up but she didn't reach it in time. When the door opened, she saw her mother standing behind Marie.

"Susan Proudmoore," Eleanor said, "I told you to wash up. Were you listening at the door?"

"Yes ma'am," Susan said.

"Well, I do believe that you will have lots of chores tomorrow," Eleanor said.

"I figured," Susan replied. Susan washed her hands in the basin and sighed.

***

"Susan!" Lia said, running down toward the dock at the lake.

Susan was skipping rocks and sitting at the end of the dock. She hoped Lia had good news because that is what she needed right about now.

"What are you doing all the way out here?" Lia asked, "I hope that you don't want to swim. The water is freezing with the snow from the mountain defrosting into the water."

Susan laughed. "I am not that mad," Susan laughed, "So do you have good news?"

"Yes!" Lia said as she wrapped her arms around Susan.

"You two are getting married?" Susan asked.

Lia was beaming. She sat down next to Susan and screamed, flailing her arms and legs.

"So what happened?" Susan asked.

"Well, Adam totally surprised me when I was working on a dress for one of the ladies on the edge of town. He told me that he talked to my father and came to an agreement.

We are going to be married and live in my parent's house until Adam and my father build a cottage not too far from here. It was so romantic. I almost started crying."

"I knew you shouldn't have worried," Susan said.

"Now we just need to find you a man," Lia said, elbowing Susan.

Susan laughed but she felt awkward. "Yeah," Susan said. Her mind lately had been on that strange man that was hooded back at the monastery. She wondered who he was. He wasn't one of the monks because he showed up just prior to them fleeing over the mountain. The mysteriousness of him made her curious.

"Susan!" Lia said, "Are you all right?"

"Oh!" Susan replied, "I was just thinking about something."

"Was that drool?" Lia said. She laughed and fell back, holding her stomach.

"No!" Susan began wiping her mouth. "It wasn't drool! Stop laughing!"

"I know! I know! I just could not help making that comment with the look on your face!"

Susan dipped her hand into the ice water and scooped a handful. It was like knives being shoved up the veins of her wrist. She took the water in her hand and splashed Lia. Lia screamed and stood up, jumping up and down.

"Susan! That's so cold!"

"Now that is funny," Susan said. She was pretty pleased with herself.

"All right, fine," Lia said, extending out her hand. "Come help me with the dress. My mother is probably waiting at the house with the material."

Susan sighed and grabbed Lia's hand as they ran up the hill. Those darn dresses they were wearing were a pain to climb in with all the lace and layered material.

***

The weather was getting warmer and closer to the hour that Adam and Lia would be united as one flesh before the Creator. Susan stood in front of the mirror and adjusted her ribbon in her hair. They had spent a couple weeks making Lia's dress perfect and Susan was a tad jealous. She admired her own dress but it wasn't the same.

I wish I could be wed to someone, Susan thought. More than ever, she wanted to know who that mysterious man was. Just remembering the stubble across his strong jaw, it made her weak at the knees. She was determined to find out who he was and debated going back to the monastery alone to see him. She stopped herself a few times, telling herself that she was mad for thinking such crazy thoughts.

"Susan," Lia said, "Come hither."

Susan went into the other room. Eleanor was in there with Mrs. Lockwood. All three of them were crying and that made Susan start to tear up. She ran and hugged Lia and they wept together.

"Oh Lia!" Susan said, "You look so beautiful. I must admit that I am highly jealous."

"I think we should head to the lake now," Mrs. Lockwood said, "They all must be ready to start the ceremony."

When they arrived, it was very beautifully decorated with various spring flowers. Deep shades of purple and pink were dominate among the hues of yellows and whites. They had requested for a monk from the monastery in Faerie Forest come to do the ceremony.

Susan walked down the aisle made by the people standing on either side to observe the union about to take place. Faces were all smiling. Marie was the flower girl and threw the petals of flowers rather than letting them glide down gently from her hand. Susan noticed that Marie was showing her fake smile rather than a genuine one.

A man was playing his violin and changed the tune once Lia began walking down the aisle on her father's arm.

Susan could tell that she had been crying. She couldn't help but roll her eyes because it seemed all Lia was doing for the past few months was crying.

She couldn't be pregnant could she? Susan thought to herself. *No, there is no way. Adam wouldn't be that stupid.* Susan put it from her mind because she knew better. That is why Adam wanted to settle down first. She was relieved that her mind was going crazy. She continued to dwell on the rugged man from the monastery. Everything about the ceremony was a haze. She knew the monk would be leaving straight after the union was complete.

When people began moving to congratulate Adam and Lia on their marriage, Susan went straight for the monk.

"May I come with you?" Susan asked.

"Excuse me?" The monk replied.

"I would like to go with you to the monastery," Susan said. She looked at her mother who was preoccupied with talking to a few of the townsfolk.

"I will be leaving in an hour," The monk said, "I will meet you down by the fountain in the town square."

"I will be there. Let me say goodbye to my family."

Susan looked around for Adam and Lia among the crowd of people. When she spotted them, she ran toward them. She wrapped her arms around them and gave them a big hug before they were consumed by people wanting to talk to them. Her mother was not too far off.

"Mother," Susan said. She ran over and hugged her mother.

"What is it?" Eleanor asked.

"I just wanted to tell you I love you."

"Are you all right Susan?" Eleanor grabbed her face. "You look ill."

Susan smiled and just walked away. She was nervous about leaving but something was drawing her to do this. She couldn't explain it but wanted to get home so she could leave before anyone could stop her. Her heart was beating fast and she could feel the rush of doing something mad.

She made it home and changed as quickly as she could. She rummaged through her dresser to pack a few sets of clothes. She carefully made sure it put back the way she left it so her family wouldn't think that she got abducted.

When she saw the monk sitting on his cart, being pulled by a donkey, she stopped. With the monk staring at her, she wondered what he thought of her sudden request. She cared not at this point whether he thought her mad and picked up her bag charging toward the cart to leave before someone noticed she left.

***

As they headed down the mountain, she admired the sun as it was beginning to set over the tops of the trees. She caught a glimpse of the spires and roof of the monastery. Her heart raced as she anticipated revealing the mysteriousness of the man she desperately wanted to know.

Susan had created this false image of a man that she desired but knew nothing about. Never did she stop to think if he would meet her expectations or highly disappoint her fantasies of the perfect man.

As they were going through the forest, wisps of dew were being formed among the trunks of the trees. They were close and could see the lights of the monastery in the distance.

"Shall I let you off by the door before I go to the stables?" the monk asked.

"No, I think I will walk from here," Susan said.

Susan was shaking because she was now beginning to think her choice was foolish. *It's too late to back down now,* she thought. She got out of the cart and began to walk. The monk waved and then continued on.

She walked up to the door of the monastery and held her hand to the handle. Susan was having some internal battle, whether she should go in or head to the stable to grab her things and head to Firestone. But where would she go?

Susan felt a strange tingling in her stomach. She looked around and saw a clear path form through the mist that was layering the forest. She closed her eyes and blinked a few times but the path was still there, clearly in front of her. She looked at the door again and decided to follow the path laid before her. There was a strange beautiful sound of a woman singing, but it changed quickly to cries of pain. She continued until she saw a bright light ahead of her.

Through a small opening in the trees, she saw a majestic unicorn lying in the lush grass much like the ones they had seen when they fled this place. The unicorn brought up her head and looked into Susan's eyes. Susan found herself creeping forward. The unicorn did not speak, but Susan heard a voice in her head say, "Peace be with you. I am Esmeralda."

"How are you getting into my head?" Susan asked, shocked that something so surreal was happening to her now.

"Fear not; I need your aid," The Unicorn's voice spoke.

"Esmeralda, how can I be sure this is really you?" Susan was kneeling beside the Unicorn now.

"Ask me a question and I will answer with a shake of my mane."

"Are you a Creature of Old?"

Esmeralda lifted her head and shook her mane.

"How are you inside my head?" Susan asked Esmeralda again.

"Do not worry, I cannot read your thoughts unless you give me permission."

"But how?"

"I know once I can hear them. When you allow me access, you can speak to me with your mind as well."

Susan closed her eyes and thought about letting

Esmeralda have access to her mind. Suddenly, she could hear Esmeralda's thoughts.

"You are dying!" Susan said, reaching out to stroke the beautiful creature's mane.

"Yes, yes. I am unfortunate to have less of my powers than my kindred, who still run freely through this forest. They still have the ability still to regenerate life. I have used what life I had left after I was released from my prison."

"Isn't there any way to save you?"

"That is why I called for you. I sensed that you were near and the aroma of your sweet spirit felt connected with mine. If you are willing to open your spirit to me, I will combine mine with yours and give you the powers I have."

"Will it hurt?"

"No, I am sure my spirit will be quite warm and gentle. You might become exhausted, but it will not hurt. I am only able to merge with you because you have hope in the Heavenly Knight which I have heard in whispers that it is called the Light. If I were to merge with you when you were in darkness, then your darkest hopes would become reality and the vanity of your mind would overcome you."

"But I don't always seem to trust in the Heavenly Knight. I often find myself discouraged and thinking of vain things. In fact I came here for vain purposes."

"Once you put your faith in the Heavenly Knight, you always have him to guide you. Nothing will separate you from his light now. You are fallen, and it is normal for you to fail in your trust, but that does not give you an excuse to fail all the time. It is your choice to trust Him."

"My brother has the spirit of a serpent. Would he have become a demon if he did not believe in the Heavenly Knight?"

"No, our power is unique to unicorns. We were specially created by the Creator to reflect His light. Life runs through our blood. We have the ability to speak to others with our minds and we also have the power of healing."

"I'll be able to heal?"

"You would only be able heal wounds that are fatal. There is even the possibility of resurrection, but that requires a willing soul to sacrifice his life for another's."

"How will I know how to use this power?"

"You will know when the time comes."

"Your mind is becoming unclear."

"Yes, we must hurry. Quickly, clear your mind."

Susan closed her eyes again and focused on hope. Esmeralda's horn began to glow beautifully bright. Susan felt her hand reach forward and gently touch the tip of the horn. Esmeralda's body glowed intensely as bursts of color filled the area like fireworks of a prism. When the light ceased, the body of Esmeralda had vanished. Susan felt warmth within her and she instantly fell asleep.

***

"My lady," said a man's voice. "My lady."

Susan opened her eyes, but could not see clearly. Everything around her was hazy and she could barely make out the figure of a man in front of her. She blinked a few times and things gradually became clearer.

"Carter?" Susan asked in a weak voice. "What are you doing here? Is this a dream?"

The man laughed. "I am not Carter," he said, "I am Christian. I am Carter's twin brother."

"Were you the man that came to the monastery to warn us of Sebastian?" Susan asked, "You wore a hood that night?"

"That was me," Christian said as he held out his hand.

Susan grabbed hold of his hand and could feel the hardness of his skin against hers. She could barely breathe as she admired the veins on his forearm when he pulled her up. She stumbled when she stood up and Christian caught her.

"I must be a little lightheaded," Susan said, holding her forehead. "How did you know I was out here?"

"Liam, the monk you rode with, came in and asked if you had made it safely," Christian said, "I had not heard of your arrival so I wanted to make sure you were safe when he told me that you were a Proudmoore. What are you doing back here?"

"To be honest," Susan said. She could feel her face get hot. "I was looking for you."

"Me?"

"I know it may sound crazy but I was. Your sister and my brother had just gotten married. And I remembered you. I honestly shouldn't have come."

Susan pulled away to leave but Christian held onto her arm. She looked at him as he smiled at her.

"Don't leave. Let's get you inside. It is starting to get cold."

He is what I imagined, Susan thought.

"Excuse me?" Christian asked, "Did you say something?"

Susan realized that her encounter with the Unicorn Esmeralda wasn't a dream and she could speak to him with her mind. She just giggled and shook her head. "No," she said.

CHAPTER TWENTY THREE

Norya

"I thought it was supposed to get warmer," Neil said, rubbing his arms vigorously. "I think I am going to be sick!" He ran over to the side of the ship.

"We are almost to Norya," Carter said.

"I have received a reply from my mother," Mianya said, "They are expecting us. She sent word that transportation will be arranged to meet them when we arrive in Norya."

Carter walked over to Neil and patted his back. He knew now to keep Neil hydrated. "It won't be too much longer till we reach land," Carter said.

"One can only hope," Neil replied, "I don't believe I have recovered since the last voyage. N…now I am cold on top of that."

"Go below deck. You might be better off down there. I believe there are blankets."

"Tiandra is below. She scares me."

"You have nothing to fear from her," Mianya said, "She is on our side."

Neil shrugged and went below deck. Carter sighed and continued to stare out over the ocean. Mianya walked up and stood beside him. Neil frustrated him but he was still trying to give him a chance.

"I sense that you struggle with patience for Neil,"

Mianya said.

"There is something about him that I want to help him change but maybe I am not the best person to help," Carter said, "The other night I woke up and thought I could see Neil watching me but maybe I was just being paranoid."

"I do find something odd about him," Mianya said.

"I want to hope for the best in people."

"That is a good quality to have, but you do need to guard yourself. I do see that Neil idolizes you and that is a snare upon him and can be very dangerous for you. This world, being in its fallen state, has men in it that hide who they really are. Often light needs to be shed on darkness to reveal its true form. Also, keep in mind we must rescue the perishing. Do not cut off ties with those that need truth."

"I don't believe I follow what you are trying to say."

"In due time you will understand, but for now, you are young. Get some rest. We should arrive in Norya by tomorrow."

***

As the ship was being tied off at the dock, Neil emerged from below. It was lightly snowing and the deck was frosted over. Mianya, Carter and Tiandra were all headed off the ship into the small port town.

"Did none of you think to get me?" Neil said.

"We weren't planning on leaving you here," Carter said.

"Should we find a place to rest?" Mianya asked.

They headed toward the pub when jingles were heard ringing through the streets. A man was shouting for people to move out of his way as a sleigh made its way down the street. It was led by a dozen blue dragons and was as big as a good-sized horse. The sleigh stopped just short of the stable.

"The dragons need some fresh pounds of meat!" the

driver shouted.

A few men threw chunks of raw meat out among the dragons and the meat was being torn apart along with their ferocious growls. Neil continued to try to warm himself as Mianya and Carter approached the driver of the sleigh.

"Excuse me," Mianya said, "Are you here by order of Queen Thalandria?"

"Well yes, I am," the driver said.

"I am Princess Mianya," Mianya said, "and these are my companions."

"We will head out as soon as the beasts finish eating."

When the dragons left nothing but bone on the carcasses, they allowed the dragons five minutes before they prepared the reigns for their journey. Carter got in the sleigh after Mianya and Neil and noticed that Tiandra was nowhere in sight.

"Where did Tiandra go?" Neil asked.

"She had told me that she would search for crystals on her own while we visit Hoarfrost Castle for the council," Mianya said, "She did not want us to lose time with Sebastian hot on our trail."

"I would never go out into the tundra alone," Neil said, "I would probably freeze to death. Remember how you were trapped in that cave Carter?"

"Tiandra is very capable of surviving on her own in harsh conditions," Mianya said. "I have faith in her abilities."

The driver made a clicking sound with his mouth and whipped the reigns. They braced themselves as the sleigh jerked forward. They were moving swiftly through the snow and sleet along the road.

They had traversed over a giant lake that had been frozen over and made their way over a few hills. When they made it to the top of the last hill, they found themselves overlooking a beautiful barren valley with a few trees.

In the distance was Hoarfrost Castle, built into the base

of the large mountain range, stretching as far as the eye can see. A great white wall surrounded the glossy buildings and towers. The spires were magnificently tall, stretching far above the low blanket of clouds. Rays of sunlight broke through the cloud breaks and hit the castle, causing it to sparkle and glimmer as if it was laden with diamonds.

Carter had only heard of the beautiful land of Norya. He had no idea that there was such beauty to a place filled with ice and snow. Even within the barrenness of the area, life was happening around them. Birds were chirping among the trees and the arctic foxes playing in the snow together. He only wished Karen would be able to see what a beautiful creation the Creator had made for man to enjoy.

"Are we almost there?" Neil said, peeking out from the blanket, "It's so bright!"

"What do you expect?" Carter asked. "The sunlight is reflecting on frozen water, enhancing its brightness."

"Is that the castle?" Neil had stuck his whole head out now. "Wow!"

"That is Hoarfrost Castle," Mianya said.

"Why would the Elves want to come to such a place?" Neil asked.

"They are not actually in the castle; they are taking refuge within the caverns behind it. From my understanding there are many hot springs within the caves that keep the castle quite warm."

"I am sure it is very comfortable," Carter said.

"Yes, I assume so," Mianya said. She looked away and stared at the sky.

"Are you anxious to see your mother?" Carter asked.

"I am," Mianya said.

"I assume she will be harsh with you," Carter said, "My mother always worries for my safety and I imagine that yours is not so different."

"You are very sweet for your concern, Carter Lockwood," Mianya said with a smile. She placed her hand on his forearm and patted it.

Mianya did not speak to Carter for the remainder of the trip and Carter wondered what was going through Mianya's mind. She had a very mysterious past and he desired to find out more. Desperately wanting to save Karen from the clutches of Baelin was his main concern.

They arrived at the main gate and passed under it, observing all the folks watching them as they emerged from under the wall. Carter had noticed that all the people from the Norya nation were robust and stocky; definitely adapted to their environment.

As they approached the castle, Carter saw a large man standing at the entrance. He was accompanied by a tall slender Elf who stood with poise. Carter could see Mianya's body stiffen and he gently patted her back. She looked at him with wide eyes and he wondered if this was right.

"Thank you," she whispered.

Carter just smiled and could feel her body relax a little. Carter looked at Neil staring at him with a frown on his face. Neil looked away when Carter met his eyes and the sleigh jerked a little when it came to a stop. Mianya sighed as the driver came around and held out his hand to help her down.

"Mianya!" King Hendor said, "Such a pleasure to see you, my girl!"

He came over and embraced Mianya in a big hug. She looked at Carter and began giggling. Thalandria continued to stand where she was with pursed lips.

"Hello, mother," Mianya said once Hendor released her.

Mianya walked over to her mother and bowed, grabbing Thalandria's hand and kissing it. She stood up and looked at her mother and stumbled when Thalandria wrapped her arms around Mianya.

"I have missed you so!" Thalandria said, "Every day

since you have been gone has been a nightmare, I felt that you would never return."

"I promise you mother," Mianya said, stepping back to look at Thalandria, "Baelin will never claim me as his own again. We cannot lose our light as we are now sealed until the day of redemption."

"Truth is good to be heard from your lips," Thalandria said.

"You must be Carter Lockwood," Hendor said, "You are very brave to face such a fiend as Baelin."

"We have not actually faced Baelin," Carter said.

"I sense the light is great within this young man," Thalandria said to Mianya.

"I noticed that as well," Mianya said, "And this is Neil, Carter's traveling companion from Allear."

"We welcome you," Thalandria said.

"Where is uncle?" Mianya asked.

"He is within the Council chambers with the other men and women," Thalandria said, "We must hurry or he shall be harsh with his words for keeping him waiting."

"What should we do with my companions?" Mianya asked.

"I have arranged a servant to assist them to their rooms," Hendor said.

Two young beautiful maids came from the doors, and bowed and grabbed the bags from them.

"These women will assist you in anything you need," Hendor said.

Hendor, Thalandria and Mianya left and headed toward the chambers where the council was being held.

"I think I want a nice hot bath," Neil said as he shivered.

"Would you ladies mind showing me around the castle?" Carter asked. "I would love to how this castle was built into the side of this mountain."

"It would be our pleasure," they both said

simultaneously.

Neil jumped onto the bed when they were shown their room. The ladies placed the bags down beside the bed and stood, waiting. Their hands were folded in front of them and they had pleasant looks on their faces.

"The water closet is through that door and the wash room is through those doors," one of the maids said. "Our tubs draw water straight from our hot springs for a refreshing bath."

"This place is really advanced in their technology," Neil said to Carter.

"I have been impressed since we arrived on this continent," Carter said.

"Go have fun learning about the castle while I enjoy a nice spring water bath!" Neil said as he ran into the wash room and closed the door.

"Where shall we take you first?" the women asked.

"I would really like to see how far this castle goes into the mountain," Carter said.

The rest of the day Carter was shown all the intricate details of the castle and how it was built. He had never seen such beautiful architecture. Although it made him miss the monastery in Faerie Forest, he knew being here was part of his journey home to take back his land.

***

"What could they possibly be talking about that has taken five days?" Neil said.

He was pacing back and forth in the room as Carter was lying on his back, staring at the ceiling. There was a light knock on the door.

"Come in!" Neil said.

"Lady Mianya requests Carter Lockwood's presence among the council," the maid said.

"What about me?" Neil asked.

"I assume that if they are requesting me," Carter said, "they are planning on wrapping up their council."

"Well if not, try to hurry the process," Neil said.

Carter was led down a dozen long hallways until he reached a large door. When it opened, the place was filled with men and women in elegant and colorful robes. There were three sections of people. Two of the sections were Elves and the third was large men and women that were obviously from Norya. A long table was placed in front of the room where Hendor, Thalandria, Mianya and a male Elf were seated. Carter assumed that he was Mianya's uncle, King Thulian, who she had talked much about.

"Welcome Carter my boy!" Hendor said as the entire room stood at his entrance.

There was a chair next to Mianya that Carter assumed was for him. He walked over with all eyes on him and stood where the chair was. When he sat, everyone else imitated him in sitting as well.

"Men and Elves, I cannot stress this enough but the time has come for us to stop Sebastian!" Mianya said as she stood up, "We must fight to save our world and rid it of the taint of Baelin once and for all. It is imperative to gather our forces, prepare to invade Allear, take the castle, and find the key that will grant us access to the Heavenly Knight's sword."

"Why should we risk our lives when he has not even attempted to come after us?" Thulian asked.

"If you believe Sebastian is not a threat," Thalandria said, "why would you vote for us to retreat to Norya for protection?"

"Do not be so irritable with me dear sister," Thulian said.

"Every day he gains more power," Mianya said. "If we do not crush him now, he will overpower the world once again. I am doing well at stopping him from gaining the crystals of power. But it will only delay him for just so long."

"If you remember correctly," Thulian said, "not all the Creatures of Old were good. Some of them did harm to the world as well. Why would we want such creatures to dwell among us once more? Mianya has already released some of the dragons which often ravished the lands those many years ago."

"Do you not remember that it was the Creatures of Old that banded together to attempt to stop Baelin?" Thalandria said.

"Baelin must be stopped now," Mianya said, "Carter Lockwood has seen his power and the affect he has on the nation of Allear. An innocent family is running for their lives because of Baelin's destruction."

"How do you know they are innocent?" Thulian asked with a smile upon his face. He was walking around the table now. "How long have you known this man? And yet you claim his words. What if this man is aiding Baelin?"

"How dare you!" Mianya said, pounding the table. "If you knew what it was to have the light within you would sense that this man has light of the Creator as well."

"Mianya," Thalandria said, "Do not be so cross."

"I apologize," Mianya replied. "Back to the topic at hand. Death by those creatures was natural and showed the effects of nature in the world's fallen state. Sebastian's murders were unnatural. Blood is a symbol of life and to play with it is in opposition to the way the world was created. That is why Baelin must be stopped."

"I believe that Mianya has the right motivation," Thalandria said.

"My men are armed and willing to stop this demon," King Hendor said. He stood up and shook his fist.

"We are fools to try!" Thulian said, still walking around the room. "We do not know if he has some untapped power that he is holding back. We do not know the ways of darkness. We are the chosen people who hold the true light." Thulian looked at Carter with narrow eyes. "How could a mere human have the light within him? Such thinking is foolishness!"

"Thulian!" Thalandria said. Her voice was bolder than before. "Stay on the topic at hand!"

"We must capture the crystals before Baelin so that he will not get any more power from them," Mianya said, "I feel that once there are no more crystals to search for, he will return to Firestone Castle. We must be ready to strike when he least expects it. He will not be easy to kill, but we must purge him from this world."

"What if he has the key on him?" Thulian asked. "The one you said you lost."

"Thulian, are you afraid of one man when we have a whole army?" Thalandria replied in a soft voice.

Thulian pursed his lips and sat down. Mianya smirked and caused Carter to smile which Thulian must have noticed because he glared at Carter.

"We must vote," Thalandria said.

"All in favor of fighting against Baelin and his forces of Allear, cast your vote," Hendor said.

All of the Noryan and Melyarian Elves stood from their seats. Two of the A'esaian Elves stood from their seats. Thalandria made a sigh of relief.

"It is settled then," Thalandria said, "We will prepare for battle. They will search for the rest of the crystals. When Mianya sends us her dove, we will strike."

"We will crush them!" Hendor said.

The council had ended and everyone had filed out except Carter, Thalandria and Mianya. Thalandria smiled and held her daughter's hand.

"My dearest daughter, I am so glad that you are alive and well," Thalandria said.

"Mother, I am ashamed, but what else was I to do?" Mianya said.

"Do not be ashamed. I only feared for your life. You

showed me no dishonor."

"I knew what he wanted. If I did not stop him, he would have even more power now. I did not suppress the light like Thulian wanted to do. Carter actually gave me something that helped me free my bondage to fear."

"Be honest with me. Did you encounter death on your quest?"

"Yes, Sebastian had me in his grasp twice. I escaped only with help from the light."

"How thankful I am that our Creator entrusted our people with his light through his grace and mercy. I apologize to you Carter. Thulian is bitter and his mind is darkened by fear. He trusts in himself now and his people have lost hope. He cannot understand why the Creator had the Heavenly Knight leave the world, and he refuses to believe that the Creator shared His light with mortal men."

"I was not offended," Carter said, "It has been an honor to fellowship with you and your daughter."

"One day he will see the truth. I only pray that the light will illumine his mind and help him see clearly again."

Mianya kissed her mother and returned to her room for the night.

I would like to thank you Carter," Thalandria said as they began walking together. "You have traveled with my daughter for a brief time but her spirit has lifted since then. I see great things in you Carter Lockwood and I know the light runs richly within your soul."

"Thank you my lady," Carter said.

Carter admired the Elves because they contained so much knowledge about the world as well as the Creator. He couldn't wait to converse more with Queen Thalandria. He turned in for the night on a positive thought after being verbally attacked by King Thulian.

***

Two weeks passed. Carter and Mianya returned from their brief quest to search for crystals in the eastern mountains of Norya, knowing Tiandra was in the west. When they had returned, they noticed there was no sign of Tiandra and noticed as well a very angry Neil.

"You never told me you were leaving to search for more crystals!" Neil said.

"You have been complaining about being cold, "Carter replied, "I didn't think that you wanted to come. It was terrible weather and quite honestly, I did not want to deal with your complaining."

"I don't complain!"

"The first thing you did when I returned was complain. Don't be offended. You just need to work on it. I don't hate you and that is not why I left. Please be more reasonable. I was trying to think of your needs."

"My needs are to be with you! Fighting Sebastian and doing interesting stuff like finding the crystals!"

"I'll return when you calm down."

Carter left the room and decided to go for a walk. He didn't like being harsh with Neil but knew if he stayed the conversation would never change. He did enjoy Neil's company even though they had nothing in common. Neil wasn't too bad of a man most of the time.

Carter found himself along the main wall, outlying the city and the castle. In the distance he saw something moving towards them. The closer it got he noticed that it was Tiandra, with her fiery red hair blowing in the wind. Behind her was another figure and Carter saw it was Sebastian and he was gaining fast upon her.

As fast as he could, Carter made his way down the wall and through the main gate. When he was in the barren snowfield that stretched for miles, Tiandra was now fighting Sebastian.

"Tiandra!" Carter yelled as he got closer.

"No fight!" Tiandra said trying to keep Sebastian from

overpowering her. "Me fight!"

Carter came dangerously close to the fight and when Tiandra saw him, she quickly removed her pack and threw it to Carter after kicking Sebastian into the snow. Carter caught the pack and looked inside, at the beautiful crystals in their many colors.

"Run!" Tiandra said.

Sebastian had finally overpowered Tiandra. When she was lying in the snow with no weapons in her hands, he thrust his sword into her chest. She gasped and lay motionless as the snow became crimson around her.

Carter knew it was no use calling out to her but he had to run. Sebastian's eyes were now on him and he turned and ran. He could hear Sebastian's pursuit behind him as the snow crunched beneath his feet.

As hope of escape seemed to be a slim chance, he lost momentum in the snow. The valley echoed as a roar came from the sky. The peaceful feeling Carter had encountered before filled his spirit once more. Out of the clouds, flew the majestic white dragon.

Not knowing what the dragon was going to do, he continued to run. The dragon swooped down and swiped at Sebastian as he ducked and rolled in the snow. Sebastian stood up again to pursue Carter. Again the dragon swooped down but now he was coming for Carter. The dragon clutched Carter's arms within his talons and flew away.

"I will find you Carter Lockwood!" Sebastian yelled.

The dragon flew toward the wall as arrows were being shot now from the archers at Sebastian who was now retreating. The dragon roared and people cleared the streets and he was placed on the ground. Without a moment of hesitation, the dragon flew away back into the clouds.

"Carter!" Mianya yelled, pushing people out of her way. "Are you all right? The alarm sounded that Sebastian was out there. What is happening?"

Carter was out of breath from running but he was also

highly emotional after watching Tiandra being run through by Sebastian. Never had he seen such evil in a man. All he could do was wrap his arms around Mianya and cry.

"Wha...," she said.

"There is a dead woman's body out in the snow!" yelled one of the guards.

"Tiandra?" Mianya asked.

"Yes," Carter said.

Now Carter was letting Mianya shed tears of sorrow on his shoulder. Carter looked up to see Neil on the wall, staring at him.

When they had calmed down, Carter handed the sack to Mianya who looked inside. She closed the bag and clutched it tight against her chest. Thalandria was out among the people now and walked over to retrieve her daughter. They all made their way inside to prepare a proper burial for Tiandra.

The next day, an ice coffin was carved in the middle of the valley where Tiandra had died. The coroner had made her flawlessly clean and beautiful, with a beautiful white flower in her hair. Before they covered her body with the ice lid, Mianya placed Tiandra bow within her clutches and laid a rose upon her breast.

"Goodbye my friend," Mianya said as she watched the coffin slide over Tiandra's body.

Mianya decided to release many of the crystals in Tiandra's honor right near her grave. None appeared in the vicinity but the flashes were magnificent, as if fireworks were going off.

Many men and women attended the funeral even though most of them had never met Tiandra. Carter was there to support Mianya but Neil was nowhere to be found.

When Carter returned to his room that night, he found Neil asleep. Mianya and Carter had planned to travel to Shalya early the next morning. Carter couldn't help but worry about the safety of Karen after what he had seen

Sebastian just do.

CHAPTER TWENTY FOUR

Mianya

Two days later, Mianya, Carter, and Neil were aboard the ship travelling swiftly toward Shalya. Neil had remained below deck the entire voyage due to seasickness again. He had attempted to purchase this strange fish to eat in hopes to cure seasickness, but it made him feel even worse.

"The roar I heard," Mianya said, "was a dragon, but how did you escape? Did you call for the dragon's aid?"

"The white dragon," Carter said, "It had saved me once before, when I was in danger on Death Mountain, it appeared and saved my life. I had never heard of any dragon like the one I saw. Most dragons when they are described are very large and bulky with similar builds. This one, however, was very long and slender. Tiny wings were on its head along with what I thought were fins as its tail. There was a peace I felt when I was in its presence."

"How strange," Mianya said, "I have never heard of such a dragon. Maybe we will encounter it if Sebastian attacks us in Shalya."

"Mianya?"

"Yes?"

"May I ask how you came to be? Humans all came from a male and female long ago, but I have heard many different stories about the Elves."

"I was grown from a pod . There is a great tree in Melyaria, formed at the beginning of the world by the Creator Himself. My mother and uncle came from the tree first in their own pods. I guess you could say that we were pollinated by both Thulian and my mother, but those were ancient days. The Creator did not want us to become corrupt like the humans, which is what would have happened if my mother and uncle continued to pollinate the tree. To save us from the corruption encroaching on our lands, the Creator gave us these pendants as a sign of an eternal covenant. That covenant was fulfilled after the knight came and rescued us from Baelin."

"Thulian is your real father?"

"I guess you could say that. Elves are different from humans in their family relationships. When I grew, I was grown from a different pod than others. There have been only three different kinds of pods that have ever grown on that tree."

"What do you mean?"

"My two sisters and I grew from golden pods. We were the only ones who have ever or will ever grow from those pods. The A'esaiah Elves grew from purple pods and they are not known as my mother's children. Melyarian Elves grow from white pods and are, in a sense, my brothers and sisters, but I hold a higher place in my mother's eyes."

"Why were you and your two sisters claimed by Thalandria?"

"We were born on her side of the tree, among the Melyarian Elves, and uncle was fine with her claiming us."

"I remember stories telling how all the commanders of Baelin's were destroyed except one. You are the one who was saved, but what happened to your sisters?"

"They chose their fate when they gave their souls completely to Baelin. They died when they turned into his demons. I was simply trapped within my demon body. I will never know their fellowship again; and although it is sad, I cannot grieve."

"I have heard that when an Elf dies, its body is returned to life. How does that work?"

"Again, it is true in a certain sense. Although the soul does not return, the body is given a new soul. Elves do not die often, but when one does, his or her body grows in a new pod that is not pollinated by my mother and uncle and the Elf takes on a new soul."

"Do you remember being a demon?"

"Yes, but I wish I didn't. Those were my darkest days."

"Will you tell me how you came to be depraved and what Baelin was like then?"

"I have never told anyone my story before. I fear to tell anyone my failures."

"We are all depraved on this cursed earth."

"Very well then, I shall tell you how I came to know Baelin. Every evening under the moonlight, my two sisters, Saerwen and Morwen, and I would go relax and play childish games in the forest to the north of our mother's castle. There was one part of the forest that was darker than the rest and all of us were too scared to go deeper into it. One night, my sisters were feeling bold and walked into that part of the forest. Meanwhile, I surveyed my surroundings. I heard pleasant laughter come from within the dark trees, but I was afraid and ran back to my room, safe inside the castle. That was the last time that I ever went into the forest with my sisters. Every evening, they returned to me perfectly the same but happier each time. I did not understand how they could be any happier than they usually were, but they were.

"One evening, weeks later, they came to me, dancing in all of their gaiety. They pulled down the satin drapes to dance with. They included me in their dance and we laughed and danced as we used to. This night was different, however. They spoke of a handsome man who spoke sweet words to Saerwen under the moonlight in the forest. Morwen fawned over him as well. They implored me to go with them into the forest and promised that he would come into the moonlight so that I would not have to go into the darker part of the forest. I agreed.

"The next evening I went and waited with them. I had a feeling that I should leave before he came, but I quenched that feeling. I resisted the light telling me what I should have done. Baelin came to us that evening. As he approached, I desired him. His beauty was captivating, and I wanted to be held in his strong arms. I lost control of myself and fawned after him, too, falling asleep in his arms as he whispered sweet words into my ear. Every morning, I would wake up feeling guilty, but every evening I would go back and do the same thing. Gradually my guilt faded.

"One evening, I explained to mother what had been happening, but she never understood what I was trying to say. It was as if I was speaking in another language. I wanted help because I did not know what to do. I was confused and lonely, and I soon began to spiral into despair. Mother watched me closely from then on. On some nights, I would enter the forest with my sisters, but then come back in a trance-like state without my sisters.

"What happened to them?"

"They were defiled because he kept them longer than me. My mother kept me under strict watch when I returned alone. When she noticed my beauty fading and my pendant beginning to burn against my skin when I wore it, she never let me enter that forest again. I was being defiled slowly and I did not know it.

"Several days later, my mother was brushing her hair and I had stepped out onto the terrace to observe the moonlight. I missed my sisters greatly, but I could not go back to that forest. I knew it would be wrong. I heard my name called from below me. As I looked down, I saw my sisters again. Their beauty was faded, but I wanted to embrace them because I had missed them so much. I pulled down my satin curtains and used them as ropes to let my sisters climb up. When they finally reached the terrace, they looked at me with wicked faces and asked me where mother was. I led them to her, not knowing their intent.

"Saerwen and Morwen followed after me as I entered mother's room. She looked at us and noticed some evil within my sisters. She looked at me with disappointment, knowing I had let them inside. I threw down my pendant as my sisters did. It symbolized rejecting the light we had grown up with. Out of fear, I ran away into the next room while my sisters remained in the room with my mother. I covered my ears, but I still heard them attack one another. The next thing I knew, my sisters ran out of the room, cackling and leaving a trail of blood behind them.

"I returned to find my mother cleaning up the blood staining her floor. 'I am sorry, mother. I was foolish,' I said to her. She looked up at me with tears in her eyes and extreme guilt came upon me once more. I went to pick up my pendant, but mother stopped me and said, 'Do not pick it up. You will not be able to bear it until you have been cleansed.' I did not believe her until it burned my hand when I tried to touch it.

"Instead of going through with the cleansing, I went deep into despair and refused to leave my bed. Tortured thoughts came into my mind. The memories of Baelin's sweet words would not leave me and my fellowship with both my mother and the Creator was broken. I felt empty and alone and missed my sisters deeply. I had a choice to make: either go through the cleansing process that mother suggested or find my sisters. As history reveals, I chose to find my sisters and gave into Baelin's way. I should have known better."

"So where did you find them?"

"I went to the forest. There I found Baelin without my sisters. He looked at me with beautiful eyes and spoke his poison. He said he accepted me as his follower, but I needed to follow him to his dwelling place on an isolated island northeast of Allear's eastern coast. I tried to refuse, but he stole me. Really, that is my own fault for going there in the first place. When he took me there, my sisters attempted to welcome me, but I felt no comfort within their presence as I had hoped. By then it was too late.

"The demon entered me and took control of my body. I was trapped within myself and had no power to speak or act. I remember looking at my sisters, also demons now. They had long, silver hair with pale skin and blood-red eyes. I was scared and wanted to be free, but I could find no hope. Baelin called Saerwen 'Phayde' and Morwen 'Payne'. I was called 'Mysery.' We sought after and destroyed anything that stood in our master's way.

"We would go out at the master's bidding, kill any innocents we came across, and steal their souls for Baelin. We gave him thousands of souls and he grew stronger. Soon, the world was in chaos, and the Elves joined forces with the humans to try to stop us. We finally gave Baelin his last source of ultimate power and he was able to take on his ultimate form: the dragon of death. He was feared by all who looked upon him. Even his own demons feared him.

"When it was time for him to complete his own personal quest for glory, Baelin sent us to begin the battle against the Elves and humans while he fought the Creatures of Old. That was the day I was thankful for. As the Heavenly Knight descended on the battlefield, all trembled in fear and he wiped out the hellish army my sisters and I had raised.

"I so longed to be free from this demonic taint, but I could not speak. I watched the knight obliterate my two sisters, and I thought that I was next, but something else happened. His sweet, gentle eyes looked into mine and I saw compassion on his face. I wanted him to be my only hope as I knew that he could be. I wanted to reach out to touch him but I was afraid to be burned by his holiness. I was so impure. He looked beyond my appearance and saw a tortured soul. I remember him speaking these forceful words: 'Your soul is alive but very weak, child. I shall cleanse this taint from your mind and body, and you will be whole because you desire to be.' The next thing I knew I was twisting in pain as the demon left my body and I finally felt clean. He had cleansed me, and I could not speak to thank him.

"My mother fought her way through the soldiers to reach me. She embraced me. I knew then that the light was all I needed and I was foolish to ever not listen to it."

Mianya began to tear up as she finished her story. Carter looked at her and felt compassion because it must have been hard to live through that and have so many years of life to haunt her. He knew how merciful the Creator was—He allowed redemption to take place in a world full of wickedness.

"It's so different to hear the story from one of the sources. Thank you for sharing with me," Carter said.

"I am positive that Baelin will not succeed. He cannot gain his ultimate power and receive that glory he desperately lusts for. Sebastian is not as strong as you may think. He is trying anything to gain his power back. His lust for it all blinds his senses."

"So you believe that Sebastian… or Baelin I should say, has another way to gain his power besides these crystals?"

"I remember hearing an old ancient ritual when I was once his servant. If any of my sisters or I were to die in some way, he would just need to find a virgin with no hope and impregnate her to birth us into the world once more."

"Has he found a virgin without any hope?" Carter asked.

"Not that I know of but I do believe he was attempting to use your Karen to fulfill that ritual. That is the only reason I could think of as to why he would take her. You also mentioned that he is trying to hunt down her family. Part of having no hope is having nothing to live for."

Carter stood there motionless as Mianya told him this. Anger was burning in his heart now and more than ever he wanted to see Baelin dead. He could not bear to see Karen be harmed in such a violent way. She was pure and had so much to live for.

"Do not worry young Carter Lockwood," Mianya said, putting her hand on his now fisted hand. "There is no way he can strip Karen of hope if she has the light within. Remember the truth. We are sealed until the day of redemption. It is a promise the Creator had established when the Heavenly Knight was victorious over death."

"That may be so, but he still has Karen and who knows what Sebastian will do to her when he realizes that he can't use her."

"Do not worry about such things. I know it is hard to think about things that you cannot control; but whether she lives or dies, you have a mission to serve the Creator. We as creation have nothing and we must submit ourselves to His will. The Creator will be glorified no matter what we do because he is the Creator and we are the creation."

Carter knew she was right but he couldn't sit around and do nothing when he now had the power to do everything to stop Sebastian. All they had to do was find the key to his destruction and in the meantime stop him from gaining the crystals of power.

***

The ship stopped at Harte to replenish its stores of food and supplies for their journey to Shalya. Mianya, Carter and Neil decided to stay in town for the night and continue their journey in the morning. It had been hard traveling at sea for Neil and Carter wanted to give him a break.

Mianya went to her room and Carter and Neil went to

another. There were only a few rooms left in the pub as a few ships had reached port along with the ship that they had taken. The room Carter and Neil had received had only one bed inside.

"I can sleep on the floor if you would like," Neil said, looking at the window.

Why does he get so weird whenever a situation like this arises? Carter thought. Neil being so uncomfortable around Carter made Carter feel uncomfortable.

"You haven't slept well in days due to the sea," Carter said, "Just take the bed and I will sleep on the floor."

"Why are you always so nice to me?" Neil asked.

"From what I know about you, you have never had any friends and I just want you to know that I have seen some change in you since we started journeying. I enjoy when you ask me about the Creator. Not to mention the time in the City of Thieves. You were brilliant with your idea on how to find Mianya."

"Thanks," Neil said as he looked out the window again, "I insist you take the bed though."

"All right but don't complain that you are stiff tomorrow from the hard wood floor."

"I think we have been in worse situations."

Carter lay down to sleep. He was dreaming of Karen and wanted to embrace her once more. She seemed real in this dream as her warm skin touched his. He could almost feel her body pulse as he wrapped his arms around her in an embrace. The dream however turned into a nightmare once he opened his eyes.

Lying next to Carter was Neil, staring straight into his eyes. Carter felt sick at the thought and jumped up, grabbing Neil by the arm and throwing him off the bed against the wall. Neil slid and hit his head on the wall. Carter didn't hesitate to grab his dagger from beside him and ran over to Neil to pin him against the wall.

"What do you think you are doing?" Carter said. He

was furious now. "Is that why you came with me? So you could be close to me? Why would you violate my body in such a way? How dare you touch me!"

Carter was so upset he wanted to cry. He didn't know what to think and didn't know what to do because he wanted to kill Neil so bad but knew it wouldn't be right.

"Carter, please!" Neil said, "It's me, Eliza!"

"Eliza?" Carter said. He was even more furious but let go of her and backed away towards the bed. He was shaking by now and so many thoughts were going through his mind he couldn't think straight.

"I love you Carter," Eliza said, "I wanted to be close to you but you kept rejecting me!"

"So you pretended to be a young lad? To trick me? And you thought that I would love you then?"

"I didn't know how else to be in your presence. You always brightened my spirits."

Eliza was crying and with herself revealed, Carter could see that it was her the whole time. *How could I be so naïve?* Carter thought. *How could I not see it?*

"I love you Carter." Eliza began to step forward.

"Stop!" Carter said, holding out his hand. "Don't come near me, you vile manipulator. Get out of my sight! I never want to see your face again!"

"But—"

"Out!"

Carter picked up a vase and threw it against the wall near Eliza and it shattered. Eliza grabbed her bag and ran out of the room in tears. Carter fell to his knees and wept in his hands.

CHAPTER TWENTY FIVE

Betrayal

As Eliza's hair grew out, she started to look more feminine. She looked at herself in the mirror and knew she could not keep up the charade any longer. She felt incredibly empty inside. Admiring Carter's physique did not satisfy her any longer; she desired more.

Eliza stayed in the room with Carter while Mianya had the other room to herself. Eliza watched Carter fall asleep. Her body was violently shaking with the desire to crawl into his arms. She laid her head down and fell into a fitful sleep.

Eliza woke up early the next morning with thoughts of Carter still swimming through her mind. She got up and looked out the window. The moon was full and bright, casting a large amount of light into the room. She could see Carter's perfect face sleeping soundly. The impulse to lie with him filled her mind and she would not deny her desires any longer.

Eliza tiptoed over to Carter's bed. She took her trembling hand and gently touched his face. He did not stir and she quivered at the feel of his stubble against her fingers. She lost control of all reason and could not resist her desire to lie in his arms while he slept.

She slowly pulled back the covers. She carefully picked

up his hand, to see if he would wake up, and then released it. It fell limply on the bed. Her body began to shake more and her breathing became uneven. She slowly lay down next to him and could feel his warm breath on her neck.

She was attempting to pull the covers over both of them when Carter's arm moved to his side and fell over. Very slowly, she turned to face him. She looked into his gentle, peaceful face. "I love you," she whispered.

***

Eliza looked across the horizon, replaying the memory through her mind over and over. Part of her was sickened by what she had done because she no longer had him. She enjoyed being so close to him even though it was wrong. There was nothing to live for but him in her mind. She wanted him to embrace her because she had no one else.

Eliza did not stop running until after she left the town. She ran south and found herself alone on the road. The sun had risen in the sky. She stopped and looked around at the barren fields. She felt empty and alone. Nothing could satisfy. She hated her life's circumstances and wanted to die. Without the love of Carter to keep her happy, her sorrow turned into despair. She had nothing but the clothes on her back.

"You failed this time," she said to herself. "You are a fool. Carter never admired you. He never treated you with kindness. The Creator was never really real. You just said so because you wanted to be with Carter."

Eliza continued on the road again. She then turned around, determined to persuade Carter, but stopped and turned around again and continued south. She did not know what would happen to her, but she just kept walking. The longer she travelled the more bitter she became as the thoughts helped her spiral downward into deep despair.

She wanted revenge on Carter for how he treated her.

She thought about how he constantly embarrassed her in front of others, and how he rebuked her when she complained. She suddenly realized how she could get him back. She knew she was close to Firestone and decided to see if Sebastian was there.

She travelled the rest of the way to Phoenix Castle. She tried to walk into the courtyard, but was stopped by the guards.

"I am sorry, sir, you are not permitted to enter the castle," said one guard with his hand held up.

"I am no 'sir.' I am Eliza and I have a special report for Lord Sebastian to hear," Eliza said confidently.

"Lord Sebastian has just returned and is very exhausted. We will pass the message along."

"There is no time. I know of a potential threat to the nation."

"I will escort you myself, then. Come with me."

Eliza followed the guard through the courtyard and into the castle. As Eliza followed him, she began to have second thoughts. She did not want Sebastian to kill Carter, but at the same time she was hurt. She wanted her revenge to be sweet and satisfying.

The guard entered into a room and Eliza remained in the hallway. Shortly after he entered, the door reopened and the guard stepped out of the room and went back to his post. Standing in the room was Sebastian, waiting for Eliza.

"Step inside," Sebastian said.

His words were kind and welcoming to Eliza. She couldn't help but admire him now. She had seen him before; but with no Carter, he seemed more desirable. He laughed and held out his hand with an evil look on his face. Eliza now became scared again. She wanted to run away and hide from everyone.

"I think this may have been a mistake," she said as she turned to leave.

"Stop!" he said.

She stopped abruptly, losing control of her legs.

"Come hither," he said in a quiet voice.

Eliza finally stepped inside the room and felt trapped. She had often seen snakes devour mice without a second thought and she felt tiny compared to him. Sebastian walked over to the door and closed it silently. Eliza stood motionless in his presence. He circled around her and looked her over.

"So, you were the one in the coliseum."

Eliza did not speak but began to tremble. She realized what a stupid mistake this was. He walked behind her now and she noticed that he stopped. He got close up to her ear and whispered, "Do not fear me. I will not harm you if you share this knowledge you claim to have. Now, what are the Elves and humans planning to do?"

"They are attempting to invade," she spoke softly as her voice broke.

"When?"

"Once Mianya and Carter find the last few crystals in Shalya."

"Carter is the one who that wild woman gave the crystals to?"

"Yes, he is the lover of Karen Proudmoore."

"Well now, what a coincidence," he said as he rubbed his hands together. "Is that why you have come here? An unrequited love?"

"Yes," she said as tears started flowing down her face. She thought that he must have special powers to sense what was wrong with her.

"Do you feel empty inside, like there is no hope for you?"

"Yes."

"The light rejected you?"

"Yes!" she screamed.

Sebastian opened the door and called for the guards. Two men came in and waited for the orders. "Take her to the dungeon," he commanded. She looked at them with horror as they advanced to seize her.

"No! Please!" she cried as they began dragging her out the door. "I have more information!"

She was desperate to tell him anything if only she would not be taken captive. She would do anything to not become a prisoner.

"Wait!" he called to the guards. "What do you mean, 'more information?'"

"They are coming for you because you have the key," she said quickly.

"Key? What key?"

"They talked about a Heavenly Knight and some sword. They said that the sword was left on earth and the knight left Mianya the key to access it. They think that you have it."

"A key? I do not recall a key."

"It was some sort of white crystal the knight gave her."

Sebastian began to tremble and Eliza thought that he was going to hit her. Instead he leaned against the wall and covered his face.

"No! I am a fool. What have I done?"

Eliza watched him and was confused. He seemed upset and wondered if he didn't have the key to his destruction after all.

"I know that you are looking for the Proudmoores," Eliza said, "They are living in Kakaran. Please, I told you everything I know. Will you please let me go?"

"No!" he said as he turned to his guards. "Take her to the dungeon. Put her in the cell nearest the Proudmoore scum. I want my prized possessions to be fairly close and heavily guarded."

"No, no! Please!" Eliza screamed as she was dragged out of the room.

As she was hauled to the dungeon she continued to scream. They threw her in a cold dark cell alone and she sat there crying until she heard another woman's voice.

"Hello?" said Karen, "Are you all right?"

"I'm fine," Eliza said, covering her face.

"I couldn't help overhearing you crying after they threw you in that cell. There is nothing much else going on. What did they put you in here for?"

"I don't know. I just told them about Carter Lockwood."

"Carter?" Karen said, walking to place her face against the bars. "You know Carter?"

"I wish I had never met him! Why do you care?"

"We were to be wed. My name is Karen. Karen Proudmoore."

Eliza's stomach churned when she heard her name. Eliza became silent and refused to talk to Karen now that she knew who she was. Bitterness ran through her like poison running through her veins. She wished she could slap Karen across the face and claw out her eyes. She glared at Karen with the deepest hatred.

"Is there something wrong?" Karen asked.

"You are the one he chose," Eliza said.

"Who?"

"Carter."

"What do you mean?" Karen asked.

"Don't worry about it. He will die soon."

"What? No, he cannot. How do you know?"

"I know because I am the one who betrayed him!"

"Why? How could you? I know who you are now. You are Eliza. Carter told me about you."

"I loved Carter! I loved him more than you ever could! He chose you over me! He will not be able to rescue you, fortunately."

"How could you betray such an honorable man?"

"Your love will never become unified. That is the goal. If I cannot have him, then I am satisfied with you not having him."

"He will come rescue me. I know he will. Do not underestimate his strength. His faith is strong."

"There is no hope left in the world. Sebastian is going to rule soon."

"You are wrong. The light is greater than any darkness."

"Look around! You are in darkness. There is no hope."

"You are a fool, Eliza."

CHAPTER TWENTY SIX

The Last Crystals

"Why are you yelling?" Mianya asked as she ran in the room.

"Eliza!" Carter said. He was still on his knees crying.

"Who?"

"Neil was not a man. It was a woman named Eliza."

Mianya knew that there was something strange about that boy who obviously now was a woman. She sensed no light within Eliza and assumed that Carter knew as well.

"Why did she do this?"

"Where did she go?" Mianya asked, looking around the room and hoping he had not killed her. The more she thought about it, she knew Carter would never kill anyone unless it was in self-defense.

"I told her to never show her face to me again. I had hoped she had the light."

"I knew she didn't have the light within her."

"You knew and you never said anything?"

"I thought you were trying to win over her stubbornness with kindness. To be a good testimony."

"I wish it never went this far. I could have stopped it."

"Do not let your mind over think this. She made her choice. Your job is to forgive. Remember the Creator's forgiveness of our evil deeds."

"I cannot believe she did this to me. I tried to explain that I had no love for her, but she desired it too greatly. She desired me more than anything. I honestly loved her as a person but she had none for me. It was all infatuation."

"Carter," Mianya said as she placed her hand on his shoulder, "let's keep our focus on keeping the crystals out of Sebastian's hands. I know you are upset, but that won't help us."

"You are right, Mianya. I can't let Eliza distract me from stopping Baelin.

"The ship should be ready by noon."

As their ship set sail later that day, Carter looked back to shore. "I hope that she finds peace," Carter said.

"I lived in peace for a thousand years," Mianya said.

"What?" Carter asked.

"Peace," Mianya said, "It seems like such a foolish thing sometimes. Especially here on this fallen world."

"I believe I understand what you are saying," Carter said, "As long as there is darkness in the world, it seems that there can be no true sense of peace."

"The peace will come. The light is stronger. The Creator has a better plan than we could ever imagine."

"There is no doubt in my mind that what you just said is true," Carter said, "I remember the words of Father Isaac; the man who trained me, and he said to me once, 'Just as the sun makes the shadows flee, so shall the light.' But one thing puzzles me: why has Sebastian not taken over the world yet?"

"At first I thought that he was biding his time, but I have come to realize that he is extremely weak. The crystal that he was encased in drained him of many of his powers."

"How do you know this?"

"Because he would not wait unless he had to. His thirst for power is too strong for him to bide his time."

"Do we have time to find them all before he does?"

"Time will be a bit rushed for us. We may not be able

to find all of them because I am much weaker after releasing so many Creatures of Old. When I use my pendant to shatter the crystals, my divine senses become weaker, but the price is well worth my sacrifice. "

"Should we split up?"

"No, you do not know where to look and Sebastian knows you are helping me now. If he finds you, he will not hesitate to kill you and I cannot protect you from him."

"What about you? He is much stronger than you are now if what you say about being weakened from the crystals is true."

"I have my ways of escaping should I choose to."

"What are you trying to say? I don't think I follow," Carter said.

"I am going to get my rest," Mianya said.

Carter watched her as she departed to the cabin below. Land was out of sight now. He looked across the vast waters and watched the sun reflect brightly upon them. He could also see the moon in the blue atmosphere.

"I wonder why the sun doesn't always keep the moon and darkness at bay," Carter said as he headed down below.

That evening, they arrived in a northern port of Shalya and found lodging for the night. Mianya fell asleep quickly and a strange dream came upon her. The dream caused her memory to come back to her mind. Those words the knight whispered to her when he gave her the key. Her mind was illuminated and knew what her role was in all of this. She woke up and held her pendant up to observe it. She kissed it gently and strange marks appeared on the metal. She looked over at Carter and said a quick prayer: "In due time, Carter Lockwood." She laid her head down once more and fell asleep, completely at peace.

***

"Mianya, we have to go!" Carter said, shaking her

shoulder.

"What do you mean?" she asked as she rubbed her eyes. She had not slept well in the past few months.

"Allearian soldiers are down below talking to the innkeeper."

"We must hurry, then!" she replied as she got up and grabbed her bag. "Out the window, quickly!"

As they crawled onto the roof, they saw the horses of the Allearian soldiers down below. Carter looked at Mianya and she nodded. They leaped off the roof, landed on separate horses, and rode off.

"This will be a much quicker way to get to the crystals," Mianya said.

Carter looked over at Mianya and met his eyes. She couldn't stop thinking about her dream and the potential she saw in Carter. *He must learn in his time,* Mianya thought.

They came to a vast, grassy plain, covered with large pieces of stone that had once been the great Shalyan wall. They stopped and looked over the massive debris covering the grassland. Here and there were areas of dead earth where Aznat bodies had been burned and Shalyans were left to rot in the sunlight.

"What is this place?" Carter asked.

"War taints this land," Mianya said solemnly.

"Sebastian?"

"He wanted the crystals the Shalyans possessed."

"The magi were powerful from what I read. How did he defeat them?"

"It was not their magic to use. They were harnessing the power of innocent Creatures of Old. It was a matter of time before it turned on them. Fortunately, Elves do not use magic. Our power is inward and comes from the Creator Himself. We are the light bearers on earth. Of course, you are now a light bearer yourself."

"I thought that humans were always able to have the

light within them."

"After the Heavenly Knight came he allowed the humans to have it, but not all are able or willing. They reject the truth that the light gives. The light reveals things that darkness tries to hide."

"What happened to the queen of Shalya?"

"She realized what Sebastian wanted. She killed herself and scattered the crystals once more. I'm sure that if she had discovered a way to release the creatures, she would have. Her heart was more noble than most of the magic users in her council."

"Your pendant is the only thing that can shatter them and release the creatures?"

"As far as I know, yes."

"How did Sebastian release the power of Baelin then?"

"I don't know how he released the power, nor do I know how he defeated the great serpent that guarded it in the deep ocean."

"What's that?" Carter asked, pointing at a shining object in the distance.

"I do believe that we have found our first crystal in this land. Let's ride." She whipped the reigns and the horses broke into a gallop.

The crystal seemed to be moving away from them. The reflection of the sun made the crystal flash brightly at odd intervals. As they got closer, they saw the crystal was being carried by a large rodent.

"There it is!" Carter called out, "It's in that creature's mouth."

The rodent looked at them with beady black eyes. It began scurrying faster. Carter saw that it was headed for a nearby hole and spurred his horse to greater speed. When he was close enough, he jumped off his horse to grab the rodent, but it slipped through his hands. Mianya gracefully jumped off her horse and ran after the rodent. She caught it just before it escaped into its hole.

"He's a little troublemaker," Carter said as he limped towards Mianya. He brushed the dirt from his clothes.

"He is just scared," she said, stroking the rodent's forehead. "Are you well? You look like you are in pain."

"My shoulder hasn't recovered from the coliseum."

"We must take it easy on you then."

"What is that rodent anyway?" Carter asked.

"I do believe this is a Shalyan hamster. They usually live underground."

"Why did it have this crystal?" he asked.

"They are scavengers. They enjoy collecting shiny objects." She pulled the crystal from the hamster's mouth and handed it to Carter so he could put it in the bag with the others.

Mianya held the rodent in the air and tickled its belly. It squeaked loudly and tried to get away. She gently placed it on the ground, and it immediately dashed to the shelter and safety of its burrow.

"They are some of the most adorable rodents in the world," she said with a smile.

"Do you think we should release this Creature of Old?" Carter asked as he looked in the bag. "Because it is the only crystal we have."

"What do you mean?" Mianya asked as she took the bag.

"Eliza must have grabbed the wrong bag when she left. We had about three crystals in that bag."

"We should release them as we get them now," Mianya said, "I do not have a comforting feeling about Eliza having some of our crystals."

Mianya reached in and grabbed the crystal, admiring its beauty. It had a strong spirit within. She knew not whether it would appear before them or somewhere else in the world. Remembering that some were dangerous and that Carter was with her, she hesitated.

"What's wrong?" Carter asked.

"They can be dangerous sometimes. When I release them, we need to ride off quickly."

Mianya took the crystal and laid it down on one of the stones from the great wall. She smashed the crystal as quickly as possible and mounted her horse in haste.

This crystal emitted multiple colors, flashing through the sky. The horses were startled and would not cooperate. They reared up, dismounting their riders, and galloped away. Mianya grabbed Carter's hand and they sprinted away as fast as Carter's legs could carry him.

He was much slower than she was. She found a hole beneath a giant piece of the old wall and both she and Carter took refuge underneath it. They could hear nothing, so Mianya assumed the Creatures of Old must have appeared somewhere else.

"Wait!" Mianya whispered as Carter began to crawl out.

A sound of a horse trotting had broken the silence. They then heard the horse stop and someone dismounted. Heavy steps came closer to their hiding place until they could see a pair of feet directly in front of them.

Mianya's breathing had almost stopped. Mianya grabbed Carter's hand and squeezed it to comfort herself. After a minute, the man started moving. He walked back to his horse, mounted it, and rode off. As the horse galloped away, Mianya started to pant.

"That was Sebastian," she whispered. "We must have drawn his attention when we released the Creatures of Old."

"How did he know we were in Shalya?"

"This is the only place I haven't looked. We must be very careful now."

"We should go," he said.

"No," she said, holding onto Carter's arm once more. "We should wait here. It is getting dark and I don't want to sleep out in the open."

"I guess you are right. We would be safer sleeping here tonight."

Mianya pulled out a few blankets from her bag and made her bed. She sensed some peace coming from Carter and thought maybe it was because Sebastian wasn't near Karen.

The next morning, they both crawled out of the hole. Carter brushed the dirt off and Mianya noticed that there was a bone from someone's finger hanging from his boot.

"Ugh!" Carter said as he picked off the bone.

"Apparently, someone was crushed under that and only their finger survived," Mianya said. She couldn't help but laugh.

"That's disgusting." Carter looked around his body and was relieved he had no more surprises on him. "Ok, where should we go?"

"I don't know." Mianya looked around thoughtfully. "Sebastian is on our tail, so we cannot afford to release the creatures once we find them."

"Let's head east."

Mianya and Carter found ten crystals over the course of the next week. They were searching for another in a dark forest when they came across Sebastian. He had the crystal in his hand and was draining it.

She looked at Carter and knew that he was not nearly fast enough to evade Sebastian as she could. "Hide in that hollow tree there," she whispered, pointing. She took a deep breath, sprinted and snatched the crystal from his grasp. She climbed up the closest tree and jumped from limb to limb, knowing that Sebastian was sure to pursue her as he had done before.

"Are we really going to do another chase, Mianya?" he called out into the darkness. "I grow tired of your games!"

"You shall not have the power you seek, demon!" she answered.

Sebastian climbed up into the trees and saw her on a

nearby branch. He darted for her, but she evaded him. He located her again and dashed for her once more, and again she barely slipped through his fingers.

"I am stronger and faster every second of every day!" he laughed. "I am smarter than before and am ready for the army you have assembled."

"You jest!" she said as she evaded another one of his attempts to grab her.

They were jumping from tree to tree and limb to limb. He made a few more attempts to catch her, but they all failed.

"So you search for the key?" he called out again.

"How do you know my plans?" she asked, trying not to become distracted. She knew he was trying to mock her.

"A hopeless bird told me."

"You will not defeat us. The light will prevail!"

"Your light is weak!" he said with an evil laugh. "Darkness consumes all!"

He finally stopped his pursuit. She noticed he had given up the chase and wondered about what he said. She waited thirty minutes then went back to where Carter was hidden.

"Carter?" she whispered, looking around nervously for any sign of Sebastian.

"Yes, I am fine. He didn't find me," he replied quietly.

"We should leave this place. It's too dark, and Sebastian could be anywhere."

When they left the forest, they watched for any hint of Sebastian. They walked a little ways before Mianya turned to Carter.

"How did he know our plans?" she asked him.

"The only person who was with us and is gone now is Eliza." He suddenly realized what she had done—and that it was partially his fault. "She did it. She betrayed us."

"It saddens me that she would betray us."

"Her foolish heart was darkened. The light was never in her like you said. I feel she was only at the monastery because I was."

"Sebastian said that he knew we were looking for the key."

"It sounded like he did not have it," Carter said.

"You may be right. He should have already known we were looking for the key that the knight gave me. Unless, he does have it and did not know what it was until Eliza told him."

"You think that he might have drained the power from it?"

"I would highly doubt that he would do that. The key had the most power I have ever seen within any of the crystals I have found. If he did drain the power for himself, he would be at his maximum power."

"I guess you are right. We must tell Queen Thalandria that Sebastian knows our plan," he said.

"Not until we have found the majority of crystals on this continent. The more we have in our possessions, the less he can steal."

"Lead the way. We must hurry now."

The one thing that concerned Mianya more than Sebastian knowing their plot was the reference to Eliza as hopeless. Sebastian had found his virgin with no hope and Mianya could do nothing to stop him from doing such a vile act.

CHAPTER TWENTY SEVEN

The Decision

After they found what they could of the crystals in Shalya, Mianya and Carter made their way to Aznat. They still had a few crystals to find before they could successfully call to arms. They found one in the house of one of the barbarian families and bartered to obtain it.

"We are so close. I can feel it," Mianya said quietly.

Carter could see she was getting serious as they found more crystals and did not understand why she was not joyful. Maybe she was worried about Sebastian being close on their trail.

"Why are you so melancholy?" he asked.

"I am just thinking about things," she replied with a smile. "The next crystal should be south, near a lake."

They travelled south until they reached a clear lake. They looked over the water and saw an eagle swoop down and catch a fish within its large talons.

"The cycle of life is an amazing thing," Mianya said. "Everything dies at just the right time."

"What do you mean?"

"The will of the Creator. He knows all and knows when its best to live and when it is best to die. I am in that will, as are you. It makes me happy to think of this world as it is now. The world before was unable to contain the light within us because of our corruption. Now we have the knight and his sword. His blood. Doesn't that excite you? We have the light within and we need to save the world with this truth. Baelin and his curse now have no power over us as it once had. Our light exposes him for what he really is."

Carter was excited when he thought of the light and its power but was also getting worried with Mianya's latest comments of death. He looked around and spotted the last crystal on the lake's shore.

"There is the crystal," he said. He picked it up, and put it safely in Mianya's bag. "We should leave now to prepare to invade Allear and take on Sebastian."

"I thank you for gathering the crystals for me," Sebastian said. He laughed as he approached them with his sword drawn. "If you give me them to me now, I will make both of your deaths as painless as possible."

"You will not have them!" Mianya said.

"My dear Mianya. I was delighted to hear your words of comfort. You are a bold one. Why not just return to me as my daughter. I do wish to have you back. I can give you a greater power."

"Never on your life!" Mianya stood ready for any tricks of his.

"It is a shame then that you have to die." He turned to look at Carter. "Thank your honorable friend. She could never bring herself to leave a helpless human to die at the hands of a killer. You will not run from me now, I am sure."

Mianya grabbed two small blades from her bag and ran towards Sebastian. The battle began. Carter saw that Mianya was extremely out-skilled and was weaker than Sebastian as she swung at him and dodged his blows. Sebastian disarmed Mianya quickly and kicked her to the ground. Carter drew his sword, ready to run into combat with her.

"Stop!" she yelled. Sebastian prepared to drive his sword into her, but she rolled out of the way. She tried to get up, but he kicked her down again.

Sebastian kept stabbing at her as she rolled avoiding the blade. She managed to kick Sebastian to the ground and threw sand in his face. She got up on her hands and knees to reach her blades, but Sebastian had wiped the sand from his eyes, jumped on top of her, and began to choke her. Instead of unskillfully prying his hands away from her neck, she dug her nails into his forearm. With another cry of pain, he loosed his grip and Mianya shoved him away with her feet.

She threw one of her daggers at Sebastian. It penetrated his leg, giving her a few more seconds to get closer to Carter.

"Mianya!" Carter shouted, "Let me help you!"

"No! Karen needs you!" she replied. "The world needs you!"

Mianya looked back and saw Sebastian picking up his blade. She began unlatching her pendant and looked at Carter as tears began to form in her eyes. She looked at her pendant one last time and then threw it to him. "Run!" she said.

Carter caught the pendant in his hands and looked at it, confused as to why she would give him her pendant. She stood motionless as Sebastian approached her with his sword. "There will be peace in my death," she said with a smile. Horrified, Carter watched Sebastian cut her down.

"Victory!" Sebastian cried out as Mianya's body fell lifelessly to the sand.

"No! Mianya!" Carter yelled out.

A loud roar filled the air, and Carter looked up to see the mysterious white dragon flying toward him. Carter looked back at Sebastian and saw him running toward him. He quickly picked up Mianya's bag and ran towards the white dragon. Sebastian barely missed Carter as he grabbed onto the dragon's tail. The dragon sped high into the air and Carter was safe.

It swooped down and caught Mianya's lifeless body within its claws. Carter was placed onto the dragon's back by its tail and he watched Sebastian near the lake cursing them. The wind was rushing past his ears so fast that he couldn't hear what Sebastian was shouting.

All Carter had left of Mianya was a bag of crystals and her pendant. He did not know that her body had been retrieved and no idea why she threw her pendant at him. He couldn't see anything and it wasn't because of the wind but it was because of the tears streaming from his eyes. She sacrificed herself so that he could live, an example of the Creator.

Carter wiped his eyes and all he could think about was her last words: "There will be peace in my death." He wondered what she meant by that. There were so many things that Mianya had told him that he didn't quite understand but she always told him to be patient and understand in due time.

Is this all that there is? Carter thought. *Death? Why did she die? Can you please answer that for me?* The dragon moaned and his scales began to glow.

Carter looked at the body of the dragon. The smooth scales felt nice against his skin. He wondered where the dragon was taking him as the cold wind beat against his face. The dragon looked at him. Carter noticed that there were tears in the dragon's golden eyes. *Maybe all this was planned*, Carter thought. *And I know this dragon must be important—but how? Thank you for sympathizing with me if you can hear my thoughts.*

Down below he saw they were passing over Allear. He recognized the castle where Karen was held against her will, and he wanted to fly in and rescue her, but the dragon continued to fly north until they reached the northernmost shore of Allear. Carter realized now that the dragon must be taking him to Norya, to see Thalandria. *Why are we going to where Thalandria is? I have no body to bring her. How am I going to face her?*

The air got colder as they reached the snowy regions of Norya and he snuggled against the warm bag containing the crystals. The dragon flew on until he had brought them to Frostwind Castle. There he landed and waited for Carter to dismount. The dragon roared loudly and flew off into the distance.

Carter was in front of the castle doors when they suddenly opened. Greeting him was one of King Hendor's attendants."

"I need to speak to Queen Thalandria right away," Carter said.

"I am sorry, but what business do you have with the Queen?" The attendant asked.

"It regards to the nation of Allear and her daughter, Mianya," Carter said.

"Come with me," the man said as he motioned for Carter to follow him.

The man led him to King Hendor's chamber, where the king sat on his throne. The king rose to his feet when Carter entered the room.

"I will summon the Queen," the man said with a bow and exited.

"Carter, my boy!" King Hendor said happily. "Come to my side."

Carter walked slowly to King Hendor. His mind was on Mianya and how he would tell Thalandria of her death. His heart was racing faster as every second went by and brought him closer to the moment the bad news must be told.

"How did the crystal hunt go?" Hendor asked.

Carter smiled and held up the bag for King Hendor to see. He took the bag and looked inside. A wide smile came across his face and his big mustache wrinkled.

"Very nice! Is Mianya not with you? I am sure she wanted to visit her mother first." He said as he swayed on the balls of his feet in delight.

Just as Carter was about to explain what happened, the doors to the king's chamber opened. Queen Thalandria walked into the room. She approached Carter and her face looked confused when she looked at Carter. He clenched his sweaty hands together to fight the emotion that filled him.

"Where is Mianya?" Thalandria said at once, "Where is my daughter?"

Carter's mouth went dry and he could not find the words to speak. Instead, he set the bag down and reached inside to take out her pendant. He held it up for the king and queen to see. As it swayed, the queen's face changed from confusion to deep sorrow.

"No," she said softly as tears started to come. "It cannot be." Thalandria fell to her knees. Placing her head into her hands, she wept. "My daughter! My beautiful princess."

Carter did not know what to say or do. He just stood there as his emotions overwhelmed him and tears came to his eyes also. He looked at King Hendor and his mustache had wet tears dripping from it.

"How could she have?" Thalandria said, choking on her tears. "I told her to be careful."

"I am... sorry." Carter said.

"How did this happen?" she asked as she looked at Carter with her tear-stained face.

"Sebastian."

"How did you get away?" She said.

"A mysterious white dragon came and caught me up into the air just as Sebastian was going to take my life."

"A white dragon? Why did it not come sooner?"

"I don't know why. But I do think she was expecting this."

"What do you mean? Why would she expect death?"

"With every crystal we found, she became more solemn and yet more and more peaceful. Sebastian was following us and finally caught up to us right after we got the last crystal in the land. She started fighting, but then stopped and just stood there. She took off her pendant and threw it to me."

"She what?"

"She continued staring at me, now with tears in her eyes. Right before he killed her, she said, 'there will be peace in my death.' She let him kill her."

"Why?"

"I don't know, my lady."

"He took her twice and the second time she did not return to me," Thalandria said to herself.

"I am deeply sorrowful on account of her death." Carter said, bowing his head in shame.

"Did you not think of bringing her body back? Is her body supposed to rot in a strange land?"

"I did not see her body when I left. I do not know if the dragon had taken it or not."

"I cannot lament peacefully without her body," she said as she started crying again. "Oh, Mianya. Oh, my daughter!"

A loud roar sounded outside. *Has the dragon returned?* Carter thought.

A man ran inside and said rapidly, "My king, there is a dead body lying on the threshold of the castle!"

"Let me see it!" Thalandria cried out as she rose to her feet. She walked out with Carter and King Hendor following closely behind. Lying on the marble steps was Mianya's lifeless body. Her garments were stained with blood. Thalandria ran to her daughter's body and wept over it as she looked into the heavens.

"How can this be?" Thalandria said.

"The dragon must have had the body."

"Thanks be to this mysterious dragon who is allowing

me to properly bury my daughter. Get my attendants to come prepare her for burial."

"Carter, you must be tired," King Hendor said. He put his large hand on Carter's shoulder. "You should get some rest."

Carter was led to an elegantly decorated room not far from the throne room. When he entered, he felt lonely compared to the massive size of the room. He cleaned himself up and laid in bed while his mind replayed Mianya's death over and over, her voice saying, "There will be peace in my death."

***

Carter woke up when he heard singing echoing in the morning air. When he walked out on his balcony, the streets were filled with Elves walking by with candles. They were singing a haunting song of lamentation. He saw four Elves, faces covered with colored garments, holding a casket laden with gold and pristine diamonds. He bowed his head and recited a prayer of hope. *May there be peace in her death. May there be peace in all the deaths of those who trust the light.* Carter thought.

The next day, Carter was called to the king's chamber to discuss the invasion. "Sebastian knows about the invasion," Carter said to King Hendor.

"How can this be? Who could have informed him?" Hendor asked.

"The man that was with us, Neil, was not a man, but a woman named Eliza. She worked in the monastery with me. I denied her love, and in her bitterness, she went to Sebastian and told him everything."

"Are we ready to leave?" Thulian said, interrupting the conversation and glaring at Carter.

"Yes, the army is assembled," Hendor said.

The men and Elves were ready and had ordered

themselves in front of the castle. All told, there were around five thousand men and three thousand Elves.

They boarded several ships and set sail toward Allear. They reached the port town of Harte and one by one the ships came in and deposited their troops.

The people of Harte were frightened and did not leave their homes for fear of their lives. The army marched through peacefully and assembled in a field nearby.

"I will ride ahead and meet you in the fields north of Faerie Forest," Carter said. He mounted his horse.

"Very well. We will wait for you and then prepare for war," King Hendor replied. "Meet us to the north of Faerie Forest."

Carter headed east to avoid the mountain and then south toward Kakaran. He passed by the cave where Eliza saved him. He rode on with great speed. Carter soon reached Kakaran and approached the door to his parent's house.

"Carter!" his mother said, "I am so glad you are well. It's been months since you have been home."

"Where are the Proudmoores?" he asked immediately.

"They own a home down the road. What's going on?"

"There is no time to speak, mother. I'm sorry. I am just glad you are safe. I feared for your lives." He kissed his mother on the forehead and departed.

Arriving, he walked inside and found the Proudmoores sitting around the table. Adam was there with Lia and he saw that she had a ring on her finger. He looked around and noticed that all were present except Susan.

"I have come to make sure you are safe. I was fearful that Sebastian had gotten to you all. Eliza betrayed us and I was not sure if she told him your whereabouts. I must leave now that I have seen you are safe."

"Wait one minute!" Adam said, "What is going on?"

"There is an army from the north headed to invade Firestone right now. Sebastian is possessed by the ancient spirit of Baelin. He is trying to take over the world and we need to stop him. I know you have not seen Karen in a long time, so I wanted to give you hope and let you know that I am to rescue her and Thomas as well.

"Thank you so much, Carter," Eleanor said as she walked over to embrace him in a tearful farewell.

"Stop!" Adam said as Carter started to leave again.

"What?" Carter was impatient now.

"Do you expect me to let you leave without letting me fight to save my own sister and brother?"

"You can't," Lia said as she placed her hand gently on Adam's arm. "What if you were to be killed?"

"I won't leave you, my love." Adam said as he kissed her forehead and looked at Carter.

"You aren't coming Adam," Carter said sternly. "I cannot protect you."

"Surely you jest." Adam laughed. "I am my own man now. I don't need you to protect me. I have the power of a Creature of Old within me if you have forgotten."

"Adam, please, don't leave me," Lia said. "Listen to Carter's words."

"Wait, Lia. I think that Adam should come," Carter said. He wanted to laugh, when he remembered Adam saying similar things when they escaped over Death Mountain. "I guess you are no boy after all." Carter smiled.

"What?" Lia asked. She looked at Carter and sighed, folding her arms.

"His strength would be helpful. His skill has improved. He is a fine young man now, Lia."

"The first wise decision you have made in a long time, Carter," Adam said, as he patted Carter on the shoulder.

Carter ignored the jab of sarcasm and motioned for Adam to follow him. They started packing supplies for the journey over Death Mountain.

"Please be safe," Eleanor said.

"Carter!" Marie got up from the table, ran to him, and hugged his leg. "Please take care of Adam for me."

"Sure, I will," Carter said as he patted her head.

Carter and Adam rode to Adam's finished house on the lake to grab some clothes and his sword. They rode west over Death Mountain. During this time, Carter informed Adam of everything that he had encountered and what he knew of Sebastian's plans.

***

Carter decided to visit his brother in the monastery to see if he was well and safe before continuing to the camp. When he reached the monastery, He was pleased to see that nothing about it seemed to have changed.

Carter and Adam walked inside. Christian saw them and his face beamed. He went up to Carter and greeted him. Out of the other room walked Susan, who stopped still when she saw who it was and blushed a little.

"Susan?" Adam asked in shock.

"Hello, Adam," she said, still blushing.

"This is where you went off to? Why?"

"What are you talking about, Adam?" Carter asked.

"She left after Lia and I got married and didn't tell anyone where she went," Adam said. "Mother was worried that you put yourself in danger since Sebastian is still looking for us."

"Why are you here, Susan?" Carter asked, his curiosity piqued.

"She is my wife," Christian spoke up as he walked over to her and held her tightly

"What?" Carter and Adam said simultaneously.

"Yes, he's my husband. When he came to warn us to leave, I saw his face in the shadows and fell in love with him," Susan said. She was bright red now and wouldn't look any of them in the eye. "I wanted to see him again because he was mysterious and I was alone. He is noble and honest and—"

"And you said I was foolish?" Adam replied.

"Adam, stop." Carter said as he turned to Susan. "If you choose to love one another and realize that the marriage is a covenant, then I am happy."

"I do choose to love him," she said as she wrapped her arm around Christian's waist and smiled up at him.

"And I choose to love her," Christian said. "But what brings you to us? You look troubled."

"We are invading Firestone Castle. We are going to save Karen and Thomas and stop Sebastian from taking over the world."

"That's ridiculous!" Christian said, "You will die. Their army is massive. News has gone out that Norya was invading and men have come from all areas of Allear to defend their freedom."

"We are not trying to take Allear's freedom. We are trying to free Allear from Sebastian's control. Do you know how long it has been since I have seen Karen? If I cannot save her, I at least want to die knowing that she lives in a safe world."

Christian didn't speak for a moment. He sat and placed his head in his hands. After a minute he stood up and walked over to Susan and kissed her forehead. "I love you," Christian said and then turned to his brother. "Carter, may I speak to you alone for a moment?"

"Sure," Carter said.

"Come with me."

They walked into the back room, leaving Susan and Adam in the room by themselves.

Susan turned to him when the door closed. "I am going to have a baby."

"What?" Adam replied.

"I haven't told Christian yet. I don't know how to tell him."

"You will be a great mother." Suddenly, Susan started crying. She wrapped her arms around her twin brother and sobbed into his shoulder.

"Why are you crying?"

"I am just so happy to see you. I am scared for you."

"This is ridiculous. Please stop crying. Why do all the women in my life cry?"

Susan looked at Adam and poked him in the chest. "You be careful! Think of Lia."

"You know I'll be fine," Adam replied, "I have the power of a Creature of Old, remember? Now that I think about it, you do too, don't you?"

"How did you know?"

"That strange connection between Creatures of Old."

She nodded and rolled her eyes. Only Carter came out by himself without Christian.

"Where is Christian?" Susan asked.

"He went out the back door to do something."

"Oh. Please, be careful," she pleaded as Carter and Adam headed for the door. "I am so happy that you are going to save Karen and Thomas." She escorted Carter and Adam outside and waved to them as they rode off north to meet the army.

CHAPTER TWENTY EIGHT

The Rescue

"It is great to finally see you here," King Hendor said to Carter as he walked into the tent. "We can start this war and stop Baelin from corrupting Allear."

"Are the men ready for invasion?" Carter asked.

"Yes, we have set it up the way Mianya told us to," Thalandria answered.

"So I am to sneak into the castle and take care of Sebastian once we breach the wall?"

"Yes, but Mianya is not alive to go in with you. Do you think that it will still be safe?"

"I have Karen's brother Adam with me. He has shown great skill in combat. We should be fine."

"Very well, we will meet you inside when we get the chance," she said with a nod and left the tent to rally the troops.

"It seems foolish to fight on the same battlefield but on the other end of the wall." Thulian said as he followed after her.

"Carter, you shall fight valiantly," King Hendor said as he put his large hands on Carter's shoulders. He left the tent after the other two.

"Carter, you really want us to just go inside the castle by ourselves?" Adam asked him.

"You think you can do that, Adam?" Carter asked.

"I know we can do it," he replied, "Let's go, then."

Carter and Adam walked outside and saw the men and Elves in formation. They mounted their horses and met Thalandria and Thulian at the front of the army.

"All right men! Move out!" Thulian yelled.

The Noryan men and Elves marched forward and made their formations across Faerie Hill. The Allearian army stretched far and wide near the walls of Firestone. Standing on the tower above the gate was Sebastian. He bore a conceited smile as he looked out over the armies.

"How foolish you are to come against us!" Sebastian called out when Thalandria's army stopped. "We will defend our land from those that attempt to take it for selfish gain. We are a mighty nation and will protect our homeland from those who oppose peace!" The Allearian soldiers cheered and smashed their weapons against their shields. "Men, attack!" The Allearian solders ran forward with their swords drawn.

"Archers ready!" Thulian yelled, raising his arm.

As the enemies closed in, Thulian dropped his arm and the archers attacked. When the Allearians approached Thulian gave the second command of attack. The two armies collided and the war began as they fought with all their might.

Carter and Adam ran into the fight, cutting into men as they fought their way toward the gate. Adam was quick, and used the power of which the serpent had spoken. The wall breaching specialists scaled the walls and opened the gate from within. Archers shot arrows at Adam and Carter as they dodged them to enter the main square of Firestone. Adam took his bow and shot down a dozen archers while Carter scanned for Sebastian.

He was nowhere to be found and they assumed he had already taken refuge in Phoenix Castle. A few of the knights sworn to guard the king approached them on horseback. Adam aimed for the chinks in the armor and shot down two of the riders. The remaining two dismounted and swung their swords. Adam was busy with a highly skilled knight while Carter was struggling against the other.

Carter was busy parrying the vicious swings of the knight. He took the offensive once Adam had disarmed and slain the man he was fighting. They had backed him against the windmill that was moving and as he was disarmed by Adam, and knocking off his helmet, the propeller cut into the head of the knight and he fell to the ground.

Fighting more knights, Carter and Adam arrived in the King's throne room. Phillip looked at them, shocked, as they killed his guards. He was trembling and fell backwards over his throne as he tried to distance himself from them.

"Take your last breath, villain," Adam said, holding his sword up to Phillip's throat.

"Please, spare me!" Phillip pleaded.

"Not on your life you vile scum!"

"Adam," Carter said as he put his hand on Adam's, "don't be merciless."

"He's the reason my father is dead!" Adam said as he held his sword back up to Phillip's throat. Adam was shaking in anger.

"Please!" Phillip pleaded again, his voice shaking.

"Adam, please. Be honorable and repay evil with good."

"Please, I'll do anything!" Phillip said as tears were forming in his eyes.

"Hold your tongue!" Adam yelled. He threw Phillip to the floor and extended his sword out.

"Adam!" Carter said as he gave him a look.

"He is coming with us, then!" Adam said as he grabbed Phillip and pushed him. "Show us where they are."

Phillip nodded. He led them down to the dungeon where Thomas and Karen had been placed last. "I do not know if Sebastian has moved them," Phillip said, "Why do you want to take our freedom?"

"Stop talking!" Adam said as he pushed Phillip forward.

"Phillip," Carter said, "We are not taking your freedom. We are attempting to free you from Baelin's control."

"Baelin? That is just a fairytale."

"You couldn't be any more wrong my King. Sebastian is possessed by the demon himself."

"You lie! Sebastian is my friend!"

"Carter," Adam interjected. "He won't listen to reason. He is hopeless to change."

They walked down the dim halls of the lower portion of the castle until they found themselves at a large, ironclad door. They went inside and descended to the dungeon. It was musty and rats scurried along the ground. As they made their way to Thomas' cell, men crowded to the doors of their cells, pleading for release.

They reached the last door. When they opened it, Sebastian stood waiting with a vindictive smile. He had three hooded men with him, each holding a captive: Thomas, Karen and Eliza.

"Carter!" yelled Karen.

"Quiet, wench!" Sebastian held up his hand to silence her.

"We have your king, Sebastian," Adam said as he held his blade up to Phillip's neck.

Phillip was trembling. Sebastian began to laugh hysterically. *What was so funny about his life being on the line?* Adam thought. Karen looked at Phillip and then back at the floor.

"You think that I care about his poor, pathetic life?" Sebastian said when he stopped laughing.

"What is this, Sebastian?" Phillip asked. His eyes were wide.

"Go ahead and kill him. I have no use for him any longer."

"Sebastian, I am your friend and your king! How could you say that? I trusted you."

"The Sebastian you knew is gone. This body is mine."

"What are you talking about? If you are not Sebastian, who are you?"

"I am Baelin, the greatest being in the world. Some call me the Lord of the Shadows and other call me The Prince of Darkness, but I call myself the King of this world!" Sebastian said.

"How could you do this?" Phillip asked.

"I was thankful that your friend Sebastian fell across my minion trapped in my old castle. If he had never found him, then I probably would have never been released. You were very easy to persuade, Phillip; pathetic, really. Once I disposed of your father and put you on the throne, it was only a matter of time before I would have killed you, too."

"Father? You killed my father?" Phillip cried out. "How could you do this to me? You tricked me and persuaded me to take Karen by force."

"That is too bad," Sebastian said. "It is your own fault for being a fool."

"Phillip, I begged you and warned you about him," Karen said.

"Karen, I am so sorry. I was fooled. Will you ever forgive me?" Phillip asked.

"Of course I will, Phillip. You were—are—one of my friends."

Adam finally released Phillip, who stood there staring at who he remembered as Sebastian. Sebastian looked over at Karen and smiled widely.

"Oh dear, helpless Karen," Sebastian said as he slowly walked over to her. He took one hand and lifted her face to look at him.

"Don't you touch her!" Thomas yelled. "Leave my sister alone!"

Thomas was struggling to free himself from the hooded

man. Sebastian walked over to him and struck him across the face. Karen screamed as Thomas stopped struggling and looked at the ground once more.

"Sebastian, enough!" Phillip yelled. "This is madness! You are outnumbered! I cannot let you harm anymore people!"

"Am I?" he said. "I have your loved ones and it would be too sad if they were to die before your eyes." Sebastian walked over to Eliza and petted her face. "I thank you for this woman, Carter. She did prove to be such a help to me. How unfortunate, though, that because of her Mianya had to die. Do you have any words for your love?"

"Carter, please, save me!" Eliza said. "I love you!"

Carter just looked at her and shook his head. "I have pity on your darkened soul, Eliza," Carter said.

"No, I am not darkened... I... I was misguided," she said.

"What a sad rejection," Sebastian said with a laugh.

"Sebastian, let Karen go, I beg you!" Phillip pleaded.

"You, shut up! I was going to use Karen for my own purposes, but thanks to Carter, Eliza came to me. I am sorry, Karen, but I have no use for you anymore." His face became expressionless. He looked over at Carter. "Two men's hearts will break at the death of one woman."

Sebastian drew his sword and started to walk toward Karen. He raised his sword. Carter started forward, but Phillip ran sooner. As the blade was about to be plunged into Karen, he pushed Sebastian, causing the blade to go into the hooded man. The man screamed and turned to dust as he was only conjured. Phillip had been knocked to the floor.

Karen got up quickly and ran to where Carter and Adam stood. She embraced Carter and started to cry into his chest. Carter wrapped his arms around her to comfort her.

"You fool!" Sebastian said, glaring at Phillip.

Phillip was still on the ground as Sebastian came towards him. He picked Phillip up by his hair and held the blade up to Phillip's throat.

"I guess I can wait for Karen," Sebastian said with a smile.

"I love you K—" Phillip's words were cut off as Sebastian took his life.

"No! Phillip!" Karen screamed as Sebastian threw Phillip's lifeless body to the ground. Tears streamed down her face as she reached out, her hands trembling. "How could you?" she said as her voice got bolder. "How could you? You... you monster! You tricked him and he never had a chance!"

"It really is a shame that he never listened to your wise words," Sebastian said. "He was really pathetic, was he not? He loved you because you were fair. Did he not know that some things that are pleasing to the eye can have deadly results?" Sebastian let out a vindictive laugh. "Now, who is next?"

Eliza looked down at the dead body and then up at Sebastian. She trembled.

"This is enough, Sebastian! Let them go!" Carter yelled. Carter let go of Karen and held his sword up. He stood in a bold but passive position, ready to move if he needed to charge quickly at Sebastian.

"I will take care of him," Adam said as he prepared to charge.

"No, Adam!" Karen said as she got in his way. "He is much more powerful than you think. I couldn't bare it if I lost you. Enough people have died on my behalf."

"Tell me, Sebastian. What are you planning to do now that your source of power is gone?" Adam spoke boldly. He had listened to Carter's journey as they traveled over the mountain.

"Ah, the crystals. I see that Carter informed you well concerning my plans to regain my power. I cannot help that you have released almost all of them, but I will choose an alternative way. I am, however, done with your silly questions. Give me her life and I may let you keep yours." Sebastian held up his hand and Karen started to be pulled to him.

"Please!" Karen screamed. She was lifted into the air and was levitating toward Sebastian.

"No!" Carter yelled.

Sebastian drew his sword and ran toward Karen. Suddenly, Carter jumped in the way and the sword went into him. Carter fell to the ground, as Sebastian pulled his sword carelessly from the body.

"What a shame," Sebastian said.

"Carter!" Karen screamed as she threw her body over his, crying uncontrollably. Adam darted forward. He took his sword and struck like a snake, but Sebastian evaded the strike just as quickly. Adam was amazed by how fast Sebastian was.

Sebastian saw Karen on the floor and lifted his sword into the air. As his blade descended, Adam quickly disarmed Sebastian. Sebastian slowly backed up toward Thomas as Thalandria and Thulian ran into the room.

"You are done, Sebastian!" Adam yelled as he slowly walked forward.

"You cannot kill him!" Thalandria yelled. Adam looked back at her, confused. Sebastian smiled and laughed once more.

"You have not seen the last of me!" Sebastian said. "I will lose a lot of power for doing this, and will have to start weak, but it is necessary."

Adam sprinted toward him. Sebastian clapped his hands twice, causing Eliza and Thomas to disappear. He cackled and clapped his hands a third time. He vanished in a cloud of smoke, just as Adam's sword reached the place where he had stood. Sebastian's empty laugh echoed through the air.

"No!" Adam yelled as he looked back at Thalandria

with anger. "You distracted me and he got away!"

"You could not have killed him! That is just the body he is using. If you kill his body, then his spirit will just find another body to take refuge in."

On the floor, Karen still cried over Carter, who was staggering breaths. "No… no…" she continued to say. Her body was covered in his warm blood. She tried to stop his bleeding as much she could, but it was no use.

"Did you get the key?" Thalandria asked Adam.

"No," Adam said, still bitter about losing his chance at killing Sebastian.

"That key will grant us access to the Heavenly Knight's sword," Thulian spoke up.

"It is the only way to kill him," Thalandria said.

"There was no key!" Adam yelled at the Elves.

"Carter! Please don't leave me!" Karen screamed. "Carter!"

Carter looked up at her and gave her a half smile. He held up his bloody hand and placed it on her lap. His eyes stared into hers as his heart no longer beat.

"Carter!" she said as she fell on his body. "My love! Please! Come back! Come back!" She began pounding on him in frustration. "You cannot leave me! I love you! Wake up! Wake up! Please someone." She looked up at the Elves. "Bring him back! Please!"

His hand fell off her lap as she fell onto him. In his hand was a bloody piece of parchment. Adam went over to his sister and tried to grab her body off of his, but she clenched onto Carter's dead body.

"No! Please, let me be with him! Carter!"

"Karen, please," Adam said, trying to hold back his own emotions of sorrow. There was nothing he could do to help her now and he felt useless.

"I love him! How could he leave me?"

"What is that in his hand?" Thalandria asked, pointing to the parchment in Carter's hand.

Adam let go of Karen. She had looked up when Thalandria mentioned something being in Carter's hand. She dove for it, thinking it was his final words to her. Adam snatched the parchment out of her hand. She screamed and clawed at him.

"Karen, you are emotionally unstable," Adam said calmly, holding it out of her reach.

"Give me that!" she demanded. "It is written to me, I just know it!"

Adam opened up the bloodstained parchment. He scanned the words and then stopped to look at Karen.

"What?" she asked, after seeing the look on his face.

He slowly folded the note. Stopping to think for a moment, he handed it to her. Her bloody, trembling hands opened it quickly. Reading the words written, her eyes widened. She opened her mouth slowly and whispered, "Carter…."

www.ingramcontent.com/pod-product-compliance
Lightning Source LLC
Chambersburg PA
CBHW070550130626
46556CB00001B/96